# ROOTS REAWAKENED

# ROOTS REAWAKENED

ROOTS RUN DEEP SERIES BOOK 1

## TRACY MICHELLE SELLARS

ST JOSEPH, MISSOURI USA

To David,
who held me when I questioned God's sovereignty.
Thank you for making God's unconditional love
and grace tangible to me every single day.

"For thou wilt light my candle: the LORD my God will
enlighten my darkness. For by thee I have run through a troop;
and by my God have I leaped over a wall. As for God, his
way is perfect: the word of the LORD is tried: he is a buckler
to all those that trust in him." Psalm 18:28–30 KJV

# ONE

*East Wharf, England*
*April 1890*

After days of searching wretched British inlets up and down the coast, his quest was at an end. He had found him. The man who had stolen what should have been his. Jonathan Davidson. A low-class charlatan with just enough pluck to play the game.

Everything would have been settled today if Davidson hadn't gone and gotten himself hitched. Word had it on the docks the girl was quite a looker. The man smiled as he ran his hands down his velvet vest. Even though the soon-to-be widow wasn't part of his original plan, it sounded as though she would do nicely for a passing fancy. Yes, quite nicely indeed.

"'Bout three months along, I'd wager," the doctor said, helping Justine Davidson to a sitting position.

*This can't be happening.*

"No morning sickness," the doctor was saying as he wiped his hands. "That's a good sign. Maybe you'll be one of the lucky ones that has it easy all the way through."

As Justine walked on shaky legs to meet her friend who waited outside the office, she thought about that word. Luck. It wasn't how she would describe her life, given all that had happened in the past year. Assuredly unpredictable. Impossibly unacceptable. Positively off-kilter. Nothing the way she had expected.

"Well?" Carrie Anne asked with raised eyebrows.

"You were right," Justine said flatly. "I can't believe it."

Carrie Anne beamed back, her freckled face in joyful contrast to Justine's wide-eyed expression.

"I suppose I shall have to tell Jonathan straightaway. He'll be home for an entire week this time. But I don't think he'll be as excited as you are, Carrie Anne. He'll be angry about the doctor's bills and the added expense of a child. You know he doesn't approve of my work at St. Alban's. He says I should be earning a wage, not giving my time away."

"If it's not too far for you to walk, why don't we find out together what he thinks." It was a statement, with a hint of a question from her thoughtful friend.

Justine gave a distracted laugh. "It's not too far. I can manage."

The shipping office had informed her yesterday that the CCS Black-stock was due to disembark this afternoon. Justine had planned on being the first face Jonathan saw. She had wanted her husband to know things could be different if they only spent more time together. He needed to know and she needed to reassure herself they could be a real couple. That was yesterday. Now she wanted to turn around and run all the way to Brookefairshire. Back home. To her papa's arms. Something warm and familiar. Something safe.

But that was an impossibility. Papa was gone. Her security lay in the hands of a husband who had only been home ten nights in their four-month marriage.

Carrie Anne hooked her arm through Justine's, propelling her down the walkway. "Don't worry. He's going to be thrilled. Children born to a young man are like arrows in a warrior's hands. Blessed is the man whose quiver is full of them. Maybe Jonathan will start to feel that way once he hears the news," her friend said hopefully.

Justine shrugged as she paused to look through the glass panes of a dry-goods store. Inside stood rows of fabric lined up against the wall like tall, willowy women sporting their best dresses. Justine imagined opening the door sometime this coming summer and purchasing muslin and cotton to begin her baby's layette.

"Mrs. Davidson!" Mr. Navin and a group of orphans she knew from St. Alban's were across the way.

Justine waved, a smile lighting her face for the first time that day. "Hallo, dear friends!" she said, holding out her hands to the children. They hugged her in return, looking up at her expectantly. It was their sweet little faces, always their faces, that grabbed her heart and tugged her in. "I don't have anything in my pockets." Justine made a great show of turning the pockets out of her dress and inspecting them thoroughly. This brought giggles behind small hands. "But I can stop by tomorrow and read you a new story."

The two women continued toward the wharf with goodbye waves, Justine's heart swelling as she thought of her own little one. Someone to keep her company during the long days of Jonathan's absence. Someone who would have a favorite bedtime story one day and want to be hugged goodnight.

She sobered, thinking of the loneliness she knew as a child. If Jonathan kept up his current pace, her baby would grow up as she did. Just one parent. Half of a whole.

The very tips of the smokestacks of Jonathan's ship were coming into view. She and Carrie Anne were making good time. Too good, in Justine's opinion. Within a few blocks, the village would meld into the busy docks of East Wharf. Soon, she would be face to face with her husband, not at all sure she was ready for the encounter.

*God, why would you allow this? I don't want to raise this child alone.*

Justine freed her arm from Carrie Anne's, one hand on her stomach, the other keeping her hat from blowing away in the salty breeze as they gazed at the *CCS Blackstock*. It was not as large as the cargo and passenger steamer that made its way with alarming speed across the Atlantic and back again. No, Jonathan's home-away-from-home looked more like a toy in the harbor next to the *Blue Flag Line*.

The *Blue Flag's* gangplank was pulled up, not yet ready to welcome its next passengers aboard. The *CCS Blackstock*, however, was releasing its crew like dozens of dusty children who had been let out for recess. Men were everywhere, shouting orders above the noise of ships clanging against the docks. Others were busily engaged in bringing down the cargo from their last stop or greeting loved ones on the pier. Justine searched the faces, looking for Jonathan, a man she barely knew. A man who would now be a father, whether he desired that title be bestowed upon him or not.

"Excuse me, ma'am," a sailor with a Scottish accent said as he wheeled by with a handcart stacked high with boxes. Justine felt that she and Carrie Anne were in the way as they watched the crew finish their work. "Let's go stand over there so we don't get plowed into." Justine motioned with her head to the side of a warehouse.

As a quarter hour passed, then another, Carrie Anne began to look doubtful. "He's not coming, is he?" Carrie Anne knew all too well Jonathan's propensity for staying away longer than his job necessitated.

The wharf was emptying rapidly as men made their way home after their long journey. Jonathan was not among them. Justine would keep her solitary status a bit longer, it seemed. "Let's go."

Turning at the end of the warehouse, Carrie Anne pulled Justine up short.

"What in the world? Carrie Anne —"

But Justine was cut off by the look on her friend's face. Justine peeked around the side of the wall and saw an image that both instantly and irreversibly seared itself onto the soft flesh of her heart. A woman stood too close to Justine's husband, gazing up at him with kohl-darkened eyes.

"Here's something you'll definitely want to take a look at," the woman said.

Jonathan quickly folded whatever the woman had handed him and seemed to stuff it up his coat sleeve. "I knew you'd come through for me." Jonathan's smile was intimate as he ran a finger down her cheek. "I'll see you tonight, my beauty. Midnight."

"I'll be waiting."

Jonathan began to walk away, whistling a merry tune. Where would he be at midnight? *Lying next to me.* Justine had half a mind to stalk after him and demand an answer. But her self-protective half didn't want one. Didn't want to be lied to and didn't want to know the truth.

"Oh, Justine." Carrie Anne laid her hand on Justine's arm. "Scriptures say a man who commits adultery destroys his own soul."

Justine didn't want pity in the form of Scripture. She didn't want an explanation from Jonathan. She didn't want this life she had stumbled into. She sank back against the warehouse, searching for a way to fix what seemed irrevocably broken.

Jonathan stopped his loping gate toward home when a blond man in a business suit placed his hand on Jonathan's arm. By the way their heads were bent, Justine could see the two were in deep discussion. She felt pulled by unseen hands, each claiming they knew the right way.

She could let betrayal force her to go home and hide out. Shelter herself from danger, from harm. She could let hope coerce her into pretending that nothing was wrong when her husband slipped away in the night. Or she could face this head-on. What would God want her to do? With sudden determination, Justine marched toward the two men. Her future with Jonathan was now or never.

Justine stopped short upon hearing the stranger's words.

"Mr. Davidson, I have come here with the express interest of giving you your portion of this little stratagem that's been cooked up. It seems the payout was bigger than either of us had anticipated. I will meet you right here at eight o'clock tomorrow morning with your money."

Jonathan's portion of what? They were barely making it month to month. Scrounging to make ends meet.

The gentleman with the wavy dark blond hair shook hands with Jonathan. "It's been good doing business with you. Allow me to purchase a cab for your trip home."

"That's not necessary—"

"Nonsense." Justine was close enough now to clearly hear the businessman's American accent. He motioned to a waiting hansom and within moments, Jonathan was headed northeast.

Justine spun on her heel and walked back to Carrie Anne, who had wisely stayed back from the forthcoming fray. If Jonathan was going to deal with unscrupulous men and associate with women of the night, let him go home, thinking Justine was there to meet him. It would serve him right to walk into an empty flat.

"'He giveth power to the faint; and to them that have no might he increaseth strength,'" Carrie Anne was saying as they slowly walked toward the village. Her recitation of Isaiah 40 swirled in Justine's mind along with pictures of learning the verse at her father's knee. His casket being lowered into the ground next to the church. Sacred vows said on her wedding day. The doctor's face upon his announcement of a baby on the way.

"'Even the youths shall faint and be weary, and the young men shall utterly fall: But they that wait upon the LORD shall renew their—'"

A loud boom sounded ahead, shaking the air with its power. A horse screamed. From behind the buildings ahead, smoke wasted no time reaching its black fingers to the sky. Men shouted. People scattered. Justine exchanged a frightened, knowing look with Carrie Anne. Both women picked up their skirts and ran toward a scene Justine had a feeling would change her life forever.

Garrett Cole stood on the pier eyeing the *Blue Flag Line*. He was ready to get home, ready to cross the Atlantic. Maybe even for the last time. He had been feeling for some time that he needed to get out of the game. In a couple of days, he would let the huge steamship return him to Waterford Cove where he could pray through what God had planned for him next.

Garrett had the desire and the means to put down roots. Yet he had no one with whom to start the greenhouse of his life, not to mention there was never enough time to cultivate a meaningful relationship. He'd learned that anything of value was hard to grow when a man spent nine months out of the year traveling between wharfs and factories and hotel rooms.

An explosion that sounded like it belonged on a warfront erupted not far from the pier. Never one to back down from a challenge, Garrett wasted no time coming upon the source. But the pageant that played out before him was worse than he had anticipated. Someone had removed Jonathan Davidson from his cab and had placed his mangled body on the cobblestone. Lifeless.

A young woman knelt by Jonathan's side, his hand in her lap. The thin gold band on her fourth finger told him what he needed to know.

Studying her slumped shoulders, Garrett felt his heart go out to the young widow. She couldn't be more than nineteen or twenty years old; just a youngster in his opinion. But her beauty could not be ignored. Though she wore tattered clothing, her shiny chestnut curls held a hint of auburn, her slender form that of a virgin. What would become of her now that she had no husband? Surely, she had a father or some doting uncle who could take her in.

He could just leave her be and move on with his life. Go back home. Erase her anguish from his mind. But he knew his conscience wouldn't let him get away with that. If she truly was Jonathan's widow, then she deserved what was due her.

Stepping through the small crowd, Garrett made his way over to her. She turned wide blue eyes on him as he came to her side, his heart taking in her look of total confusion and shock.

A cab careened around the corner and two constables jumped out of their conveyance. Garrett backed away and stood with the onlookers while the accident was inspected, the unconscious cabbie taken by ambulance and Jonathan's body placed in an awaiting wagon. Some officers took testimonies while others began to investigate the shattered remains of the cab. A cab Garrett had hired for Jonathan Davidson.

Raking his hand through his hair, Garrett considered his options. This had not gone as expected. A final errand, a few days roaming the English countryside, then homeward to Virginia to begin laying a new foundation for his future. Now this. He couldn't leave without telling Mrs. Davidson of the situation. But would she care now that her husband lay dead?

As the bystanders slowly dispersed to their evening engagements, Garrett placed his hat on his head with conviction. This was not over yet.

Justine lay in the darkness on her lonely bed and listened to the sounds of life outside the window. Couples laughing, enjoying a walk in the evening's fresh spring air, men hurrying home to be with their families after a hard day's work. Justine laid a hand on her stomach, wondering what she would one day tell her child about his father.

This morning had been the funeral. The calendar showed it was her twenty-first birthday, a day for commemorating life. It had become a day of bereaving all that would never be. Even when she had laid her father to rest, she hadn't known such a feeling of solitude was possible. God was with her, yes, but still she felt deserted and alone.

Growing up without a mother, Justine had learned to be content with fewer interactions than other children. But her father had been a kind man, always there when she needed him. Then when Jonathan came along, she knew she would never feel isolated again.

Now it would just be her and the babe growing within her. How would she support the two of them? Perhaps the laundry where Carrie Anne worked would hire her. But who would take care of the baby while she was away for ten hours a day? An unbidden image sprang to mind. She shuddered at the thought of having to give the baby to the orphanage, even though she knew the children were well cared for. If it came to that, she could content herself by visiting the child every day and overseeing his care as much as possible.

Guilt washed over her as she pondered the unwelcome thoughts. She hadn't succeeded at being a good wife, one that a husband would want to come home to. Now it looked as if she was already failing motherhood. She sighed as she turned over on the lumpy mattress and faced the dark wall. Reason and sense told her she should be hungry, should eat for the baby's sake. Her stomach had another opinion.

Was Jonathan really gone? It seemed surreal. Had he been less than faithful to her? She would never know for sure. Who had wanted him dead? No enemies came to mind. Maybe if she could see and touch some of Jonathan's things, she could remember their few good days together. The thought beckoned her as she got up and lit the lantern.

Carrie Anne had located a box of Jonathan's and added to its contents the things that had been found on Jonathan's person. Justine brought it to the rickety table near the stove. Lifting the lid, she saw Jonathan's coat on top. It had been damaged by the explosion but remained intact. She withdrew it and inhaled the scent she had come to associate with her husband. A mix of sea and man. She reveled in holding something that had held her husband and kept him warm on the days he was out on the open water. But who else had held him? A painted lady on the docks? A woman in every port town? The thought made her put the coat back in the box.

She sank into a chair as the heartache she had tried to hold at bay while in the company of the small group of mourners came bubbling to the surface. Rocking back and forth, deep penetrating sobs wracked her body.

All of a sudden, a gush of something warm between her legs caused her to stop swaying. Justine gasped as she stood up, lifted her dress, and saw blood making a trail down her leg. With a cry of realization, she ran to the chamber pot.

In an anguished voice she ground out, "God, what are you doing?"

The box forgotten, Justine barely had the strength to stumble across the cold floor back to her bed and fall into an exhausted sleep.

# TWO

Garrett dismounted his rented horse and tied its halter to a ring in the stone wall. He found the number he was looking for and, lifting a hand, knocked on the knotted wood door. When no answer came, he pounded a little louder. Maybe Mrs. Davidson had gone to the market or to stay with family.

A man on the street stopped his velocipede next to Garrett. "If yer lookin' for Mrs. Davidson, you won't find her 'ere. The husband is dead and the woman is gone."

"Gone, you say?" Unease swept through him at the thought that he may not be able to catch up to her before his ship left. "Where to, might I ask?"

"Brookefairshire. At least, that was 'er first stop. Then she's a-leavin' fer good." The older man straddled his bicycle and scratched his balding head.

Interested as Garrett was to find out how this velocipede differed from those that he kept in storage back home, he needed to stay on task. Garrett's eyes searched the man's face for signs that he was serious. "Surely you can't mean she's gone?"

"Aye. Took me old heart by surprise, it did. That girl wot be the best thing that e'er happened to St. Alban's Orphanage." He lifted his hat. "Mr. Navin's the name. Now if you'll be excusin' me, I best git back."

"Wait." Garrett laid his hand on the older man's arm. "Do you know where this Brookefairshire is?"

"Sure thing. You can git there by horse in an hour. Take this 'ere road north a bit and look fer the crossroads. There be a sign pointin' the way." And with that, the man pedaled away on the cobblestone.

A quick glance around the street told him no one was watching, so Garrett tried Mrs. Davidson's door and found it opened easily. It took only a moment to sweep his gaze over the empty cupboards, barren table, and stripped-down bed to confirm for himself the girl indeed no longer resided there.

With determination of the task at hand, he shut the door firmly behind him, mounted his horse, and raced north.

"For your trouble, sir. Half now and half when we journey back." The cabbie had been more than happy to receive fair compensation for his morning's work. It was a large amount subtracted from Justine's purse considering what precious little remained. Only enough left to buy her a few meals and a steerage ticket aboard the *Blue Flag* this afternoon.

But it was worth it. She had awoken this morning and steeled herself against the day. No longer would she sit by and wait for tragedy to come knocking on her door. She was done being a pawn in this grand game of chess God seemed to be playing with her life. Justine's walk up the gangplank of the massive ship docked in East Wharf would topple the chessboard, send all the pieces scattering, and put her in charge of the next move.

"Twasn't any trouble, miss." The cabbie held out his hand.

"I should be ready within the hour. If you please, meet me at the bank. You'll find it located across from the only pub in the village."

The sound of fading hooves marked her cadence as she walked down the drive. The home she had grown up in sat at the edge of a thicket on the outskirts of Brookefairshire. It may have been a foolish errand, but her heart drank in the sights before her. She intended to press each image she saw this morning so firmly in her mind that in the long days ahead, she could recall them with ease.

The oak door that she and Papa had hung together. The stone and mortar he had laid piece by piece. The vegetable garden where each summer she had worked so happily.

"What's that yer wantin', little miss?" A creaky voice startled Justine. An old woman had opened the door a crack while Justine bent at the flower bed. "If ye's 'ere to collect the rent, come back on the morrow."

"No, ma'am." Justine rose and began to back away.

"Well, get on with ye, then!" The door slammed shut.

Justine realized then that upon coming there, she had hoped to be invited into the cottage. Maybe sit down to tea in the front room one last time. Breathe in the air that may still hold a trace of her father's scent—pipe tobacco and butterscotch.

Quickly, Justine plucked a crocus from the flower bed that lined the front of the cottage. A memento of her childhood, the happy days with her father. Its beautiful purple and white petals had yet to open and now never would.

She would press it in the pages of her Bible, and one day, maybe when she needed it most, she would find it and be transported to this place. But she must kill the flower to remember. She must put to death her past to open a door to the future. Sometimes, she realized, death must come to bring life. She fingered the fragile petals as she walked to Brookefairshire.

"Blast it all," he said under his breath, slamming the door behind him. "That's what I get for trying to be a gentleman."

Two days he had waited. Waited while the girl buried her husband. Waited until he thought he would go mad.

Her residence was near empty and he knew his chances of accomplishing his goal were growing slimmer by the moment. She had obviously moved out, but to where was the question. This was not going quite as planned. He had not, however, become a successful businessman by displaying a lack of persistence. He would not be easily waylaid. The first line of business was done; Jonathan was dead. That had been easier than he expected. Now if he could get his hands on his money, all recompense would be paid. But he would not receive his due without getting close to Justine Davidson. And by the looks of her, that was sure to be a pleasure.

☙❧

With her trunk stashed away at Carrie Anne's place, Justine had nothing to encumber her walk. Nothing save her heavy heart.

A familiar nudge inside made her bristle. Justine had always taken matters of pain or consequence to the Lord. She fairly laughed aloud at the thought. Ludicrous! Why should she turn to God now when He had taken everything from her? Everything. Justine had nothing left, no family and not even enough money to see her through a week when she arrived in America. Why would she turn to a God who was strong enough to save her child, strong enough to keep Jonathan faithful, and yet had chosen not to?

When she saw the blood last night, her heart had hardened like the candy she'd often made for her father. Except that sweet offering always made an ordinary day seem special. Now the bitterness in the back of her throat threatened to choke the very life of her soul.

In that one horrid instant, everything she knew to be true had been altered. She still believed in God, but no longer in His faithfulness. God, in all His sovereignty, had come into question. Like the tick of a clock moving forward, she couldn't turn the hand back on the uncertainties that filled her mind.

Disregarding the troubling thoughts, Justine looked up from the cobblestone to see the building she sought was just ahead. Past the market, where friendly faces had greeted her for twenty years. Past the churchyard that held her parents' graves. And there, just inside the joint bank and law office, was her father's most trusted friend.

Her eyes drank in her surroundings before she opened his door.

This would be her last look at all she had ever known. Was she strong enough to face the unknown, to head into a new life? She would have to be. She would go to America and survive, even thrive, amidst anything that came her way.

"Miss Torvald!" A man at the front desk jumped to his feet. "I mean, Mrs. Davidson. Beg pardon. I'll fetch Mr. Flanning, straightaway."

A portly man came into the reception area, wiping his forehead. "Mrs. Davidson!" His face looked startled. "I received word only moments ago that you had vacated your flat and were nowhere to be found." The older man mopped his brow again. "And yet, here you are!"

Justine was taken aback. "Did you need to see me, Mr. Flanning?"

"Yes, it is a matter of extreme import. Won't you come into my office and take a seat? Ah, this really is a to-do." He proceeded to shuffle papers on his desk and adjust his spectacles repeatedly.

"Mrs. Davidson," he finally began, "as you know, your father did his banking business with us all the years he lived in our fair town."

Mr. Flanning cleared his throat, and Justine shifted anxiously in her chair wishing he would say what was on his mind.

"And as the only lawyer in the area, I had the privilege of acquiring your father's business in that department as well."

Justine sat back ever so slightly. Her father had hired a lawyer? Whatever for? Gregory Torvald had been a simple tradesman with an uncomplicated life.

"You may be surprised to learn that your father was an extraordinary saver. I know he gave you a comfortable life in our little village, but he was considering your future most of all. He wanted you to be provided for if he was not here to do it. There was a fairly standard clause put in his will that stated you were not to receive the monies until you turned twenty-one." Mr. Flanning passed a document across the desk. It contained a figure that outweighed Papa's yearly wage many times over.

"You're serious?" Justine faltered. "I mean, I can't believe it." Justine held the paper to her chest and closed her eyes. "Oh, Papa."

"This number includes the sale of your father's home to a landlord who has been snatching up properties around Brookefairshire."

The stony heart that had taken up residence in Justine's chest softened slightly as she pictured her father's face when he came home from a hard day's work. Tired but happy. Effort he had made for her. This went beyond the small keepsake she would press into her Bible. This was love and every time she used the provisions, she would think of him.

"My deepest condolences regarding your husband's passing." Mr. Flanning was now breathing calmly. "I refrained yesterday from treading upon your grief. But this morning, I sent a messenger to East Wharf—" Mr. Flanning sighed. "Well, at any rate, I am quite pleased to have found you, young lady."

Justine adjusted her skirt around her lived-in boots. "I am sorry to have caused you trouble, Mr. Flanning. I must tell you it makes me feel nearer to my father, knowing he cared for my future in this way." She paused, biting her lip. "I know this may seem unusual, but do you have it within your accounts on hand to give me the sum today?" When he looked doubtful, Justine went on. "You see, I am planning on boarding the *Blue Flag Line* this afternoon."

Mr. Flanning seemed to be thinking. "I will say it's highly unusual, but your father was a true friend to me." He stood. "Wait here, Mrs. Davidson. I'll see what I can do. Here's a copy of Gregory's will for you to read over and sign. You'll find everything is legal and binding."

Justine added her signature to the short document, lost in thoughts of her father when the door reopened. Justine glanced up to find Mr. Flanning placing a thick envelope and a heavy bag on the oak desk in front of her.

How could it be possible? Justine felt over the edges of the bills and fingered the coins, finding it even more difficult to comprehend what her father had done for her, now that she saw the money. With this amount, she could do so much more than make ends meet when she got settled in her new land. Possibly even purchase a small apartment in which to reside.

Another throat clearing brought her back from her musings. "Mrs. Davidson, might I make a suggestion?" He continued at her nod. "This is quite a sizable amount of money. Perhaps you could make arrangements with the captain of the *Blue Flag* to see it safely to America. I would hate for it to be stolen or lost. After all, your father's gift should be protected."

"Yes, I believe that would be a good idea," Justine said faintly.

"Your father was very dear to me. I will hold you both in special memory. Go with God."

Justine went through the motions of saying goodbye to a few more familiar faces in Brookefairshire but her heart was divided. Sectioned off, piece by piece. Surprises, defeats, and questions had carved it like a great jigsaw puzzle, too complicated to put back together. Most distressing of all, the corner piece was missing. The one that held the sides together and kept the whole thing from completely falling apart. This afternoon she would be out to sea, between shores and homelands, never to feel at home with God again.

# THREE

The *Blue Flag Line*'s colors of red, white, and blue flapped in the afternoon breeze outside the shipping office. It waved its tricolored banner, a symbol of the country she was leaving behind and the promise of a land built on Stars and Stripes. Waterford Cove, Virginia. Even the name of where they would dock held a note of adventure. Promise. New life. Justine squeezed Carrie Anne's hand as they took their place in line.

"I still can't believe you came with me." Justine sat down on her small trunk. She was feeling weak this afternoon and couldn't staunch the bleeding that had begun last night. "You know you're keeping me afloat, don't you?"

"I knew the moment you came to my door that this was going to be a big day. I prayed about it all morning while you were in Brookefairshire. When you came back," Carrie Anne shrugged shyly, "I knew what I had to do. This is my chance, too." She laughed lightly. "But who would have thought that my friend, Justine Davidson, the girl who doesn't have the word 'change' in her vocabulary, would be the one to suggest this." She motioned to the sign posted outside the *Blue Flag*'s office. It listed several classes of tickets with varying prices.

"I've been thinking, and I've made up my mind, so don't try to stop me." Justine went on before Carrie Anne could protest. "I've decided to pay for cabin class tickets. For both of us."

"Next in line. Step this way, ma'am."

Saved by the ticket agent. "Two cabin class tickets, if you please." Justine's hand shook as she reached to count out the money from her father's gift. He would be proud of her today. Brave. Confident. Independent. She reassured herself this was the right thing to do.

The timing couldn't have worked out better. The ship was heading west and soon East Wharf would be in the past. She had nothing holding her in England and everything to look forward to in America, the land of freedom. Freedom from memories. Freedom from heartache. Freedom to take the reins of her life. Freedom from the unanswered questions that insisted upon repeating themselves over and over in her mind.

"Make that three first-class, sir." An American accent. Broad shoulders. Dark blond hair.

"Pardon, me. Do I know you, sir?"

"Ma'am. Miss." The blond hair dipped twice before them in a gentleman's bow. "Garrett Cole from Waterford Cove, Virginia. At your service."

Shouldering his way beside the two women, his presence demanded attention. "I'll be escorting these women on the voyage. Please put their room as near to mine as propriety would allow. I'll see to it they make it safely over the pond." Mr. Cole gave the man the necessary money.

"We can take care of ourselves. We don't need charity." The nerve of this man, assuming benevolent care of complete strangers.

"Forgive me. I should explain myself further. And I will." He glanced behind him at the lengthening line of passengers. "Right now, both of you need to fill out the paperwork and sign here and here."

In short order, an exceptionally regal-looking document was placed in each of their hands. Justine stared at its official seal. Her ticket to a better life. Then tags were distributed for their baggage and they pushed the trunks next to the growing stack.

"Really, Justine. You shouldn't be doing that. It's too heavy for you."

"Carrie Anne!" She hissed. It would be mortifying for this stranger to know about her delicate situation.

"Sorry," Carrie Anne mouthed silently. She was smiling now as the unlikely threesome made their way out into the sunshine. Her friend no doubt looked upon the situation as some grand provision from her heavenly Father. Not having to pay for passage would certainly leave them with more money to gain their fresh start in America.

"Are you quite alright, madam?" Concern was written in Mr. Cole's brown eyes. "May I take your bag for you?" He reached to remove it from her shoulder.

"Thank you. No." She held her purse closer to her side and side-stepped the man, wondering at this turn of events. This man, this Mr. Cole, was certainly the one to whom Jonathan had been speaking with on the pier the day the *CCS Blackstock* came into harbor. The one who had paid for a cab to take Jonathan home. The cab that had…*Oh, dear.*

Not one for fainting dead away, Justine nonetheless grabbed Carrie Anne's arm for support. They had just become indebted to and taken under the custody of a man who might possibly reveal everything she wanted to know about her husband. Even the circumstances surrounding his death.

He couldn't believe his luck. It looked like Mrs. Davidson would be on the guest list for the *Blue Flag Line*. It surprised him to hear around town she was making so bold a move. Although he had not expected it, her coming to America, and Waterford Cove at that, went along quite nicely with his plans. And there she stood, almost as pretty as the young thing with whom he had spent last night. Mrs. Davidson would certainly outshine that harlot if he could get her out of that brown work dress and into a decent gown.

On his arm in Virginian society, Mrs. Davidson's clear peach complexion and slim figure would steal the show. The highlight of her ensemble though, would be her innocence, her vulnerability, giving him easy access to her trust. Smiling to himself, he rubbed his hands together in anticipation as he entered the ticket office.

She may have eluded him briefly, but for as long as her life remained, he would not be far behind.

Mrs. Davidson had the kind of eyes a man could get lost in. In all Garrett's born days, he hadn't encountered their equal. Realizing he was staring, he dropped his gaze and readjusted his overcoat.

"Anything you ladies need, I'm at your disposal for the length of the trip." He noticed the way Mrs. Davidson always clutched her purse tightly to her side. What did she have in there that warranted protection?

"Mrs. Justine Davidson," she said. "And this is Miss Carrie Anne Barnes. We'll be accompanying each other on the journey." Mrs. Davidson said the last with an emphasis she surely intended. Independent, this one was, but she also held the look of a fledgling bird, trying out its wings for the first time. A little frightened, a little excited, a little proud. If she fell from the nest, Garrett couldn't promise he wouldn't try to pick her up and rescue her.

"I know who you are, Mrs. Davidson. I saw you the night of your, um, your husband's accident."

Her answer was said more coolly than he would have hoped for. "Yes, I recall. Truth be told, I also saw you speaking with Jonathan that evening on the pier." Passengers were milling all around them, some even beginning to board, but Mrs. Davidson seemed to pay them no heed. Instead, she went on. "Did you happen to mention that you were a friend of my husband's?"

"I didn't mention it, but I will now. Jonathan was, well, not a friend, per se. More of a business acquaintance. Come. Walk with me. It'll be nearly a week until we can use our land legs again."

Now that he knew he'd be in the company of this lovely lady for a spell, Garrett felt himself relaxing. There would be plenty of opportunity to sit with her and relay his message. First, let her enjoy the amenities of first-class. Sit back, take in the sea air. Chat with her friend, Miss Barnes. Drink root beer maybe for the first time. It was the least he could offer to so fragile a creature in what was surely a time of grief. If he couldn't use the money God had blessed him with for someone such as Mrs. Davidson, who could he use it for?

Each woman took the arm he offered her and they strolled along, dodging little girls in white dresses, impatient mothers scurrying after them, and fathers wiping sweat from their brows while they saw to last minute details.

"Sir, we must thank you for your kind generosity."

"It was my pleasure, Miss Barnes, and the least I could do to ease any grief our friend has endured upon her husband's passing."

"You are too good, sir. As the Apostle Paul says, 'My God shall supply all your need according to his riches in glory by Christ Jesus.'" Miss Barnes patted his arm.

Garrett glanced at Mrs. Davidson's hand—which was not patting him—tucked next to his side, marveling at how well she fit next to him. Silently chastising himself, he stood up tall and looked straight ahead, knowing he could not in good conscience have such thoughts toward a newly widowed woman.

"Sir, you mentioned you hailed from Waterford Cove," Miss Barnes was saying. "If it be the Lord's will that we establish ourselves in your fair town and do not venture further up the coast, do enlighten us to its virtues and to how you've come to live there."

"With pleasure, Miss Barnes." Garrett's heart swelled with pride, thinking upon his city's many amenities. "We have lately seen a great boom in our economy, mostly due to our industrial progress. But I assure you, we're not all smoke stacks and factories. No, indeed. You'll find a quaint city center, fine arts and entertainment, and there's even talk of a university coming under construction late this year." He steered them round and came face to face again with the ship. "Yes, ladies. I content myself in knowing Waterford Cove has everything you could hope for as you make your transatlantic crossing. As for myself, you could say I'm in the investment business."

As he took in the ship's great bearing, Garrett sincerely hoped that the women would soon agree with his assessment of Waterford Cove. The town certainly had its welcoming arms stretched out for anyone who came to its shores. From the poorest of the poor to the highest of elite society, Waterford Cove could make anyone feel at home. He wondered where these two ladies would fit in. Garrett pondered where his place was as well.

He wasn't an immigrant, setting foot on foreign soil, but being away from family and friends for extended periods of time always left him feeling out of sorts and slightly left out. It was hard to admit that even when he wasn't at home, life went on without him. His mother would be knee-deep in her volunteer work, while his father, president of Waterford Cove Holdings, was never at a loss of things to occupy his time. And if Garrett calculated the dates right, his sister, Anica, should have already delivered the first grandchild of the family by the time he got home. A little niece or nephew to dote on might be just the antidote to his glumness about not having a family of his own.

"Look! It seems the line on the gangplank is lessening. I can't wait to get a look at the inside of the ship." Miss Barnes's exclamation caught his ear, but Mrs. Davidson's reaction captured his attention. It was the first time he had seen her smile and he felt beguiled. Garrett would have to watch himself around this one. Even though he outclassed her by a mile, her worn clothing and more humble roots couldn't mask her determination and beauty. By land and sea! What was he thinking? She had been a widow less than a week. As soon as his business was complete, he would do well to put Mrs. Justine Davidson far from his mind.

The welcome dinner aboard the *Blue Flag* held the grandeur of an affair put on by the royal family. At least that's how it felt to Justine. Carrie Anne readily agreed. Granted, this ship held both cargo and passengers, but the women found themselves surrounded by more opulence than had been available in busy, humble East Wharf.

Upon seeing the ship's accommodations, Justine had to admit she liked how the other half lived. She could hide her boots and skirt under the table now and imagine that, even if just for one evening, she fit in with these people. It was a heady feeling. Even though she was not feeling quite herself, she was comforted all through dinner simply by feeling the brush of her purse against her leg. Her father's money would never buy her a place among high society in America, but all week long she could enjoy this luxury.

"Justine," Carrie Anne elbowed her. "You okay?" She eyed Justine's plate. "You've barely had two bites of your oxtail soup and I've never seen you turn down dessert."

Mr. Cole was eyeing her uneaten food as well. "Where are my manners, ladies?" He placed his napkin on his plate. "You are no doubt anxious to get a good look at the sea now that we've set our prow toward Virginia. And after that, you can settle in your room for the evening. Shall we?"

"How very solicitous of you, Mr. Cole." Justine narrowed her eyes but nevertheless steadied her bag against her shoulder and allowed him to escort them out to the deck.

Justine didn't hold his arm this time. There was something about the situation that told her she shouldn't trust Garrett Cole's warm eyes and inviting smile. The coincidences were accumulating. She could now add how Mr. Cole had labored all evening to convince them Waterford Cove was where they needed to put down roots.

"Ladies, I will look forward to giving you the grand tour of the ship after breakfast. Would you care to meet me for the morning meal al fresco? I can swing by your room around eight?"

My, but he was persistent. But what man wouldn't be who had something valuable to gain? "We shall see, Mr. Cole," Justine said as they came to their cabin door. "Good night." Her mind and body demanded rest. Yes, that was all she needed. Rest. Then she would wake up, make sense of this muddle and go forward with a fresh, clear mind.

In Justine's sleep-deprived mind, the sound of the door lock clicking into place held a kind of finality to it. It brought with it the totality of her losses. Justine turned to find Carrie Anne getting ready for bed and suddenly the room seemed claustrophobic. All thoughts of rest escaped her. She needed fresh air, and now. As she reached to unlock the door, a knock sounded on the other side, causing her to step back. "Who's there?" she called.

Mr. Cole's voice said from the hallway. "It's Garrett Cole, Mrs. Davidson. May I have a word with you?"

Wondering what the man could possibly have to say since she had only taken leave of him a moment ago, Justine hesitantly opened the door, thinking solitude might be the better option.

Tipping his hat in greeting, he said "I noticed you've kept your large bag with you since we boarded and wondered if I could take it to the captain for you for safe keeping. You never know the gents who may roam these corridors." He glanced up and down the hall then gave her a disarming smile. "Better safe than sorry, they say."

Garrett's proposal caught Justine off guard. His wavy blond hair had a windblown look and at the moment, he looked more like a lovable big brother than someone who was trying to use his charm to gain the advantage. Who knew if he could be trusted? He said he had been in business with her husband, but Justine was raised by a father who taught her to use wisdom and discretion. Something told her this was one of those times. If she was going to be alone in a new world with only one friend in sight, she'd have to hone that particular skill even further.

"I was just on my way to talk to the captain to see if he'll put it away safely for me," she quickly decided that was exactly what she needed to do. Grabbing the purse from where she had dropped it near the door, Justine told Carrie Anne she'd be back shortly. When she stepped out into the hallway, she locked the door behind her.

She preceded him down the hall that led to the staircase at the far end of the ship and decidedly ignored him as he tried to catch up to her. This Mr. Garrett Cole seemed to be a wealthy business man. What on earth could he possibly want with her? Other than the hefty sum of money she now carried. Did he wish to enrich his coffers further? She would have to be on her utmost guard. Perhaps he was the sort of man who made his living preying upon lonely widow women.

Her anger at the way this man was trying to take advantage of her bubbled to the surface, and she whirled around to face him as they reached

32

the ship's deck. How unfortunate that at this very moment, his brown eyes held the glint of the setting sun that turned them to transparent amber.

Bringing her suspicions to the forefront once more, Justine had to remember his true purpose in "helping" her.

"Mr. Cole, if that is your real name, I will have you know that I am familiar with what kind of man you are. Once you knew I had money to be stolen, it appears you intend to follow me all the way to America. You've taken advantage of my weary state and caused Miss Barnes and I to be indebted to you when you purchased our passage without permission. And now you are stalking me on this ship and we've barely left port!

"Your charms, Mr. Cole, are lost on me. I see through your schemes and will *not* be taken advantage of by the likes of you. You will have to choose another victim because this woman is too smart to be fooled."

With that, Justine stomped off in the direction of the captain's office.

Garrett stared after her retreating back with something akin to awe and dislike, all rolled into one. What money was she talking about? And how could such a sweet young girl like that whittle a man down to nothing with just a few sentences?

Still, there was something he liked about Mrs. Davidson. He didn't know much about her, but he wouldn't mind getting better acquainted. She may have made some hasty assumptions about him, but he wasn't worried. He would find a way to set the record straight. Somehow, he had to, if he was ever to explain the real reason he was following her.

But now that he had been beaten down with her presumptions, his interest was only further piqued. A girl with a little gumption was a rare thing. Maybe it was because the women he knew in Virginia were only out to impress the right people in society, which had the unfortunate side effect of compelling their spunk to fly right out the window.

Such passion as he had just witnessed held real appeal and he looked forward to his next encounter with Mrs. Justine Davidson. But getting on her good side would take a wing and a prayer.

# FOUR

The man tugged down the sleeve of his shirt, scowling at a faint yellow marking on the cuff. He couldn't wait to get home and have a decent laundress care for his clothes. Dragging himself from pillar to post on account of vagabonds like Davidson was enough to wear a man out.

The captain had delivered his trunk to his cabin, and he knew under the carefully folded suit, lay his favorite vest. He was of the opinion that its deep green velvet set off his eyes quite nicely. He would use his charms to catch Justine Davidson's attention. He'd done it hundreds of times before with other women. He had an entire week to introduce himself to the lady and edge his way into her good graces. Each day he would be one step closer to what was rightfully his, what should have been his from the beginning.

"More root beer?" Garrett Cole motioned to the waiter with three raised fingers and a question to Justine. Her first glass of the bubbling, amber liquid made her nose sting and her taste buds sing. It also helped to settle her stomach. After a few cautious sips, she conceded she was hooked.

She nodded her consent at the grinning Mr. Cole who seemed to read the enjoyment on her face. She hated to be trumped, figured out so quickly. She had never had the knack of quickly whittling away someone's outward shell to expose who they really were when no one was looking. It appeared Garrett Cole had cracked her exterior by being able to read her expressions. They had only known each other in the week that the *Blue Flag* had been on open waters, but he was rapidly making inroads to where not many had gone.

Justine tried to continue perusing a three-week-old copy of the *Waterford Cove Tribune,* ignoring Carrie Anne and Mr. Cole's banter. She noticed Carrie Anne also didn't deny the pleasure of a second bottle that was delivered in grand style to their table overlooking Waterford Cove's harbor.

"That sounds delightful. What do you think, Justine? Mr. Cole was just saying that he'll take us out on his bicycles sometime."

Justine had heard every word. "We'll see," was all she would commit to. Not only did she fear getting up on one of those contraptions, her bleeding was becoming alarming. She checked it often and was surprised each time at the amount. Straddling a piece of metal and exerting physical strength didn't seem like the best idea. Especially with Mr. Cole as their escort.

"Even if we don't go on two wheels to see the city, you ladies will have to let me take you on a tour once you get settled." Mr. Cole's warm look took them both in.

Justine averted her eyes, instead searching the shore as though she could make out specifics from her vantage point. Getting closer by the moment, there she stood: America, a land that was undergoing as many changes as Justine was. New people. New discoveries. New heartaches. New hope.

Justine folded the newspaper and tried to get the last of the sweet soda pop on her tongue without looking too unrefined. She stood and prompted Carrie Anne to do the same. "Mr. Cole, thank you for the unusual treat. I don't think I'll be forgetting it anytime soon." She turned to Carrie Anne. "We really should see to getting our things ready."

Garrett stood as well. "It's been a pleasure, ladies. When we see each other at the farewell lunch, please allow me to give you the name of a few reputable boarding houses. It will do my heart good to know you two will be well settled until you find a permanent residence."

Justine turned her face to feel the salty mist as she and Carrie Anne walked slowly away. Justine had spent much of the week in her cabin, resting and worrying. Was it normal to experience these symptoms? These feelings?

"He really is a nice man," Carrie Anne said. "I do wish you wouldn't rebuff him. He's trying so hard."

"That's just it. Why does he always have to be around? Be so solicitous? We barely know the man, yet he's like a shadow I can't shake."

"But why would you want to? I don't understand you, Justine." Carrie Anne shook her head and turned the key to their room. "I hope you can see how God has provided everything we've needed so far, and then some. And Garrett Cole is a part of that."

"As is Eric Waverly." Justine slowly lowered herself onto her bed, careful not to plop as she would have done before the miscarriage. She thought of the dark-haired man whom they had met on deck a few days ago.

"Mr. Waverly certainly is interesting." Carrie Anne opened her trunk and began packing. "If you ask me, he's the one who is always following you like a puppy."

Something in Justine's heart pulled slightly. Invisible strings that told her she was still alive. Still a woman who enjoyed the interest of a charming man. Thinking of Eric Waverly's charisma did that to her.

"Speaking of Mr. Waverly, I saw him when I went to speak with the captain about my father's money. Mr. Waverly said he would look for us on deck when we begin to disembark this afternoon."

Justine was grateful she was able to divert Carrie Anne's attention away from the subject of God's provisions. Carrie Anne may have experienced the loss of father and mother, but she had never lost a child and a husband. She didn't have to lie on her bed night after night waiting for the threatening darkness to crush her. Carrie Anne's hurts were in the past and the Bible verses she flung at Justine caused the emptiness to press all the harder.

Carrie Anne finished organizing her trunk and sat down to read her Bible. Justine turned her face to the wall. After a moment, she felt Carrie Anne rest her weight on the mattress.

"Listen to this. It's a verse that really helped me when my folks passed away." Justine could hear the crinkling of pages. "'Blessed be… the God of all comfort; Who comforteth us in all our tribulation, that we may be able to comfort them which are in any trouble—'"

Justine quickly rolled over and sat up to stop the disturbing flow of words. Her eyes flashed at Carrie Anne, heaving the betrayal she felt toward God onto her friend. "He wouldn't have to comfort me if He hadn't stolen my family, would He? Why would God allow this?" Justine got up and opened her trunk. "No, don't answer that."

Maybe if she kept her hands busy, she wouldn't have to think and remember. She saw Jonathan's box and her Bible lying at the bottom where they had sat untouched all week. Opening the box now or anytime soon wouldn't bring Jonathan back. Reading the Bible wouldn't undo any loss she had encountered. She refused to let her wounds fester. She would bandage them up and remain untouched by the pain. Justine haphazardly covered up the box and the Bible with her other earthly belongings just as she had covered her heart with indifference.

"I'll leave you with your thoughts because I know you don't want to hear this right now," Carrie Anne said at the door. "But remember, whenever you are ready to come back to God, He will be waiting for you with open arms." With that, Carrie Anne slipped from the room and locked the door from the outside leaving Justine to navigate the deep waters of loss by herself.

Justine sat back on her heels with a huff. *Carrie Anne's wrong. I haven't left God. He left me.* Instead of continuing her hasty packing, she stood and went to the mirror and put her thoughts on today's farewell lunch. She thought of how she could put up her hair for the occasion and wondered what Eric Waverly would think of the new style.

"Waverly." Garrett regarded the dark-haired man who joined him at the ship's railing as passengers waited for their turn to disembark. "Seems I'm not the only Waterford Cove resident who gets to sleep in his own bed tonight."

"Too true, Cole." Eric Waverly crossed his arms and leaned his back against the railing. "Now if I can just make some of my own luck by ensuring I see more of the two lovely ladies you've been keeping company with this week. And speaking of beautiful women, what about your sister? Maybe I'll swing by your place and take her for a spin around town." Garrett clenched his teeth as Eric nodded at Justine Davidson and Carrie Anne Barnes who had come up from below deck.

"Anica will be thrilled I'm back." Garrett hoped Eric would catch his implied meaning that he would be around to protect his baby sister from the likes of Eric Waverly. "The baby is due any day now." There. That little piece of information would keep the predator away.

Eric shot him a sideways look as the women drew near. Carrie Anne's bright, freckled face looked excited and nervous while Justine's appeared pale and solemn. Garrett noticed she hadn't eaten much in the times she had joined him for meals. He sincerely hoped she was hale enough to not get turned away when she applied for citizenship. He knew many immigrants who didn't pass their health inspection were sent back home.

"Ladies, you're welcome to join us." Eric Waverly took over the conversation as soon as the women were within earshot. "We should get our turn to step foot on Virginian land soon." Eric went to stand directly in front of Justine, turning his back on Carrie Anne and Garrett.

"Did you think about what I said?" Garrett heard Eric say. "I do hope you'll take me up on the offer. I don't think you'll receive a better one."

Garrett covertly watched Justine respond to Eric's magnetism.

"I think we will, Mr. Waverly. Thank you for recommending it. I'm sure our stay there will be more than comfortable."

Garrett's ears perked up. Where would she be staying? He had offered several options for boarding houses at lunch, but couldn't get the women to commit. Trying to look nonchalant, Garrett interjected himself into their conversation. "Mrs. Davidson, I'd be delighted to know where I can find you. There's something I need to speak with you about." Garrett noticed that Justine had her much-protected purse with her once again.

"Next! Next group to disembark!" shouted a sailor as he strode up to their little group. "Come right this way. Quickly please."

If he didn't know where Justine was going to be staying, this was his last chance to deliver his message. Why had he not taken a moment in the last week to give Justine what was hers? The answer to that was simple. Garrett knew when he told her, she'd have no reason to ever see him again. And he wasn't ready for that just yet. Perhaps he was lonely. Perhaps the state of his heart held an ulterior motive for accompanying these women. Garrett had seen no harm in that. Until now. His last chance was fading. And fast.

The wind off the ocean and the sight of the dock in turn sent Justine's hair fluttering around her face and heart fluttering in her stomach.

As Justine neared the railing, she noticed Mr. Cole was leaning casually against it with one hip it as if he hadn't a care in the world. Perhaps he didn't, other than the slight annoyance she could read on his face as Eric Waverly spoke to him. Garrett seemed to have it all. He hadn't mentioned a wife during their brief meals together but he had told of his parents, upstanding members of Waterford Cove's community. Justine couldn't suppress the jealousy that rose up within her. In her experience, it was always the ones with money who had the good life while commoners like her were given the leftovers.

While Justine silently judged the man, the steamship continued to teem with activity. Sailors rushed about doing their last-minute preparations and other crew members readied the mail that the *Blue Flag Line* was delivering from far away shores.

"Anica will be thrilled I'm back. The baby is due any day now." Mr. Cole kept his eyes on Justine as he spoke to Eric Waverly.

*So, he does have a wife waiting for him.* And a baby about to arrive. Justine's gut twisted painfully at the reminder of all she would miss out on.

Yet even as he spoke about his family, Garrett Cole had the audacity to gaze openly at her. Wasn't it rude to stare? Americans must certainly not think so. She would soon be one of them, so she had better get used to it.

Thinking it would be impolite if she turned the other way, she steered Carrie Anne toward the two men, responding to Mr. Waverly's greeting.

Eric Waverly soon had her attention, speaking of The Dunsmore Inn, a boarding house he had recommended. Mrs. Dunsmore was evidently a long-time family friend and owed him a favor. He implied he would negotiate a very reasonable rate. Justine placed both hands on her purse so as to keep from fidgeting while they spoke. This man's opinion of her mattered a great deal. He was well connected in Waterford Cove and she wanted to show respect not nervousness for his regard and generosity.

Mr. Waverly's back was to Garrett and Carrie Anne, but Justine could see their expressions clearly. Her friend's freckled face was turned toward the action, waiting and watching, while Garrett seemed to be focused on the exchange between Justine and Eric. Justine hoped she was putting on a face that matched the women of Garrett Cole's circle, showing him that she could make responsible decisions and actionable plans.

Garrett Cole's eyes landed on her bag then flicked quickly away, causing Justine to grasp it more tightly. The man had a tendency to disconcert her in a most alarming way. Even though he had been the perfect gentleman, she couldn't help but wonder if he really was following her for an ulterior purpose. Justine would do whatever it took to ensure that no one took her father's gift.

Now Mr. Cole was trying to worm his way into the conversation, questioning her as to where he could find her once they landed. Justine was glad she didn't have the chance to answer. It was time to say goodbye to the *Blue Flag*, the gallant ship that had taken its duty of transporting her from shore to shore so seriously.

"Mrs. Davidson?" Mr. Cole said as she got into the smaller watercraft that would take them to the pier. "Did you hear what I said? I'd love to know where you will be staying. There's something I need to discuss with you."

Tiny alarm bells sounded in Justine's mind at the question and her self-preservation came to the forefront. She ignored Mr. Cole's persistence, instead focusing with some difficulty on finding her footing and then her seat. She was surprised at how much this little boat was rocking compared to the giant of a ship she was just on. Her head began to swim. She put her hand to her temple and tried to focus on the horizon. That had helped some when they had been in rough seas.

Eric Waverly cleared his throat and caught her eye, casting her what appeared to be a look of warning. Was he trying to tell her to be careful around Garrett Cole? How well did the two men know each other? She had only seen them speaking twice on board, once at the railing just a few minutes ago and once when she and Carrie Anne had been taking a walk with Mr. Cole on the upper deck. Eric Waverly had stopped their promenade and introduced himself. Eric had a face she could trust. Mr. Cole, not so much.

"I did hear you." If Mr. Cole knew their exact location and if he was after something, he would have perfect access to it. Justine glanced at Carrie Anne whose face didn't give her a hint whether to answer him or not.

"Mr. Waverly has told us of a nice place to stay." Justine decided to leave it at that. Her head was swirling now. Oh, please let me not be sick. The dock was only five yards away. She closed her eyes and clutched her bag to her stomach.

Garrett knew a young beautiful woman alone had to protect herself from the dangers of the world, so he chose not to take Mrs. Davidson's behavior personally. If it was his sister in this circumstance, he hoped she would do the same thing.

Her closed eyes sent him a clearly worded message as they bumped into the dock and a shoreman tied their small boat so it wouldn't drift away.

*If only she understood this is for her own good,* Garrett thought as he helped get their trunks onto the dock. He had done hundreds of business dealings over the last ten years and he wasn't about to let this mysterious beauty get his goat. He *would* finish the job.

Miss Barnes came to his aid as the two women were helped out of the boat. "We will be renting a room at The Dunsmore Inn on West Elm Street." He noticed Mrs. Davidson dig her nails into her friend's arm. "Mr. Waverly knows the proprietress."

"That's right. Leave it to me to make sure you ladies are well taken care of. I'll be around in a few days to check on you." At that, Eric waved and walked away.

Garrett sighed silently in relief at the man's retreat, then watched as the two women reached for each other's hands and stood looking at the sights before them. He could only imagine what they must be feeling as the next chapter of their lives opened up. Garrett was grateful they had each other.

He let them have their moment and turned his attention to hail a cab to take them to their accommodations before heading home.

"Ladies, please allow me the pleasure—" Garrett's words were cut short at the look on Mrs. Davidson's face. She looked a little green and was leaning forward slightly. He had seen that look before, having traveled with fellow seafarers who didn't fare so well on the open seas. Knowing what to do, Garrett reached Justine just in time.

"Let's get you sitting down." The words were no sooner out of his mouth when Mrs. Davidson lost what little she had eaten at lunch on the wooden boards at their feet.

"Oh, I don't feel so well." She sat down on the trunk.

Garrett shed his overcoat, not caring that it would surely be ruined if it encountered any of the vomit. Miss Barnes seemed sympathetic as well and offered to clean up the mess while he gently laid his coat over Mrs. Davidson's dainty shoulders.

"I'll be right back," Garrett said walking over to the cabbie. He wouldn't be sick as well. He. Would. Not.

It was a good thing he hadn't become a doctor like his uncle. He never would have made it. Taking a deep breath of sea-coated air, he asked the driver to wait for a moment and tried to gain some measure of control over his traitorous stomach.

Once he felt comfortable to return, he realized he had left the situation during a time of need. His mother would be appalled. She had raised him to put another's needs above his own, as Christ instructed. To do unto others as you would have them do unto you. He quickly walked back and noticed Mrs. Davidson was trying to curl up on her trunk. Unbidden, he wished instead of his coat that she was using as a blanket, he could offer her the warmth and comfort of his arms. Before his thoughts could become scandalous, he took action.

"Here's what we're going to do," Garrett looked decisively at Miss Barnes, hoping she would see the wisdom in his plan. "My parents will be happy to have you and Mrs. Davidson as their guests until she is back on her feet. We can send a note to Mrs. Dunsmore to expect you in a few days."

"That sounds very sensible. And very generous. You're sure your folks won't mind?" Miss Barnes asked. "You don't mind, do you Justine?"

Justine opened her eyes a crack and shook her head.

"They'll be delighted," Garrett assured them both. Miss Barnes got her friend into the conveyance while he saw to their trunks then climbed into the awaiting carriage.

"Jonathan," she mumbled. Garrett's heart clenched as he understood what she was saying. This little lady had just lost her husband, then traveled across the sea to an unknown future. The least he could do was assist her in any way possible. Home wasn't more than ten minutes from where they were. He figured he could hold his breath at least that long.

She felt so weak. Justine lay on the cushioned bench of the enclosed carriage and realized she was shaking all over. The smell from her vomit combined with the smell of the horses made her stomach roil in protest. The latter brought to mind the day Jonathan died. She closed her eyes and tried to conjure his face in her mind. Oddly, that was

44

harder than she thought. She opened her eyes wide in sudden panic, her chilled body sweating profusely as she grasped at the fading image.

Aware that Mr. Cole and Carrie Anne were looking at her, she said softly, "I will be all right, I assure you."

"Miss, perhaps you caught a malady aboard the ship. My parents always have a guest room ready. There you can stay until you are feeling well enough to move to the boarding house. I pray this is to your liking?"

Justine studied Mr. Cole to gauge his sincerity, but found only compassion written on his face. Since he had a wife at home and a new child soon to arrive, it couldn't hurt to have him drop them off at his parents' house. He would soon be gone, anxious to see his wife, and Justine was sure to never see him again.

"I thank you for arranging the forthcoming hospitality," Justine said in a weak voice. He was being kind. She could at least be polite in return.

"Quiet yourself. You need to rest."

At least he could determine when to leave her alone and for that she was grateful. She felt Carrie Anne take her hand and was once again thankful for her friend's presence.

Justine dosed as the carriage passed through the town, continuing on until they reached what she heard Mr. Cole tell Carrie Anne was Bay Street. Justine didn't sit up in time to see the Cole mansion looming ahead on a small crest surrounded by acres of grasses and wooded land.

The carriage made its way up a smooth drive and Mr. Cole commanded the driver to get them as close to the porch steps as he was able. A man whom Mr. Cole called Louis came to assist when the motion of the carriage mercifully stopped.

When she tried to sit up, a new wave of nausea swept over her, and she let out a low groan.

"Mrs. Davidson. Don't be alarmed. I am going to carry you up to a guest room. You don't even have to open your eyes if that helps you feel better."

Justine gave a small nod at her consent for this handsome stranger to carry her into his parents' home. Perhaps she did trust him a little after all. Just a little.

45

# FIVE

Just as Garrett hoped, Mother met him on the massive stone steps with a welcoming smile and then sprang into action the moment she became aware of the need. Garrett carried Mrs. Davidson through the double front doors and followed his mother up the grand staircase to the second floor.

Charlotte Cole opened the door to the first room on the right. His mother had chosen well; the room was large and held a mahogany canopy bed as its centerpiece. A purple and white coverlet brought a delicacy to the bed, while white wallpaper covered with purple crocuses adorned the wall. Matching mahogany wardrobes, vanities, and mirrors added an air of richness. A pair of carved chairs sat in front of the bay window overlooking the countryside. Yes, his mother knew just how to make their new guests feel welcome.

He could hear footsteps coming up the stairs and maids bustling in behind him. One of them pulled the covers back so he could lay down his charge. Her eyes had taken on a sunken look, her face pale and drawn as he placed her gently on the generous pillows.

Garrett turned at the sound of regal footsteps approaching the bedside.

"My dear boy! How good it is to have you home again! Surely you must find another occupation, one that allows us to see more of you.

All this sailing about has me praying for you night and day! Give your mother a hug."

Garrett's heart warmed at the sight of the precious lady. She was truly the only woman of high society he knew who valued people more than things. If only he could find a wife with such character.

"Mother," he said as they embraced warmly. "It is good to be home. Allow me to introduce Mrs. Justine Davidson from England." Garrett glanced at the woman on the bed and found her resting with her eyes closed. It looked as though she had fallen asleep. Probably the best thing for her. Garrett took his mother's hand and led her from the room.

"Let's allow her to rest, Mother. She must be exhausted. But her companion awaits us in the parlor. Louis had Mr. Smythe settle her there. You will enjoy her, I believe. She's a delightful young woman."

The parlor was bathed in sunlight and felt cozy and warm compared to impersonal hotels. The pale-yellow walls and cream-colored settees reflected the late afternoon sun and set the room fairly aglow. Surely Mrs. Davidson would perk up in this cheery atmosphere. Perhaps he could arrange for her to be brought down when she awoke.

"Mother, this is Miss Carrie Anne Barnes. Forgive me, miss, but I am afraid I do not know from where you hail."

The fair-skinned, redheaded girl answered in her English tone, "My parents passed last year. We lived near Bristol."

"Why, son! Isn't that where you journeyed on one of your recent business trips?"

"Yes, it is, Mother. I spent nearly a fortnight doing business in and around Bristol. Miss Barnes, might I ask you how you came to be in East Wharf?"

"I have been working at a laundry. That's where I met Justine. Mrs. Davidson, I mean. She used to bring up the washing from the orphanage, every now and again." The girl seemed embarrassed to have to acknowledge her low status and flushed from the neck up.

Charlotte Cole took over in her kind, compassionate way. "Don't worry, my dear. It was not a shameful thing to support yourself after your parents passed away. On the contrary, what you did was quite noble. Other women may not have had the courage to move to a different place and find employment. You are to be commended for it."

Leave it to his mother to smooth over a situation and make a person feel important. She was a Christ-follower and it showed in her every word and deed. He had learned much from her example, and yet still felt he had quite a bit of room to grow. Just thinking about it made him long to sit under the teaching of his pastor and soak up the Word of God. It was Wednesday, so in four days' time, he would get to do just that.

Although Garrett had left Mrs. Davidson in the care of his family's trusted servants, he wanted to check on her. He certainly hoped she wasn't contagious. He had given Mr. Smythe, the family's butler, an order to retrieve his uncle, Dr. Jeffrey Cole. Garrett would make a stop in the office to talk with his father, then reassure himself Mrs. Davidson was all right.

"If you ladies will excuse me, I'm off to find Father. Mother, Miss Barnes, I am certain to see you at dinner shortly." As Garrett made his way from the room and into the grand foyer, he could smell a succulent dish being prepared even now in the vast kitchen at the rear of the home. He rubbed his hands together in anticipation of Cook's culinary talents.

Walking down the hall, Garrett poked his head into his father's office. The older man looked up from his ledger and stood with a smile.

"Garrett, you're back. Welcome home, son." The two men shook hands and took a few minutes to catch up on what Garrett had missed while he was away.

His father spoke of the bank then inquired of Garrett's travels. But something in his father's face said the man wasn't telling him something.

"Father, I can read you like a book. I know there's something you are keeping from me." Garrett lifted his eyebrows in anticipation.

James Cole settled himself behind the massive desk once again and threaded his fingers together. "I didn't want to have to tell you this, son, but it appears Waterford Cove is bowing under the pressure to use child labor to keep up with production in its factories."

Garrett felt his face grow hot at his father's unspoken meaning. Garrett knew all too well that he himself had played an important role in this horrific reality. He paced in front of the window and wondered what he could have done differently. Garrett had made a career of getting new inventions into factories so they could be produced and used by his fellow Americans. But the mass production often brought about harm and fatalities. Children should never be involved in using the dangerous machinery. It could prove disastrous.

Feeling both ashamed and compelled to stop contributing to these atrocities, Garrett thanked his father for letting him know and made his way back to the hallway. He shifted his thoughts to Mrs. Davidson's situation and dearly hoped she hadn't come down with something serious. Perhaps it was only a bit of lingering seasickness.

Garrett stepped onto the inlaid floor of the foyer and grabbed the end of the staircase's curved banister to propel himself up the stairs. Maybe one day God would see fit to give him a home of his own. A wife and children. Oh, how he longed for the day. Yes, he slept in the big house when he was ashore from his business travels, but he could only hope those escapades would not endure forever. His love for invention drove him to faraway destinations and kept him constantly occupied. But he would gladly set it all aside for a life that held more meaning than any invention he could hold in his hands. A life that included someone that shared his purpose. Someone he could love and who would love him in return.

His footsteps seemed a bit heavier as he climbed the last of the stairs to the guest room. But when he opened the door and noted Mrs. Davidson was sitting up in bed, his despondency passed. He drew in a deep breath at the sight of her. She appeared to have washed her face and her cheeks had more color than before. Her hair hung in curls around her shoulders and she was sipping tea. He wasn't a doctor, but from his perspective, it appeared she was recovering quickly.

"Mrs. Davidson, I see you are feeling better." Garrett said as he stepped into the room.

She looked up and her soft expression immediately vanished. How long would this woman mistrust him? Probably until he spoke the truth to her. While she was in his home, they would have opportunity to talk and he'd finally be rid of this particular bit of business.

"Thank you for calling on me, Mr. Cole. And yes, thanks to a bit of rest and something sweet in my stomach, I find I'm feeling much more myself."

Garrett inclined his head toward her as she spoke, just to hear the soft lilt of her English accent. By Jove, what had gotten into him? This woman was a widow. And a widow nonetheless to a previous business acquaintance.

Clearing his throat loudly and letting his gaze sweep the room, he said awkwardly, "Well, then, Mrs. Davidson, I have ordered a doctor to see you shortly. I believe you will find his bedside manner most approachable. If you are feeling well enough, you may join us for dinner in an hour or dessert in two."

With that, he shut the door behind him, determined to not let a beautiful young widow get into his head.

Justine stared after Mr. Cole's broad back as he left the room. If this man had a wife and child on the way, why did it seem as though he hung on her every word? And why had he called on her instead of his mother? It seemed terribly inappropriate for him to even still be there. Perhaps he would simply join the family for dinner and then take his leave to be welcomed home by his own family. Then Justine would have the privilege of not having to worry if he was after her father's money.

Justine sucked in a gasp. Money! Where in all the ruckus had her shoulder bag gone? That was why he was in the room. To distract her so he could steal her bag. Blast it all. She stood up from the bed and a maid bustled toward her.

"Madam, if you need anything, I will fetch it for you."

"You don't understand! I must find the bag I had with me when I got off the ship. Have you seen a brown linen bag about this big?" Justine put her hands about a foot apart to show the size of the item.

"Yes. Now, don't fret. It's over here in the wardrobe."

Justine nearly wilted with relief and though she felt a bit weak, she made her way across the lushly carpeted room to a wardrobe boasting carved lilies.

Throwing its doors wide open, she rummaged about until she found the item. Looking in the bag, she consoled herself with the knowledge that indeed, no one had touched her inheritance.

Just then a knock came at the door. The maid answered to reveal a handsome gentleman.

"Good afternoon, miss. I'm Dr. Jeffrey Cole. I see you are up and about. Does this mean you're feeling better?" He placed his black bag at the end of the bed. "The missive I received communicated otherwise."

Justine couldn't be certain her incident on the docks wasn't related to her miscarriage. She looked at his kind face and knew she couldn't lie to the man. That would never do. But to allow him insight into her situation was altogether uncomfortable, to say the least. But what else could be done about it? There she was in a stranger's home, taking their hospitality. The least she could do was be truthful with the doctor they sent.

But that didn't mean she had to come right out and say it. No. Let him examine her and if he drew his own conclusions, then so be it. She would only speak the terrible words if she had to.

"Justine Davidson, sir. Pleased to meet you." Justine lay back down on the comfortable pillows. "I was feeling poorly when we were on our way to America." It felt odd having a stranger examine her. "I think I was suffering from seasickness."

It wasn't a total lie. Her stomach had rebelled frequently over the past week but she also knew she had lost quite a bit of blood aboard the ship. Hadn't taken the time to rest after first losing Jonathan and then her little one. No, she wouldn't even think like that. It was in the past.

Dr. Cole gently probed here and there on her weary body. Wait, did he say his name was Dr. Cole? "Sir, might I ask how you are related to Garrett Cole?" As soon as she had spoken the words, she wished she could snatch them right back.

The doctor quirked an amused eyebrow in her direction and Justine felt sure he knew what she was thinking. She wanted to reassure him that her question in no way expressed an interest in the businessman.

Before she could come to her own rescue, Dr. Cole did it for her. "You may find this hard to believe, but I'm Garrett's uncle." At the surprised look on her face, the doctor tipped his head back and laughed. "I am indeed only a couple of years older than my nephew. It seems I was a little late joining the family. Garrett's father is my brother." He seemed amused at his own story, which put Justine at ease.

"Do you think I will make a recovery, sir?" Justine asked, bringing a serious tone back into the room with her question.

Dr. Cole sighed. "I'd say a little rest and a lot of hearty food and you'll be your old self. As long as you don't overdo it, you should be just fine." The handsome doctor paused, then looked up to meet Justine's eyes. "You have suffered much as of late, have you not?"

His kind expression and understanding tone caused Justine's defenses to almost tumble. She braced herself against the pain and waited for it to subside. She looked him straight in the eye and could do nothing but confirm the truth.

# SIX

The tinkling of crystal drinking glasses and quiet laughter greeted Justine as she made her way down the steps after a lengthy nap in the guest room. Knowing she wouldn't have to face Garrett Cole again after tonight only gave her a small measure of comfort. Her earlier confession to the doctor made her feel more drained than all of the physical side effects of a miscarriage combined.

But she was in America, a place where she could replace old memories with new and begin again. Something hollow inside her heart echoed. She quickly pushed the feeling away, knowing full well what it was. The empty space where her Lord used to reside now gaped like a cavernous black hole. The vacant part of her heart that used to be full of joy.

It made her sad, true enough, but she would not let pain and disappointment be the master of her life. It was time to put all that behind her and find happiness. Even if she had to create it for herself. And she would. She would never be let down again. She'd see to that.

Justine entered the vast dining room hesitantly, not knowing if it was appropriate to approach unexpectedly. She needn't have worried. Welcoming smiles beckoned her into the room. Then she saw the food; the scents and sights of the scrumptious meal alone would have lured her to take a seat at the table.

"Why, Mrs. Davidson, do come in. We saved you some dinner, and dessert is to be served in the drawing room shortly. Won't you sit down?" A middle-aged woman with soft brown eyes and dark blonde hair pulled into a fashionable up-do welcomed her first. "I'm Garrett's mother, Charlotte Cole. We are so pleased to have you and Miss Barnes join us."

Justine sat in awe of the congenial atmosphere in spite of the rich furnishings of the home. She had always equated snobbery with the rich. Perhaps she had judged too quickly.

"Dear, meet my husband, James Cole. And of course, you already met his brother, Dr. Jeffrey Cole."

Justine felt her face grow hot at the last revelation. How she hoped the doctor would keep her secret. First impressions had powerful, lasting effects.

She tried to cover her discomfort with what she hoped was the correct response. "Truly a pleasure to meet you. We're so grateful for your hospitality." Justine saw Carrie Anne nod from her seat next to the doctor.

Justine lowered her gaze as small talk once again scampered its way around the table. Carrie Anne and Dr. Cole seemed intent on their discussion while Garrett regaled his parents with stories from aboard the *Blue Flag*.

While she listened, Justine examined the plate set before her that was piled with all manner of delectable food. It was the first time she remembered being hungry since the dominoes of her life began to topple over. The roast chicken breast and creamy mashed potatoes caught her eye first.

Before she could move on to a roll and perhaps some fruit, a servant announced dessert and coffee.

Not wanting to be rude, Justine followed the friendly gathering into a beautifully appointed room. Rich colors of green and gold accented everything from the settees to the gas-burning, gold-plated sconces on each wall. Suddenly feeling out of place, Justine glanced around, wondering what proper etiquette was. She was, after all, just a girl from a modest home in a far-away country.

She backed up against a wall that held paintings probably worth more than her father's entire home and tried to assimilate everything around her. This opulence, this excess was what she had been missing her entire life. Justine Davidson needed this. And she vowed to herself right then and there that she would have it.

Garrett had watched Justine as she shoveled food into her mouth at the dinner table and now as she tried to blend into the green and gold wallpaper in the drawing room. Only when the coffee and lemon meringue pie made an appearance did her face light up. For such a small woman, she sure did pack in the food. On the other hand, he too had eaten his fill tonight. He should take it as a good sign she had her appetite back after this afternoon's episode.

He caught himself staring at her as he mused but tried to find somewhere else to look when she turned his way. Miss Barnes was settled into conversation with Mother while his father and uncle stood at the huge window talking business, to be sure.

Garrett made his way to where Mrs. Davidson stood and offered her the nearest settee. She perched herself on the edge and looked like she might bolt at any given moment. Perhaps the time had come to inform her of his news.

But Mrs. Davidson spoke first. "Mr. Cole, how is your wife? I must say I am surprised to find you still here with her in such a delicate state."

If the next invention he promoted was a flying machine, Garrett didn't think he could have been more surprised at her question. "My, my wife?" he sputtered, spilling a bit of coffee down the front of his clean dress shirt.

"Why, yes. I heard you mention to Mr. Waverly that she was due any day now." Mrs. Davidson's brows furrowed as she awaited his answer.

A light clicked on in his head and he chuckled loudly at the realization. The entire group turned toward the pair.

"Do let us in on the joke, Garrett," his father said.

"Mrs. Davidson thought Anica was my wife!" He hooted even more boisterously.

"Oh, dear," Mother said from where she stood talking with Carrie Anne. Looking around quickly at the group, Garrett realized no one else had found this humorous and he sobered immediately.

Mrs. Davidson's face was the last one he took in. Instead of seriousness, something akin to horror and embarrassment was written there.

"If you will excuse me, I thank you for the dinner." She fairly flung her dessert onto the nearest table and ran from the room, her brown skirt catching on her heel as she went.

☙❧

"Oh, Justine. It cannot be so bad." Carrie Anne patted Justine's shoulder as the two sat on the bed in the guest room they were to share.

"Carrie Anne, you heard him on the boat. He said he was looking forward to seeing Anica and the new baby. Not his wife, indeed. This faceless Anica is probably his mistress and that is why he found it so amusing." Justine buried her face in her hands and wished all of this would just go away. Instead of being at home in England with her father, she was in a strange land with people she didn't understand and who didn't understand her. If that weren't bad enough, she felt so inadequate when compared to her pristine surroundings. She would have to somehow repair her best skirt, which now had a huge tear in the hem brought about by her hasty escape. It made a dramatic contrast against the gorgeous coverlet on which she sat.

A soft knock on the door came and she thought it might be Mr. Cole coming to apologize. It was the least he could do after humiliating her in front of his parents and uncle.

But it wasn't the broad shoulders and honey-colored hair of the man who appeared in the doorway, but the petite form of his gracious mother. The woman's smile put Justine at ease immediately.

"Please excuse my son. He sometimes forgets how he was raised. I am sure he only found humor in the situation because Anica is my daughter, Garrett's sister. She and her husband are expecting their first child any day now. They will be coming to stay with us for a few months, beginning tomorrow. I only wish it were Garrett who had found a wife and had the blessing of family." Charlotte Cole said this last statement as she looked at Miss Barnes.

Justine felt an immediate jealousy. She supposed the two of them would make an adorable couple. It was just as well.

Justine wasn't sure what the future held, but one thing she knew with certainty: Mr. Cole was an enigma she didn't want to solve. Tomorrow morning, she would find the boarding house that Eric Waverly recommended and make a new way for herself. She would take control of her life, protect her father's money from plundering hands, and most of all, guard her heart against men like Garrett Cole.

Justine rolled to her side and found she had a perfect morning view out the bay window to the landscaped gardens beyond the house. They were alive with color and beckoned her to their sanctuary.

She washed her face quickly in the fresh water left in the basin, careful not to wake a still-sleeping Carrie Anne. As she slipped into her torn skirt, she noted her bleeding was much less today. But she wouldn't dwell on that. At the vanity, she gathered up her hair, trying to make it look like Charlotte Cole's from the night before. When she couldn't copy the effect no matter how hard she tried, she shook out her curls and tied them back with a simple ribbon. She didn't know how her poverty and lack of society upbringing could make her stand out any more. A quick glance at her work-worn hands gave her the answer.

Justine sighed just loud enough that Carrie Anne turned her way and rubbed the sleep from her eyes. "Justine?"

"Don't worry. You can keep sleeping. I'm just going to take a walk in the gardens. I'm feeling somewhat better. Maybe when I get back, we can depart for the boarding house."

Not wanting to overdo it, Justine made her way carefully down the steps, through a hallway and finally out a set of double doors and onto the grounds that led to the garden.

An ivy-adorned archway led the way down a path past fragrant cherry blossoms, bold and beautiful tulip beds, and dainty bluebells just opening their faces to the world. Justine made her way to a bench under a tree that promised to unfurl all of its leaves in time to provide shade on a sunny day.

She smiled to herself at the way she had babied the little flower box outside her old home in East Wharf. It certainly paled in comparison to this botanical masterpiece. She could spend hours here, and wished that were possible. But this was not her home, and she needed to make her way from this place today. It saddened her that she would have to forfeit getting to know Charlotte Cole in order to avoid a certain someone's presence.

Guilt niggled her heart at the judgmental thoughts she was having toward Garrett Cole. Could she have jumped to conclusions about him too soon? His parents were so loving and kind. They had made her feel more than welcome in their home. Justine supposed it was possible that meeting Garrett in England had been a coincidence. Her fingertips brushed the velvety petals of an azalea. It was possible that it was a fluke that Garrett had spoken with her husband right before he placed Jonathan in the cab, wasn't it? And that he was the one to pay for Justine's passage. And ask to take her bag more than once…Oh, she wanted to believe she could trust him.

A clearing of the throat drew her attention to the man of her thoughts. Thinking for sure he could read her mind, Justine turned her face away to study a daffodil as if it were the most interesting thing in the world.

"We need to talk," his deep voice announced. "Come. Walk with me."

Garrett braced himself for the forthcoming reprimand but found only coolness awaited him. Mrs. Davidson must certainly think him a cad for his behavior last night during dessert. He couldn't blame her if she chose not to speak to him, but speak to her, he must.

She rose slowly and fell into step beside him. "Last night, my laughter was inexcusable. I had nothing to gain by embarrassing you like that, and I deeply apologize. I am hoping this will make up for my boorish manners." He formed his lips into his most charming grin and pulled an envelope from his shirt pocket. He handed it to her with a flourish.

She gave him a suspicious glance and took it. "What is this?" Her look of mistrust was one he was coming to recognize.

"Just open it. I do believe you will find its contents most interesting."

They walked slowly as Mrs. Davidson broke the seal and unfolded the letter inside. He watched her eyes scan the page. Fear and frustration, along with another emotion he couldn't name, each made an appearance on her face.

"Is this why you followed me?" she asked in an accusatory tone as she stopped on the path.

Garrett was completely taken aback. Thankfulness, shock, astonishment, glee. These were things he expected. Why, the woman seemed almost angry!

"Mrs. Davidson, if you will look at the sum noted right there, you will see you are a fairly wealthy lady now."

"Wealthy? Is that your interest in me? First, you deal in secretive business with my husband. Then surely realizing I had just inherited money, you proceeded to follow me onto the boat. And you have finagled me into staying at your home. Now I see all along what your plan was. Well, I'll have you know, I will not be coerced into some sort of romantic liaison with you so you can get your hands on this too. I don't even know what this money is. Jonathan and I had next to nothing." Before she turned her back to him, he saw the pain etched on her face.

Deciding to take the gentle approach when everything in him screamed to fire back at her, he laid his hand on her shoulder. Big mistake. She turned and pierced him with those blue eyes of hers. They turned icy in an instant, a quality he found most intriguing. By heaven above, this woman enticed him. Although her misunderstandings ran deep, it made him want to rise to the challenge. Just for another chance to see her spunk, he decided to string her along a little bit more.

"This money was part of the business arrangement your husband and I had. There was nothing secretive about it. However, before I will feel comfortable giving it over to you completely, I feel I must make you more fully aware of the situation."

Mrs. Davidson looked at him with one chestnut eyebrow raised, as if by pure expression he would relinquish the information of the circumstances. Not so fast. A nice dinner over candlelight would be a much more delightful approach.

"I find my calendar quite full today and tomorrow, having just arrived back in Waterford Cove. But tomorrow evening I would ask the pleasure of your company, along with Miss Barnes, at Rue De Flores on Madison. You are sure to be charmed by such an elegant location. While the three of us partake of French cuisine, I will be able to answer all of your questions."

Before she could reply, he flashed a smile, hoping to disarm her defenses.

"I don't see that I have much choice in the matter," she said. "All right then. You may pick Miss Barnes and me up at The Dunsmore Inn tomorrow at seven o'clock." Mrs. Davidson tilted her beautiful chin into the air as she stated her last sentence. She would be furious to know she only made herself more desirable to him in doing so.

Garrett hid his triumph under a calm smile, tipped his hat, and made his way back to the house. As he did so, he walked by the large beech tree in the center of the garden. It always caught his eye when he took the time to come out back. There, engraved in the bark were the names of lovers coupled together for all time. JAMES + CHARLOTTE. BRET + ANICA. Then a single word. GARRETT. How lonely it looked all by itself. Perhaps one day, he would be able to etch someone else's name next to his own. As he walked toward the house, it surprised him to admit he hoped that someone would be Justine Davidson.

# SEVEN

As a maid scurried about the charming guest room packing up her and Carrie Anne's belongings, Justine glanced around one last time. There was something about this home that drew her. The lush surroundings made her humble home as a child and then as a wife look like pure poverty. She had never lacked for food, but this luxuriance was astounding.

Ducking back into the room after everyone had gone, Justine made quick work of locating the bag with her father's money inside and hastily wrapped it in an old blanket. She dug to put it on the very bottom of her trunk, somewhere where no prying eyes would look. She consoled herself with the knowledge that later today it would be safely tucked away at The Dunsmore Inn.

The cherrywood banister felt as smooth as glass under her hand as she made her way slowly down the stairs, not simply for the sake of her body, but for her mind as well. The figure Garrett had shown her in the garden early this morning could change everything for her.

She had slept more soundly last night than she had since the day of the accident. That, plus the refreshing breakfast and time with Carrie Anne had helped her keep her perspective about this so-called money from Mr. Cole.

And now, here was another chance to relax. This was the first time she'd had the privilege of sitting in the bright, rich parlor, but as she settled in with Mrs. Cole and Carrie Anne, she was glad to feel the room's calming effect on her bruised heart and the tea's strength-infusing qualities.

As she listened and responded to Charlotte's questions about Jonathan's death and life in England, Justine thought the older woman was the most gracious person she had ever met. She exuded a quiet confidence, leaving Justine with a longing to be filled up with the riches that Charlotte possessed in abundance. Joy. Faith. Love.

Justine's soul felt impoverished. Her husband's passing and the miscarriage aside, she knew the Lord's absence in her life was what had caused this rift in her spirit. There was no doubt in her mind that God was real; she had seen evidence of Him every day of her life. But everything she had learned about the Lord had come into question under the lens of her losses.

She cast a thoughtful glance at Charlotte's smart-looking shirtwaist and skirt. Justine wondered if the older woman would help her prepare for tomorrow evening's affair. Justine certainly had no flair for getting her hair just so or choosing the right outfit. She almost laughed out loud. She only owned a few ratty pieces of clothing. Yes, she certainly would need some help if she were going to arrive in style at the restaurant.

"Mr. Smythe has informed me the maids have finished packing your things. I will have your items safely delivered to the boarding house whenever you are ready," Mrs. Cole was saying. "Oh, don't worry, dears. I see that look in your eyes. I had Louis go over there this morning and see to it that a suite with two beds is ready and waiting for you." Charlotte seemed more like a young woman than a middle-aged mother with her cheerful banter. Her heart was so light, it seemed it could lift the spirits of anyone who was in the room with her.

"Thank you for that. Mrs. Cole, I also want to thank you for having Dr. Cole come and examine me yesterday. You must give me his address so I can offer him payment for his services."

"Don't be silly. Jeffrey is a member of the family, and I know he was happy to oblige. And please call me Charlotte."

Charlotte put her finger to her cheek and tapped the smooth skin thoughtfully. "You know, by way of saying thank you, perhaps you two would like to come one over one night and have dessert with the family and challenge him to a game of whist. He loves to play, but I am afraid everyone in the family knows his tricks, so he never wins. It would be a delight to see him have a new match."

Justine had never played cards in her life and felt the need to explain such. To her great surprise, Carrie Anne piped in.

"If Justine cannot play, I would be happy to," Carrie Anne said with her eyes on her hands. "I miss playing. It is how my parents and I passed many a winter's night."

Charlotte placed her hand on Carrie Anne's, and Justine could see again the woman's constant effort to make everyone feel at home. "I am sure he will be delighted. It's Thursday now. Instead of just coming for an evening, why don't the two of you join us for church service on Sunday and then come to stay for the afternoon?"

Justine was about to protest. Church? *I don't think so.*

But Carrie Anne piped up too quickly. "Thank you, Charlotte, for such a kind invitation. Can we bring anything to the affair?"

A Sunday morning service would be torture, Justine was sure. Trying her best to suppress a sigh, she mentally detached herself from the subject and looked out the window.

"Just your beautiful selves. Might I offer our driver's services to escort you ladies to your new home?" Charlotte peered at her guests while taking a delicate sip of the fragrant, spiced tea.

Justine thanked her then plunged ahead with the topic that was foremost on her mind. "Ma'am. I mean, Charlotte," she stumbled. Realizing she was probably making a fool of herself when she so wanted to impress this woman, she cleared her throat and tried again.

"Charlotte, this morning your son invited Miss Barnes and me to a dinner out tomorrow tonight to discuss some business. It seems he knew my husband and has some details to share with me."

"Oh, how wonderful! Where are you three headed?"

"Rue De…Um. I can't remember." Justine inwardly rolled her eyes. She really needed to learn how to carry herself when with those of high society. At the current moment, she knew she looked and sounded more like the hired help.

"Rue De Flores! Oh, how delightful!"

Still uncomfortable, Justine said, "I was wondering if you could tell me where I might find an appropriate dress for the evening. I am afraid I came to your fair country with meager belongings."

If it were possible, Charlotte's face lit up even more. "I have most of the day free. Why don't I take you and Carrie Anne shopping? Justine, are you up to going out and about? I promise not to make you walk very much at all. I just need to be back by dinner. That's when Anica and Bret will arrive. I don't know if you remember that I mentioned my daughter and her husband are going to be staying with us for a spell? But we have plenty of time. Why don't we grab a bite to eat first and then find you the perfect attire?"

Her excitement was contagious and soon all three women had Louis driving them to Charlotte's favorite boutique.

As they made their way to a street lined with fancy shops, Justine felt her unease with polite society evaporate like the morning dew on a warm spring day. And spring it was. All around her, Justine couldn't help notice the beauty of creation. She felt her heart clench at the thought of the wide canyon that stood between her and God. It seemed so vast, as if nothing in the world could bridge the gap.

Taking a deep breath, Justine decided to halt her vacillating thoughts and join the here and now. Nothing would be solved by brooding over difficulties that had no resolution.

Charlotte and Carrie Anne were giggling over the way a new hat wouldn't fit quite right over Charlotte's chignon. "I tell you, I try to keep up on the latest fashions, but even the most modern woman can't do it all," Charlotte said with a twinkle in her eye. "I'll just bet that my lady's maid can get this to work out better than I can."

Justine thought Charlotte's ensemble looked just fine without a hat, but Justine was wise enough to know that what a person wore was part of fitting into the upper class. It all seemed so enticing. To come into a room in the latest fashions, accompanied by people who were respected in the community sounded like a dream Justine wouldn't mind pursuing. Maybe tomorrow at the fancy restaurant she would get a taste of that kind of life. But just how did someone from the outside get inside the circle of such people?

"Forgive me, Justine. I got carried away with these accessories. We need to find you and Carrie Anne here something wonderful to wear."

"'Tis no worry, Charlotte. I was just looking at these dresses here. What do you think? I truly need your help in this matter. As you can see, my current style is sadly lacking."

"This one, although nice," Charlotte said, fingering the sleeve, "would be considered a simple day dress. I was thinking of something more along these lines." She led the way to the front of the store where wide windows overlooked the street. Beautifully adorned carriages rolled past while women who looked well-suited to Waterford Cove's upper crust sauntered into the bank across the street to handle their own financial affairs. Yes, this was the life Justine wanted.

Charlotte gestured to the dress on the mannequin in the window and Justine caught her breath. It had to be the most stunning gown she had ever laid eyes on. Clearly, she couldn't afford such a masterpiece, but maybe the storekeeper could suggest a less expensive version. Its green puffed sleeves were accented by the most delicate trim, while the waist was gathered high beneath a sweeping neckline. All that fabric glided to the floor in a flood of satin and ended in layer upon layer of lace overlay. Justine simply couldn't take her eyes from the beautiful creation.

Carrie Anne silently examined its intricacies while Charlotte went to retrieve the clothier. She returned with a round woman whose red hair was piled so high on her head, Justine thought for certain it would cause the woman to lose her balance at any moment.

"Mrs. Woods, my friend Mrs. Justine Davidson. She would like to try on the dress you have in the window."

Mrs. Woods swept her hawk-like gaze over Justine's clothing, her look more than doubtful. But Charlotte in her charm had Justine in a large dressing room within moments.

As the silky fabric slipped over her Justine's skin, she felt something inside of her come alive. The mirror in the small space captured every angle her hungry eyes wanted to see. Justine's mind compared her inheritance to the price of the dress. Nodding her head decisively, she knew this was it. The exciting beginning of her new and different life.

❧

The Dunsmore Inn was nothing like Justine had expected. The boarding house was a large Victorian that stood apart from the other homes on a side street about a mile or so from the wharf. Its sweeping front porch and two-story turret made it look more like the home of a successful businessman instead of a place where you could rent a room.

Justine tilted her head back in the late afternoon sunlight and thought perhaps this was just one more piece of good fortune in this new life she was making. Still dressed in her torn brown skirt, she couldn't wait to get settled in her room and change into one of the new outfits she'd bought this afternoon. Not only did Justine walk away with a dress for dinner out, she now had a day dress, a nice shirtwaist and matching skirt, and something suitable for church on Sunday.

Her purchases hadn't made as big of a dent in her funds as she had originally thought they might. Justine was sure Charlotte's relationship with the store's proprietress had something to do with that. Charlotte had also told the store owner to charge the items to her own personal account, saying Justine could exchange her money when it was convenient and pay Charlotte back.

Joy zinged in Justine's heart at the thought of wearing such beautiful pieces of clothing. The only thing lacking now was what to do with her hair. She had so much to learn.

Justine knocked on the door of the charming inn and the two friends were greeted by a middle-aged woman dressed to the nines. Her ample curves filled out a dress that was so festooned with lace and flounces, it looked impossible to sit down in. The woman's hair was streaked with gray, but was arranged in a fashionable sense. Jewels accented her neck and ears. Justine tried not to stare.

"Come in, come in," the woman crooned. "You must be Miss Barnes and Mrs. Davidson. I am Angelina Dunsmore, your new landlady. Welcome to the Dunsmore Inn."

Justine set down her packages and looked around the Queen Anne style home. Unlike the Cole's house, which although richly adorned, felt homey at the same time, the boarding house made Justine feel as though she should stand perfectly still so as to not disturb anything.

"I must say, you two certainly don't look like my typical boarders, but Eric Waverly stopped by to say you would be coming, and my oh my, isn't he just the most dashing young man? I'd do anything for him," Mrs. Dunsmore gushed. "He asked me to give you a discount and the man who brought your bags asked them to be put in my best room. But before we get you settled, might I ask if you two are employed?"

Justine cringed at the woman's implication that she and Carrie Anne didn't have enough money to stay in her prized home.

"I can assure you I can make payment for our room." Justine didn't want to admit she had yet to hear what the cost would be.

Carrie Anne cleared her throat self-consciously and said softly, "I, however, cannot promise the same. Having just arrived, I will need to find work and a more affordable place to live."

"What sort of employment do you seek, miss?" Mrs. Dunsmore scrutinized Carrie Anne with her sharp eyes, and Justine began to have pity on her friend until Carrie Anne looked up and confidently addressed Mrs. Dunsmore.

"I can clean and cook. Since you offer room and board, might you be in need of a hand in the kitchen or perhaps with the laundry?"

Justine couldn't help notice the note of hope in Carrie Anne's voice as she spoke. Justine found herself holding her breath, waiting for Mrs. Dunsmore's answer. It would be so wonderful if Carrie Anne could find employment here rather than somewhere far away. She needed her friend close by.

Mrs. Dunsmore held her nose high as she spoke, but it seemed the two friends would like her answer after all. "The room I've put you in has two beds. You may stay with Mrs. Davidson over the week's end.

Come Monday, I expect you to pay back your short stay with a day in the kitchen. If at that time you prove your worth, I may consider hiring you. But don't get your hopes up, young lady. We shall see what shows on Monday."

"Thank you, ma'am." Carrie Anne and Justine exchanged glances as the landlady in all of her skirts rustled up the polished staircase and led the girls to a second story room. When the door swung open, Justine realized with glee that the sitting room was in the turret she had seen from the street. The room also encompassed two generous beds, large wardrobes and gas lamps. It was tastefully decorated in pink, green, and white and even had an attached bath with a claw foot tub. She couldn't believe this was happening.

After Mrs. Dunsmore discussed the rent, which seemed acceptable, and the rules of the boarding house, which seemed reasonable, the woman took her leave. Justine immediately went to the middle of the room and spontaneously spun Carrie Anne in a circle.

"Can you believe our luck! Just look at this place. I never could have imagined it would be this opulent. Makes my place back in East Wharf look like a hole in the ground." Justine stopped short. "Why do you have that look on your face? Surely you can't object to all of this?"

"Come sit with me. I think we need to talk." Carrie Anne led the way to the turret where two chairs awaited them. She pulled her plain skirt around her slim frame and settled herself on the white, slip-covered chair. "As grateful as I am to have a place to lay my head, I feel quite uncertain about this situation. Justine, you know I don't have the money to stay here. Even if Mrs. Dunsmore extends employment to me, something about this doesn't feel quite right."

Justine took her friend's hand in her own. "Look at me, Carrie Anne. You're always saying God is looking out for us. Perhaps this is His way of providing for you after all you've been through. You know you deserve it."

"That's where you're wrong, Justine. I don't deserve anything." Carrie Anne withdrew her hand. "Everything I have is a gift from the Lord. Everything. He's the One I look to in good times and bad. 'For the

LORD thy God, he it is that doth go with thee; he will not fail thee, nor forsake thee.' Don't fool yourself, Justine. Look at all this around you. Look at our time with the Coles. These are things directly reflecting God's faithfulness to me." Carrie Anne paused and looked Justine straight in the eye. "And to you. They reflect the Lord's favor, but we can't claim the right to any of this."

Justine stood abruptly and clapped her hands. "Enough of that. We have ample time for each of us to take a bath before joining Mrs. Dunsmore for dinner."

Justine went to her packages and began to unwrap them from their tissue paper as she heard Carrie Anne's soft sigh behind her. Justine shook out a perfectly fitted shirtwaist and skirt and laid them next to her green gown.

"Tomorrow night, Mr. Cole will be by with his driver to pick us up at seven o'clock. You can help me put on this beautiful dress and we can even try our hand at doing each other's hair. What do you say?"

"All right. I'll look at these next four nights as a gift from the Lord. But I am not making any promises about what happens after Monday."

"It's a deal. I'll hang the dresses while you run a bath. Then after dinner we can talk about what we want to do tomorrow before we go to our first elegant meal among Virginian society!"

It was time to make his next move. Running a comb through his thick hair, the man stood in front of the full-length mirror, admiring his reflection. There wasn't a chance Justine Davidson would ignore him tonight. She had avoided him on board the *Blue Flag* till he feared he may look frenzied when he did manage to corner her. The handful of times he had been able to speak with the lovely widow didn't come close to the connection he had hoped to make.

But like the tide that brought them to Waterford Cove's shore, he would slowly draw her closer and closer. Beginning tonight.

# EIGHT

When Garrett pulled up in front of the charming boarding house, the lights from inside shone with a welcoming ambiance. He hoped Justine would find happiness there. He certainly didn't know everything about the beautiful young lady, but one thing was for sure—he was more than drawn to Justine Davidson.

No, make that two things he knew with more certainty than he'd had in a long time. After his father had told of the worsening situation with child labor in the factories of Waterford Cove, other than Justine's lovely face, he could think of little else. Every time he pictured little hands catching in a perilous machine, he felt a physical pain in his chest. Someone had to do something. And it started with the factory owners. But did he have enough influence, the right pull, to change anyone's mind? To many of the owners, it sadly boiled down to the bottom line. They didn't care who got hurt in the process.

Garrett drew up short at the front porch, one shiny, boot-clad foot on the first step. With his hand on the post, he paused to consider the pendulum of his thoughts. They were back on Justine.

"Justine." It was the first time he had spoken her first name out loud and it tasted sweet on his lips. Perhaps it was her recent losses that made him take notice of her. Or maybe it was the unique circumstances with her finances that intrigued him. Still, it could be her beguiling blue eyes that drew him in each time she spoke.

He knew all of that to be true and if he was honest with himself, he saw her as a potential mate. What a cad he was! The woman was not too long into her grieving and here he was mentally meeting her in front of a church wearing his best suit. Maybe his problem was that there were no promising prospects on the horizon. He would do well to get this business arrangement over with tonight and then focus his attentions elsewhere.

Taking the stairs two at a time, Garrett knocked on the door promptly at seven o'clock. Mrs. Dunsmore greeted him first, and as she peered up at him, her bird-tipped hat nearly slid off her head.

"Oh, Mr. Cole! How delighted I am to make your acquaintance again. I haven't seen you since the Mickelson wedding. Won't you come in?"

She gestured grandly with her portly hand as Garrett made his way into the entryway of the home. He should have known he couldn't avoid an encounter with the matron. Although considered on the outskirts of those with the best financial reputations, she nevertheless was part of that crowd. She had a distant uncle with a duke's title she laid claim to and thereby proceeded to invite herself into all manner of society's circles. It wasn't her lack of pedigree that bothered Garrett. The woman's high regard for herself made everyone else feel they were lacking after only a few moments in her presence.

"I was hoping you would have arrived just a bit sooner. Punctuality is the mark of a true gentleman. Wait here while I let my newest tenants know you're here."

Mrs. Dunsmore hiked up her heavy skirts and sashayed up the staircase at an alarming speed, probably eager to get back to him to hear the latest news on his sister. That was the other thing that ate at him about the landlady. Always sticking her nose in where it didn't belong. But, he supposed with a sigh, a new baby was always of interest to someone and that in itself didn't make a person a gossiper.

Choosing not to sit in the parlor while he waited, Garrett instead went to the window and gazed out at twilight beginning to descend on Waterford Cove. With as much traveling as he did, it was such a treat to be able to spend time with family and friends. Maybe that was another reason he was looking at Mrs. Davidson as more than an acquaintance. He spent so much of his life roaming about on business he never had time to meet his future bride, and even less time to court her.

Turning at the sound of rustling and whispers at the top of the steps, Garrett found himself gazing up at the most amazing sight. While Miss Barnes had traded her dark wool skirt for a simple cotton dress, Justine had donned the loveliest of gowns. Its deep green hue made her chestnut locks shine in the light while her fair skin looked as rare as porcelain.

Never could she say that she was simply a lonely widow woman from humble roots. Justine's inward light shone as she joined him. He was fooling himself to think he wanted to avoid this woman after their business was concluded.

"Allow me to escort you to the carriage," Garrett said as each lady took an arm, hoping to avoid the inquisitive Mrs. Dunsmore. Fate had seen better days.

"Why, Mr. Cole, you wouldn't dream of leaving before giving me news of your sister, would you?"

"Of course not, Mrs. Dunsmore. I can assure you Anica is doing fine and the baby will make its imminent arrival any day." Garrett guided the women to the door and called over his shoulder. "I'll tell her you asked after her. Have a pleasant evening."

Turning his attention to the ladies at his side, Garrett smiled down at each in turn. Best to give both women equal attention.

"Why, ladies, you look positively radiant this evening," Garrett complimented as they coursed down the street on their way to the restaurant.

The two women sat across from him, their attire setting them apart from the other. While Miss Barnes was clearly an attractive woman, Garrett found he could not stop looking at Justine. It was as if some magical transformation had occurred. Her hair was swept up in curls and loops, much different from the simple bow he normally saw her wear. Her lips seemed fuller, her eyes brighter and her cheeks a bit pinker. Graceful gloves went from the tips of her fingers to her elbows. No one at the restaurant would ever suspect where she came from or why she was there. Perhaps getting primped for the evening was helping to take her mind off her troubles.

Garrett hoped he could offer Justine a nice evening after all she had been through. *Even more,* he thought as Louis brought the carriage to a stop, *I can offer her financial security for some time to come. That is, if she'll get out of her own way long enough to hear what I have to say.*

Justine put a hand to her stomach as she followed the maître d to their reserved table at Rue De Flores. Seating herself beneath the candlelit chandelier, she squelched her fears and replaced them with forced confidence. If she was going to make a new life for herself, now was the time.

Carrie Anne, however, didn't appear fazed by their surroundings, even though her attire vastly differed from the rest of the patrons. Yet, her friend kept mostly quiet, most likely because she knew the evening's agenda.

Garrett Cole was another story entirely. He was still on his kick about the amenities of Waterford Cove. Justine only half listened.

Yesterday's early morning conversation ran through her mind, as did mental pictures of the figure he had showed her. Could it be true? It seemed such a large amount of money. Her late husband had been a simple man, though a hard worker. Was it possible he had managed to acquire this large of a sum without her knowledge? And if so, how did he get it? She hated to cast more distrust on Jonathan, but could he have come by it in an unseemly way? If it had been obtained illegally, she knew she wouldn't be able to accept the money.

So many questions. And the brown eyes of the handsome man across the table from her seemed to hold all the answers. Now it came down to a matter of trust. Wishing she could offer a prayer for guidance, Justine decided it was time to find out what was what. This thing between her and Mr. Cole needed to be sorted out. The sooner the better.

"Mr. Cole, you wished to meet with me this evening to discuss the business you had with my late husband. I must say I have lived in a state of perplexity at what you showed me."

Justine was forced to await his response as a waiter took their order.

While Garrett was placing his, Justine noticed people looking over at their table. Were they sizing her up or was it just her imagination? After choosing a three-course meal, Justine turned her attention to Garrett's response to her inquiry.

"Jonathan made a very wise investment and the number I showed you is the dividend that is being returned."

"Wise, you say? He never once told me of these *investments* you speak of. He was a simple worker on the *CCS Blackstock*. What could he possibly have invested in? And with what money?" Justine fiddled with her linen napkin. "We didn't have anything extra set aside." Justine knew she sounded exasperated and tried to keep her voice low. The answer to this mystery seemed just out of her grasp and yet she was afraid to hear any more.

"Judging by your response, I assume you knew nothing of Jonathan's business dealings. I can see now what a shock it must be to know your husband was doing something you were not aware of." Garrett looked thoughtful. "He had a good head for business. I was looking forward to what we would work together on next."

"How well did you know him?" Carrie Anne spoke another question Justine wasn't sure she wanted the answer to.

"I first met Jonathan several years before his death."

At Justine's bewildered look, he went on.

"You see, I am the mediator between those in our world who dare to dream and create the latest inventions and those who want to proliferate their funds." He shrugged as if his was a common job. "I travel abroad to join the two together. If an investor, such as your husband, lays money on the line for a specific invention, and that invention in its completed stage is sold, the royalties and cash profits from such a sale are passed back to the original investors in the form of interest."

Garrett's voice continued, though it sounded a long way off. "I had traveled to East Wharf to give Jonathan his share of a most successful invention he had put his money on almost two years before, although he was involved in many others that were profitable as well. I only wish I could have given him the money face to face." He took a long drink of water. "But being a fair businessman, I felt it only right to offer you, his widow, the royalties and interest his investment has earned."

The room had gone perfectly still around Justine. She no longer heard the din of the dining room, and Carrie Anne's hand on her gloved arm felt miles away. The world narrowed itself into one single thought: Jonathan had deceived her. Had hidden from her who he really was. Had never truly let her know him.

Never once had he mentioned being an investor. Never had she seen the financial fruit of his "business dealings." Even if she could somehow wrap all of this with a nice tidy bow, there was the woman she had seen him with. What else would be revealed about Jonathan? She didn't want to know. The simple truth was her husband had lied to her, most likely repeatedly. What a fool she had been.

Justine picked up her spoon and slowly stirred the soup that had been set before her. Her husband's duplicity marched through her mind in a series of images. The day she had met him shortly after her father died. Jonathan's hand in hers as he led her over the threshold on their wedding night. Time after time as she stood looking down the street when he didn't come home as promised.

A large hand covered hers and she set down the spoon. She looked up into the caring face of Garrett Cole. Dare she trust that this man had told her the truth? She had two choices. Either accept what he said and take the money or deny her husband's betrayal and refuse the money altogether. At that very moment, she didn't want to do either. But her sensible side broke through.

Taking her hand back from the man before her, Justine smiled shakily at him. "Mr. Cole, I thank you for tracking me down in order to bring me this information. You have been most honorable in your quest and you are to be commended for that. Please understand my shock and anger at this situation. Never was I aware these transactions were happening and I—" Justine broke off.

"We understand, Justine," Carrie Anne said, glancing at Mr. Cole. "You must feel you didn't know your husband at all."

"I need a moment to process this privately. Do excuse me." Justine made herself take slow steps from the room and found solace on the deck overlooking the pier. Ships dotted the murky water, deep and dark as her heart.

She had thought her father's death would have broken her. But then she had met Jonathan and believed their love would see her through.

Anyone would have assumed Jonathan's death and her subsequent miscarriage would have been the end of her, but again, Justine had found a way to press on. She had boarded the ship to America and had been brave through it all. But this, this news was the greatest shock of all. To have trusted someone with everything only to learn they hadn't reciprocated. If she and Jonathan had been as close as she had hoped they would be, he never would have kept this from her. It made their whole marriage seem a farce, and she wanted to run down the street and keep running until she could get away from these awful feelings.

To compound the problem, she felt God had deceived her too. He made Himself out to be a faithful God, but to look at the turn of events her life had taken made it clear to Justine that He was not who He said He was either.

It was one thing to marry an almost stranger for the sake of security. But to think I was in love with a man who was really a liar and an imposter…That had another effect all together. It was a blow to learn her husband was as unfaithful as the God she used to serve. She wished she had never met either of them.

A warm hand at her elbow caused her to come crashing back to reality. Justine turned, expecting to find Garrett, but instead looked up into familiar green eyes. The eyes of Eric Waverly. He looked especially handsome tonight, his crisp white shirt sharply contrasting with his black hair and smooth tanned skin.

"Mr. Waverly," Justine greeted him. "What a surprise to see you here." What was it about this stranger's touch that made her feel like she was in a trance?

He kept his hand on her arm while he spoke. "Waterford Cove might be a growing city, but it's still easy to find who you are looking for."

"You were looking for me?" Justine suddenly felt uncomfortable.

"I saw Mrs. Dunsmore earlier today, and she told me of your plans tonight. Remember, I told you I'd check on you to see how you're getting settled. Wouldn't want a lady in need to be in want of something I could provide."

Justine looked through the French doors to the candlelight within. Was she safe out here with this man? He certainly had the most handsome face she'd ever seen. Eric Waverly was of those men women noticed, the kind of man with a certain presence to him. She was certain he could have any woman he wanted, yet he was there because he cared about her. She was struck by the thought.

Justine managed to reply, "You certainly didn't need to come and find me, although I do thank you."

"Forgive my rudeness for interrupting your evening with your friends. I couldn't rest until I saw for myself that you were being cared for with the highest regard. Please know I am always at your service." He said this with a little half bow. "Won't you sit down?" he said as he pointed at a table for two on the porch. "You do know, don't you, that you have the most enticing accent? But when we met on the *Blue Flag*, I never got to hear exactly where you are from."

Looking out over the pier, Justine somehow found herself telling this man of the recent loss of her husband and father. He really was quite easy to talk to.

The french doors leading to the restaurant suddenly flung open as Garrett burst through. Justine stood up at the sight of him.

"Mr. Cole. I was just going to come back inside." Justine felt the need to explain herself.

Garrett nodded to her then turned to her companion. "Waverly. What are you doing here?" he asked coolly.

"Never been better, Cole. Thanks for asking," Eric said sarcastically. "This nice young lady and I were just having ourselves a pleasant chat out here in the breeze. Won't you join us?" Eric's compassionate kindness toward Justine had turned seethingly cold to her dinner escort.

"No, thank you. If you will excuse us, we shall resume our evening." Garrett began to take Justine's arm and turn her toward the dining room. She felt bad leaving Mr. Waverly, but by the way she was being propelled toward the door, it didn't look as if she had much choice.

What would a well-to-do woman with a prestigious reputation do in this situation? Remembering her beautiful gown caused Justine to feel more the part she was playing, so she politely looked over her shoulder and dipped her head in acknowledgment. Hopefully that would suffice. But if she ever saw Eric Waverly again, she would be sure to thank him properly for his solicitousness.

The warm, spring air blew softly against Garrett's face as Louis steered them through Waterford Cove's quaint streets. Normally Garrett would have stopped to marvel in the sights and scents of the new season, but Justine's crestfallen face led him to make haste getting the ladies back to the inn.

"Mrs. Davidson?" Garrett broached the silence. "Please understand that when Jonathan made his investment with me, he was not yet married to you. I had no idea of your lack of knowledge of such dealings. Jonathan was always so excited about the latest invention I was seeking backers for. He did choose wisely, however, and as you can see, it paid off."

Justine clasped her hands before her and he could see they were shaking.

"I have half a mind to be mad at you, Mr. Cole. But I'm going to choose to take you at your word." Her voice was small as she spoke, but Garrett took heart that at least she believed him about the money.

The paltry explanation he'd offered in light of the betrayal she felt didn't feel like enough of an effort to Garrett. He needed to do something more.

"Mrs. Davidson, would you do me the honor of allowing me to escort you and Miss Barnes on a tour of the town? Say, after breakfast tomorrow?" Garrett saw Justine hesitate, so he rushed on. "I deeply apologize for any part I may have played in this entire scenario. I want to try to make it up to you. What do you think?" He held his breath, waiting for her response.

Justine looked at Miss Barnes, who gave a slight nod, and he knew he wasn't going to get one wink of sleep all night.

# NINE

Why, oh why, did we agree to go with that man today?" Justine was more than flustered as she pulled her new day dress from the wardrobe.

"Here, let me help you put that on." Carrie Anne made a fuss over getting Justine into the gauzy material and buttoning it up. "If I remember correctly, more than once you've asked me *why*. Could it be you think I am wise, my friend?"

Justine could see from the twinkle in Carrie Anne's eye that she was teasing. Yes, this was the second time she had asked Carrie Anne the answer to a difficult question. The first had been on the ship in their cabin. Other questions of why still remained unspoken. Why had God allowed all these bad things to happen to her? Why did it feel as though He had deserted her? She shook her head and knew that even now she was no closer to an answer.

Putting on a light air, Justine laughed at her friend's banter. "Yes, as a matter of fact, I do, O Wise One. But this time, I suppose the question is not quite as serious." Justine paused before the mirror and inspected her new dress. It was unlike anything she had ever owned. Her bleeding was subsiding and she noted the dress's pale yellow accented the color she was beginning to get back to her cheeks. "Although, Mr. Cole could be a threat I am not perceiving. He's too handsome for his own good and the circumstances under which we met seem too coincidental."

"Sit and let me do your hair." Carrie Anne was proving herself quite capable with pins and ribbons. "Let's put it in a simple bun and allow some curls to frame your face. As for Mr. Cole, he's quite the gentleman. And I will be with you so you have no fear of being alone with him. If he proves himself less than trustworthy, why we'll just find ourselves another tour guide," she said with a smile on her lips.

Justine was grateful for Carrie Anne's light humor this morning. It let her rest from the carousel of thoughts that whirled round and round without end. Yet as soon as she remembered they were off of her mind, there they were again. Foremost this morning was her anger at Jonathan, anger she knew would never be resolved. It wasn't as if she would ever hear from his own lips why he had betrayed her. And what of the other investments Garrett had mentioned? What had Jonathan done with all that money? Had he spent it on women and other worldly passions?

"We'd better get downstairs," Carrie Anne said. The near-summer air beckoned through their open window but Justine and Carrie Anne each grabbed a light shawl, just in case Mr. Cole planned on taking them near the water.

Garrett pulled up to the Dunsmore Inn just as they were coming down the porch steps. "Good morning, ladies. And what a pleasant day to be taking a ride. Do make yourselves comfortable."

Justine noticed he had taken the liberty to have fresh blankets put in the carriage in case they got chilly. She also spied a picnic basket which made her curious as to where they might be headed.

As Louis started the horses, two small children caught Justine's eye. Dilapidated clothing hung on their skinny frames as they scurried around the side of the house. They couldn't be more than seven or eight years old. The carriage moved down the road and Justine turned her head and watched until the two disappeared out of sight behind the inn.

Garrett wished at this precise moment he could read Justine's mind. As she watched the two street urchins, her face showed compassion mixed with something he couldn't quite name. Repulsion? Pity? Longing?

"You might be interested to know, Waterford Cove is home to many a homeless child. Parentless children who are forced to steal or work in a factory if they have any hope of getting a scrap to eat."

"Surely there is some place they can go?" Carrie Anne put in.

"There is a small mission my mother has in mind to organize, but it will only be able to feed so many. There is no permanent home for these children. The nearest orphanage is a good thirty miles away. And even if a child could make the trip, they would most likely be turned away." Garrett had often wondered at the plight of the less fortunate and how he fit into the big picture. Didn't Christ say that true religion started with helping the widow and the orphan? And that what you did to the least of these, you did to Christ Himself?

Garrett felt a twinge of something stir in his heart, something that had been there a long time. It was a feeling he got every time he took a moment to be quiet and really think about what God wanted from his life. Deep down, Garrett knew he had been living for himself. Going after what felt good in the moment. A choice transaction. A fulfilling disbursement. Chasing after what he wanted, not what God wanted.

But as he looked at Mrs. Davidson across the carriage, he knew he'd doubtless glean more compensation from one of her smiles than from any one of his career successes. There was joy in helping her overcome her grief. And maybe that was exactly where he needed to start. Helping those around him. He smiled to himself thinking what Mother would say. She would be proud.

He caught Justine's eye and noticed her intense stare. He hoped she didn't think he was smiling at the plight of the poor.

"You say these children work in factories, Mr. Cole? There must be some sort of law that governs against such a thing. An age eligibility?"

"One could only hope. Right now, the factory owners will usually take whoever they can get for a cheap wage. Most don't rightly care who works or who gets hurt on the machinery; they just want to see a profit. It's sad, but true."

"Truly, I thought America was a place where people could make their own way, be who they wanted to be without tyrants ruling their every move. A place where people were treated with fairness. A land with laws that benefited everyone. Even children."

Again, Garrett felt unmistakable guilt press upon him. The unavoidable reality was that he was liable for contributing to these heinous circumstances. Some of the machinery was, after all, due to the financial connections he had made between inventors and investors. Without the investors' money, the machines would not be here today. To make it worse, Garrett was living off of his own portion of the successes.

"Where are these factories located, Mr. Cole?" Carrie Anne asked.

"I was going to take you ladies down to a shopping sector on the south end of town, but if you're interested, we can take detour and head north to the industrial district first. We both have an acquaintance who owns one of the factories."

"Who? I've only met a handful of people in Waterford Cove."

"Why, Mr. Waverly. Didn't he tell you what he did for a living?"

At the mention of the dark-haired man, Justine instantly turned a bright pink. Garrett hoped that didn't mean she had taken an interest in Eric. Though she still must be grieving her loss, Garrett wondered what might become of his and Justine's relationship over time. Blast! There he went again, jumping ahead without thought to the consequences. He needed to learn that when God put the right woman in front of him, his heart would know.

"Yes, I see. Mr. Waverly. He was such a gentleman last night. It is hard for me to believe he owns a factory where children could be hired and possibly injured."

Garrett could see how Justine would think that. He had seen more than one young woman fall under Eric's green-eyed spell. Lord, don't let Justine be one of them.

"I cannot say if he does, in fact, employ children, but since I do see him on occasion, I will be sure to inquire."

They passed along through a few average-looking neighborhoods, but the further north and east they traveled, the smaller the houses became and more and more bedraggled-looking people populated side streets and front steps.

When the smoke from the factories was just ahead, the atmosphere seemed to change yet again. Houses turned to shacks and people shouted at each other over the top of their carriage. Garrett hadn't been up here in ages, and he was most appalled by the stench and poverty.

He glanced at the two women to gauge their reactions. Carrie Anne sat looking out the window, her lips moving in what seemed to be silent prayer and Justine's eyes had gone wide.

"This isn't exactly what I had planned to show the two of you today. But all the same, I am glad we came. It certainly gives me a new perspective on not only my life, but these people's lives as well. I wish I knew how to help them." On impulse, Garrett told Louis to stop in front of Eric's factory. Garrett jumped down from the carriage and made his way over to a dirty young woman with a baby on her hip.

"Miss, is there any way I can make your day better?"

If God was calling him to help, why not start now?

Justine sat in awe, watching the exchange between Garrett and the young woman. Her clear, bright eyes stood out in contrast to her soiled hair and face. The babe on her hip cried softly into her shoulder while Garrett talked to them. She saw Garrett pull some coins from his pocket and hand them to the woman. The woman's eyes grew round and she smiled, revealing several missing teeth.

Justine immediately felt disconcerted. As she looked into the face of the young woman, she knew that could very well have been her. If she had become a single mother who worked at the laundry, she knew she wouldn't have been even able to afford her old flat. Where would she be right now if Jonathan and her father hadn't left her some money to live on? She would have eventually had to pay rent and try and make ends meet while taking care of an infant. But what if she couldn't physically do the work? What if she had gotten sick and couldn't work at all? Is that what happened to this woman? Did it all just turn upside-down for her one day?

Justine couldn't help but think that maybe God had been watching out for her after all. Even so, she still wrestled with the thought that if He hadn't taken away her family in the first place, He wouldn't have had to help her. She had been doing just fine and did not appreciate His intervention. In fact, she was very angry at Him for it.

She turned her attention back to Garrett. *Is there any way I can make your day better?* What a way to bless someone! Justine admired the man for his compassion. This wasn't exactly a nice part of town. Yet there he was in his fine trousers and pressed shirt offering money to a stranger. Yes, there was more to Garrett Cole than met the eye.

"Waverly!" Justine heard a voice call. She peered through the carriage window and saw that Garrett had spotted Eric exiting his factory.

"I wondered if I might see you here today. What might this spring day for hold for you?" Garrett motioned for the two women to come and join them.

Eric seemed surprised to see them step down. After last night at the restaurant, Justine had not expected to see Mr. Waverly again so soon. He stood there in a fine suit of dark gray, his black hair neatly combed into a fashionable style. Eric certainly was a handsome gentleman, but his attire seemed out of place in this workmen's district.

"Mrs. Davidson, how good to see you again," Eric said as he grasped Justine's hand in his own.

"Mr. Waverly, how do you do? Thank you again for your concern last evening. You remember Miss Carrie Anne Barnes? We were together aboard the *Blue Flag.*" Justine motioned to Garrett. "And Mr. Cole was just saying this factory belongs to you. Pray tell, what do you manufacture?"

Eric gestured grandly toward the large building behind them. Smoke billowed out into the clear blue sky, clouding an otherwise beautiful day. "This, my dear, is where the sewing machines are made that produce your gorgeous gowns. We import the finest materials to make the machines, then transport them all around the world. Without my factory, you would be stuck sewing by hand every night."

He said the last with a laugh that didn't sound quite right to Justine's ears. Nonetheless, she could easily ascertain the pride he felt as a businessman.

"Eric, I was hoping to talk to you about a new invention I heard about yesterday. I thought of you, since it involves textiles. Would you care to meet this week to discuss it?" Garrett looked to the other man with expectancy.

Eric turned to face Garrett squarely, fire shooting from his eyes. "Cole, when you took that deal away from me, I swore to you I would never work with you again, and my answer hasn't changed."

As Justine watched the exchange, she felt an intense dislike for Garrett coming from Eric and she involuntarily took a step backward. What had happened in the past between the men? It really wasn't her business to know, but her curiosity was certainly piqued.

"Mrs. Davidson," Eric addressed her, calm and confident again. "I received an invitation to a lovely charity ball soon. This coming Friday, to be exact. I wondered if you would do me the honor of accompanying me?" He quirked his eyebrow and put on what was surely his most charming smile, obviously hoping Justine would accept.

At first, Justine was caught off guard. But what could she say at the proposal of an evening among Virginia's most prominent citizens? And it was for a charity. Feeling Garrett's gaze bore into her, Justine chose to ignore his stare and accepted Eric's offer with a dainty bow. With that, the date was set. And, as she noticed, so was Garrett's jaw.

Unbelievable. Eric Waverly was just doing this to goad Garrett. Eric knew all too well how to get under his skin, and he was helpless to do anything about it. Well, maybe not completely helpless. He had Justine with him today, and despite her pending date with Waverly, Garrett would make the most of their time together. He wanted to fault Justine for her poor judgment in companionship, but he knew all too well Eric's dispensation for charming the ladies. Garrett would have to gently warn her.

With that unpleasant conversation now behind them, Louis steered the horses southward, parallel to the shoreline, and into a lovely shopping district. The tall gas lights and cobblestone streets gave the area a European flair. To Garrett's delight, Justine sighed in pleasure as she stared at the passing sights and sounds that made this area so unique. He hoped being there might quench some of the girls' homesickness.

First, Louis stopped in front of a quaint curiosity shop. Justine and Miss Barnes quickly asked to go inside. Garrett followed at a distance, then leaned one shoulder against the doorframe and watched the proprietor show off his most unusual pieces.

"This one here is quite special," Mr. Dandurand was saying. Garrett knew the man well. When Garrett was a boy, he had often accompanied his mother on shopping trips. He remembered pestering her until she gave in and let him explore Bijoux d'Artisan while she shopped nearby. Mr. Dandurand was a genius with jewelry and trinkets, forever hiding some secret within their intricacies.

"Open it up and see what you see," Mr. Dandurand prompted Justine.

Garrett felt a sense of satisfaction as he watched Justine exclaim over the unique necklace. He walked over to see it more closely. At the end of a long gold chain hung the shape of a fawn with its legs folded underneath it. On the neck of any woman, it would be a striking piece, but Justine had found its almost invisible hinges and opened it reverently.

"It's a locket!"

"The idea for this came to me one night when my *épouse* and I were reading from Psalms. *Nombre quarante-deux.* Number forty-two."

"'As the deer panteth after the water brooks, so panteth my soul after thee, O God,'" Justine whispered. Garrett peeked over Justine's shoulder to see the work of art. Sure enough, on the back, engraved in rolling script, were the words *Psalm 42:1.*

Carrie Anne wrapped an arm around Justine and gave her a squeeze. Justine handed the piece to the proprietor. The girls moved to inspect other items underneath the glass as Mr. Dandurand put the necklace away.

Soon they made their way across the street to a shop whose window display held a beautiful wedding gown. Not for the first time did

Garrett wonder what it would be like to be married one day. Did the Lord even have that for him? His mother was constantly trying to play matchmaker to find him a good mate. The problem was, they were just "good." He wanted great. Was Justine that "great" he searched for? Probably not. Garrett had learned from past relationships that when he thought something was a good idea, it usually wasn't.

Carrie Anne and Justine headed inside the shop and he followed close behind. This was one of those stores where a man could lose a month's pay without even blinking. He hoped Justine was a frugal one. At the moment, she and Miss Barnes were exclaiming over a pink get-up with too much lace for anyone's good.

"Just look at the neckline, Carrie Anne." Justine's breathless tone told Garrett she was head-over-heels for the gown. Maybe he should step in before she did something she would regret.

"Ladies, it's just about lunch time, and I thought we would walk around the corner to a nice little park. What do you say?" He quickly opened the door for them and gestured outside.

Louis was waiting close by, so Garrett grabbed the picnic supplies and the three walked to the park. They settled on a blanket under a canopy of white apple blossoms. The scent was heavenly.

"Can you believe I already have an invitation to a ball?" Justine said as she laid out the sandwiches. Garrett hoped she was talking to Carrie Anne because he knew his reply wouldn't be what she wanted to hear. "What will I wear?" she went on.

"I should think with the inheritance from your father, you could buy something special for the event," Carrie Anne said.

Garrett saw Justine give her friend a quelling look before prattling on about her upcoming date. Garrett tuned her out, instead focusing on Carrie Anne's comment. So, Justine had come into some money from her late father. That filled in some of the gaps he had about this lady.

But wasn't her type the kind he was always trying to get away from? And here he had thought differently of Justine Davidson. But no. She was all show on outside with nothing substantial inside, thinking only of how to spend her money and wondering what her gown would look like. She cared about who would be there and what they would think of her. Yes, this was the reason he wasn't married yet. This is how they all were. How very disappointing.

On the other hand, perhaps she was just caught up in the novelty of this new world. After all, he had seen her home back in England. A straw mattress, a one-room flat. This was her moment to live the life she'd never had. That must be the case. He should be willing to believe the best.

He was even amenable to giving Eric Waverly another shot at partnership. But it seemed Eric still held a grudge over that lost investment years before. It was clear the man held nothing but contempt for Garrett.

He pictured Justine and Eric together at the ball, merrily waltzing across the room in one another's arms. Garrett wasn't sure if it was that particular thought or something that had to do with Eric's refusal to do business with him, but he was confident of one thing: Garrett Cole would make certain he was in attendance at that ball.

# TEN

Packed back into the snug carriage, Justine was grateful they didn't need to pass the factories as they made their way toward the inn.

As Louis expertly maneuvered the horses, Justine's thoughts wandered into territory she knew wasn't neutral ground. Even though it was uncomfortable, she couldn't deny the tugging on her heart when she thought of those less fortunate than her. Is that what it truly was? Just fortune, everyone playing their hand at life, some getting lucky, others drawing a card that forced them to live a life of poverty?

With her father's inheritance and her recent knowledge of Jonathan's extracurricular endeavors, Justine found herself on the other side of the poverty coin. While in England, making their market budget stretch through the week had at times proven difficult. Now here she was in a beautiful carriage, escorted by a man of influence, and shopping for gowns that made her heart thump with pleasure.

She knew she should be grateful for the turn of financial events, but it did feel sometimes as though the money had been handed to her in trade for her father's and husband's lives. She shook her head, refusing to let tears well up in her eyes at the irony of it all. God certainly had no favorites, just as the Bible said.

Another carriage pulled up beside theirs, much to close for comfort. Justine recognized Mr. Smythe, the Cole's butler, poking his head out the window. He motioned for Louis to pull over.

"Smythe, whatever is the matter?" Garrett addressed the man.

"Anica. The baby comes and she wants you to be there. We don't have much time; come quickly."

Anica was having her baby at the Cole home? That's right. Justine remembered Charlotte saying Anica and her husband, Bret, were to arrive the same afternoon Justine and Carrie Anne had settled into the Dunsmore Inn. It seemed an odd thing to do, but perhaps Anica felt more comfortable with her mother nearby while she awaited the arrival of the baby. But why would she want her brother there? Justine had never had a sibling; maybe this was more normal than it felt.

"Ladies, would you mind terribly if I didn't take the time to drop you off at the inn? It is out of the way by quite a bit. I'd like to be there to greet my new niece or nephew. I know a shortcut from here that will get us there quickly." Garrett seemed quite excited about the prospect of becoming an uncle. Justine could hardly refuse his request just because she was ready to put her feet up for a moment.

"Of course, Mr. Cole. Do whatever works best for you."

Soon they were stopping in front of the Cole mansion. Garrett's mother stood framed in the doorway. Her face was aglow with joy and suddenly it hit Justine what would soon take place. What would never take place for her. She couldn't walk inside where the joys of new life would suffocate her. She would have to look at the newborn, probably be asked to hold him, and all the while, hear how wonderful it was to have a new addition to the family.

"Carrie Anne, you go on ahead. I'll catch up to you in a bit," Justine said quietly and escaped quickly around the back of the house.

∞⟨⟩∞

"Miss Barnes, please make yourself at home. I'm going upstairs to check on my sister." Garrett began to exit the carriage, but noticed Carrie Anne seemed to have something to say. Since she was a woman of few words, he decided it must be important.

94

ROOTS REAWAKENED

She cleared her throat. "I was wondering," she said in a soft voice, "if I might accompany you. You see, back in Bristol, my family was good friends with a midwife. I helped in many a delivery. It would be a joy to assist the doctor."

This little mite had the stomach for such a thing? He wouldn't deny her request, although he doubted her ability. Despite the fact that her strawberry-blonde hair and green eyes were quite becoming, her shy demeanor often caused her to be overlooked. He would have to make more of an effort in the future to include her in conversation.

"By all means, please come inside. You remember my uncle from when you were here last?" At his question, Miss Barnes' face turned pink.

"Yes," she squeaked out.

"Well, come along then, I am sure he's inside. You two can get better acquainted."

Garrett led the way up the steps to the grand double doors of the home and gave his mother a quick squeeze before ushering her and Miss Barnes into the foyer and closing the door behind them all. Today he would become an uncle. He was happy for Anica and her husband, certainly, but part of him longed for it to be his own child being born. Would he ever see that day? At this stage in life, he was beginning to doubt it. But then again, if God wanted him to have a family, He would supply a wife. Garrett just needed to be content in his current circumstance. Just how long he could remain satisfied had yet to be determined.

The doctor was just coming down the stairs when the group walked in. Jeffrey's eyes lit with delight when he spotted Miss Barnes. Perhaps there were some unspoken sparks between the two. Garrett felt his gut twist in jealousy and had to force away the feeling before shaking Jeffrey's hand. It seemed everyone around him was moving on with their lives while his stood perfectly still. "How is she, Jeffrey?"

"Anica's doing quite well. Didn't want her uncle hovering over her every minute. But I suspect she'll deliver within the hour. She'll be glad to know Mr. Smythe found you." Jeffrey turned to Carrie Anne. "But I didn't expect to have the pleasure of your company as well."

Amazingly enough, Miss Barnes didn't turn fourteen shades of purple when she accepted his uncle's chaste kiss to her hand. Women. What a mystery.

Carrie Anne began to speak to Jeffrey of her midwife experience so Garrett left the twosome to chat and went to find his mother, who had settled in the parlor.

"Mother." Garrett accepted her into a warm embrace. Her hair, normally perfectly coiffed, had sprung a few leaks. Even so, she was beautiful, her heart making her outward appearance shine. "Where's Bret?"

Charlotte Cole gave her son a bright smile that matched the yellow décor of the room. "Oh, you know your brother-in-law. He wouldn't be anywhere but his wife's side during a time like this. She is near the end, too, and soon I will be a grandmother. Oh, I remember the day I became a mother. You came in such a flurry. You always were ready to take on the world. And now the next generation has begun." His mother rubbed her hands over the goosebumps accumulating on her arms. "I wonder if it'll be a boy or girl?"

They were good things to reflect upon, but Garrett's mind was divided. Where was Justine? Why hadn't she joined them in the house? Should he chase after her or check on Anica? Better to stick to the task at hand. And he wouldn't mind seeing his sister, although he would have to make it brief in the birthing room. After all, he knew his tendency to get queasy at the sight of a prick of blood.

"Would you like to come with me, Mother? I'd like to give my love to Anica." Together they went up the stairs to a lovely guest room at the end of the hall.

"Knock, knock!" Garrett opened the door a crack and caught a good view of Anica's strained face. Her blonde locks stuck to her face as she perspired profusely. He was so used to seeing her composed, it was difficult to see her in pain.

Opening the door all the way, he could see maids bustling about with linens and water, and noticed that Jeffrey and Miss Barnes had made their way to the room before him. They were collaborating at the foot of the bed.

"Garrett," Bret looked especially relieved to see him.

"Garrett! Come pray with me," came Anica's breathless request.

Okay, he could do this. *Just don't think about the blood.* His sister needed him to be strong right now. Garrett made his way to her bedside and held her damp hand.

"You're doing great, sis. Just hang in there. Bret, would you like to join us in prayer?" Bret came over, as did Jeffrey and Miss Barnes. Together they bowed their heads and asked the Father's blessing on the labor and the new life.

Garrett gave Anica a quick kiss on the forehead with a promise to be nearby to congratulate her when the baby arrived. "And if you need anything, just ask. I'll do whatever I can."

He and his mother bid Anica farewell, and Garrett softly shut the door to the birthing room. Miss Barnes seemed to be in her element, and Garrett hadn't seen that look on Jeffrey's face since they were teenagers.

Sighing, Garrett descended the stairs with something else on his mind than the budding romance between his uncle and Carrie Anne. He needed to find Justine and somehow knew just where to look.

*How could I be so stupid?* Justine had thought making the journey to America and leaving her past behind would make everything all right. But it hadn't. She still mourned the loss of her father. She still felt estranged from God. She still couldn't believe she had been pregnant in the first place then left alone to deal with the loss of her unborn baby. No, this whole idea had been harebrained from the beginning. Maybe she should go to England, back to what was familiar. No, that wouldn't solve anything either. She felt trapped by her feelings, and she wanted out.

Justine navigated the pathway through the gardens at the Cole home. She slowed her gait and tried to drink in the peaceful surroundings. Fountains trickled their music while fruit trees displayed their spring splendor. Ivy covered walls and trimmed hedges surrounded the vast outdoor masterpiece, encompassing her in a peaceful embrace.

Yes, peace, that's what I need. But where to find it? A nearby bench beckoned her to sit. From this west end of the garden, she couldn't see the house or any of the servants roaming about. She felt secluded and her heart somehow needed that. On the verge of tears but refusing to give in to them, Justine began to whisper her anger toward God. It was time to tell Him what she thought of His plans.

Justine knew she wasn't quite ready to call Him Lord again, but she figured addressing Him as God would do. "God, where do I even begin? I feel so betrayed by You. You and Jonathan. You could have spared my family's lives, but you didn't. Jonathan could have been forthright with me, but he chose to do things in secret. And because of both of your actions, here I sit, alone, in a new country.

"I blame You for my empty womb, but I also admit it was partly my own fault. I could have taken better care of myself. I could have eaten and drank but even that You could have changed by sparing Jonathan's life. What is the purpose of all this? I know You discipline those You love, but this feels like harsh chastisement.

"I'm so angry! To be honest, I don't even want to talk with You. If You want a relationship with me, You're going to have to do a miracle."

Justine sighed and opened her eyes to find Garrett Cole standing over her.

Justine's face went pink when she finally saw him. Garrett hadn't meant to eavesdrop, but as he neared the garden wall, he heard her praying on the other side. Then it seemed his feet had a mind of their own and before he knew it, he was standing in front of her, watching her sweet face show the agony of her heart. Now he braced himself for the coming blow.

But instead, the young widow stood up and turned her back to him, covering her face with her hands.

This time it was his arms that had a mind of their own. He gently turned Justine toward him and wrapped her in his embrace. And instead of pulling away, it seemed she melted into him and her sorrows became his own.

Garrett Cole wasn't a man given to tears, but this woman's anguish cut straight to his heart, and he found his throat thick with emotion. Justine's prayer had disclosed a piece of information he otherwise wouldn't have been privy to—a baby had been lost and Justine thought it was partially her fault.

There was no sobbing and after a minute, Justine began to pull back. "Would you like to talk about it?" Garrett asked in a compassionate tone as he released her.

She lifted mournful blue eyes and an overwhelming need arose in him. A desire to snuff out the pain he saw there. A yearning to tell her that she could go on. That it wasn't her fault. Nor God's.

"Thank you for what you just did," she said as she averted her eyes. She must surely be embarrassed by his eavesdropping, not to mention their embrace, innocent though they both were.

"My pleasure. You should know I came when I heard you praying." Her gaze jerked up at his admission.

"Then you…"

"Yes. But I must say, you are doing the right thing by bringing your cares to the Lord."

Justine sighed and looked up at the canopy of sprouting, new leaves above them. "No one else knows this, but that's the first time I have prayed since, well, since I lost the baby. My faith died that day."

Garrett patted her shoulder reassuringly. "Ah, but *you* are still here. And though you may not know why you have been made to suffer so, God still has wonderful plans for you."

She shook her head, causing curls to jump out of her neatly arranged hair. "How can you say that? I thought His wonderful plans included all the things that have been taken from me." This time her sigh sounded resigned.

"I don't have the answers, Mrs. Davidson, but I can be a listening ear." Garrett's smile turned charming as he tried to show his sincerity. "I've been known to be a pretty good listener. I can also promise to pray for you." As he looked down at her, he saw a tiny light flare in her eyes.

Garrett meant what he said. He vowed in that moment to be faithful in prayer for this woman. He would also begin to pray that today was the beginning of a deep friendship with Justine Davidson.

# ELEVEN

A baby's healthy cry from a faraway room greeted Justine as she and Garrett entered the house. Charlotte Cole bounded down the stairs with tears on her cheeks. Her husband, James, was right behind her. "It's a boy! Can you believe it, Garrett? We're grandparents and you an uncle! What a day the Lord has made. And we will rejoice in it!"

As Charlotte prattled on, Justine's mind went to the day the Lord had made when she had lost her baby. She imagined herself the new mom, with family and friends gathered near to witness new life, celebrating alongside she and her husband. How terribly unfair! Would she always feel this sudden impairment of her soul at the mention of a baby? If she was this upset at just hearing the news, how would it be when she actually saw the little miracle?

Maybe that was it; Justine knew life was a gift and a miracle, and maybe the day her baby died, God had simply decided not to complete what He had started.

Justine found it impossible to offer her congratulations. But it would be rude to leave, so she stood quietly to the side.

Out of the corner of her eye, she saw Garrett looking at her and she knew what he was thinking. *Poor Justine*, right? The one who had killed her unborn baby. *She'll never know what it is like to be a mother.* Yes, those were obviously Garrett's thoughts after overhearing her prayer.

She chanced a glance in his direction and found something in his eyes that made her heart question her conclusions. His gaze bored into her with an intensity she had never known. What was it she saw there?

Charlotte was saying something to her, so she dragged her focus to the matron.

"Dear," she said with her hand on Justine's arm, "would you like to meet Anica and her family? I'm sure they would love to meet a friend of Garrett's."

Charlotte linked arms with Justine, and without waiting for an answer, steered the way up the stairs and into the birthing room.

The sight that greeted them took Justine's breath away. Seeing a loving family should have made her heart break, but somehow the joy she saw there allowed her to be happy for them. They, people whom she had never met. Maybe there was hope for her after all.

Garrett came in right behind her and placed a hand at the small of her back. It made her feel safe and secure. She looked up at him and hoped he read the gratitude in her expression.

Garrett tipped his head toward Justine then led her to the bedside to meet his sister.

"Anica, Bret, congratulations," Garrett said. "What's his name?"

Bret spoke up. "We decided to name him Caleb after Caleb in the Bible. It means *whole heart* in Hebrew. We want our son to remember to always give God his whole heart."

Justine watched Anica's and Bret's faces and introduced herself rather than chance a look at the baby. Jeffrey and Carrie Anne were in the corner gathering the supplies. They had their heads bent in conversation as they worked and seemed oblivious to anyone else in the room. Justine marveled at the way they seemed to take to one another.

Garrett had Caleb in his arms and before Justine could stop him, he handed the baby to her. The look in his eyes said he knew how hard this was for her, but that she needed to do this. Not for Bret and Anica. But for her. She timidly took the infant and cradled him against her chest and gazed down into the beautiful face of the little boy. Her own son would have been born in a few months' time. Maybe one day God would see fit to bless her again in that way. No, she shouldn't assume such a thing, or even hope. It would only get snatched away like everything else.

Mrs. Dunsmore met Carrie Anne and Justine as they entered the inn after dark that evening. After a thorough scolding that included a repetition of the Dunsmore Inn's rules, the landlady led them into a drawing room at the front of the home. Its large bay window held a view to the street, bathed in the soft glow of moonlight.

"Since you missed dinner tonight—and I expect that not to happen again—I will have a tray brought in with something light from the kitchen." Mrs. Dunsmore clicked her fingers to signal a nearby servant. The girl snapped to attention and ran to the kitchen like her skirt was on fire.

"I'll tell you, it is so hard to find decent help these days. It'll be good to know I can count on you Monday morning, Miss Barnes. I expect you to be in the kitchen at dawn, and if you prove yourself to be worthwhile, well then, I'll just have to see about hiring you." Mrs. Dunsmore shook her head, causing her jowls to flap in the non-existent breeze. "But I'll have you know, young lady, I will not tolerate you giving out the scraps to the poor. Why, just this morning, two ragamuffins came around back and I caught one of the kitchen girls giving them the leavings." She huffed and fiddled with the lace on her sleeve.

Justine glanced at Carrie Anne, recalling the sight of the street children they had seen earlier in the day. Were they the same two who got scraps of food from the Dunsmore Inn? They had to be. Was that the only food they ate all day? What if Mrs. Dunsmore caught the kitchen maid again? The children could very well go hungry. Something must be done about this.

Justine cleared her throat. "Mrs. Dunsmore, I appreciate the food you ordered for us this evening. But generous as that was of you, I would much rather see it go to those who need it. We have had our fill for today. Why don't you save it for those two children in case they come around again?"

"Oh, they'll be back. They've been scrounging food from us for the last two years, and I've had it. I won't just give away what I've rightly earned or what someone else has paid for. Besides, there are so many street urchins, one meal isn't going to make a dent in the issue. Better just to leave them be and ignore them the best we can. The dirty, filthy things." Mrs. Dunsmore brushed at a non-existent crumb on her vast skirts.

Justine felt too tired from their busy day to argue, so after kindly refusing the food, she and Carrie Anne made their way up the stairs to their suite with their purchases from the morning in tow.

Justine's full plush bed beckoned her when she opened their bedroom door, and she realized just how long of a day it had been.

Carrie Anne had not been her usual quiet self when Louis had taken them back to the inn. She yammered on and on about Jeffrey and how wonderful he was, how he was the gentlest man she had ever met. It sounded like her friend was truly smitten. But Justine knew doubts lay just beneath Carrie Anne's infatuated surface.

"What do you think, Justine?" Carrie Anne questioned as she readied for bed. "Be honest with me now. Am I being as foolish as I'm afraid I might be?" Carrie Anne slipped into the bathroom to grab a hairbrush, giving Justine a moment to ponder her question.

What did she think? The thought of Carrie Anne settling down with someone so quickly gave Justine a panicked feeling. Yet another person in her life was about to be snatched away. But she loved her friend too much to say that. And it wasn't really what Carrie Anne was asking.

Carrie Anne returned from the bathroom in her robe and sat on her bed, pulling the brush through her hair with long, even strokes. "He's so wonderful, you know? Maybe a little too wonderful."

"You mean, you don't trust him?"

"Oh, no. Even after our few interactions, I'm already assured he's a godly man." Carrie Anne set the brush on her lap and looked at Justine. "He's got everything going for him. A doctor. A fine family. Money to spare, I'm sure. We come from two different worlds, you know? What must he think of me?"

Jeffrey fit the mold of almost everyone they had met so far in Waterford Cove. Well-to-do. Influential. Lives full of promise. Justine wondered if the differences in their classes might come between Carrie Anne and Jeffrey if they pursued a courtship. But judging by the way they looked at each other, Justine didn't think either of them would give any credence to other people's opinions.

Justine realized she hadn't responded when Carrie Anne said, "You were a married woman, Justine. Give me your thoughts on this matter."

How could Justine ignore her friend's pleading tone? But to hear that her state of matrimony was past-tense hit Justine in the stomach like a kick from a horse. But now was not the time to focus on her own problems. She had a friend who had been there for her and now she would return the favor.

"I admit I was a little jealous today of you and Jeffrey. I saw the way he looked at you and can unequivocally say, I don't think Jonathan ever looked at me like that. I think he loved me, but in retrospect, I think I wanted to be married so badly, that I sort of settled for someone I thought could bring me what I was searching for. But no. I don't think you're being foolish. And I don't think he cares one wit about your social status. Trust me."

"I've never had a romance before. Not that this will probably turn into that," Carrie Anne said as she finished brushing. "I'm not usually pessimistic, Justine, but the differences in our lifestyles are obvious. Just look at me! I should be reasonable, and forget I ever met Jeffrey."

Carrie Anne crawled beneath the covers, so Justine followed suit in the other bed and blew out the light. In less than a minute, Carrie Anne's soft breathing could be heard.

As the day's busyness caught up with Justine as well and she closed her eyes, she said thank you for the new life born today and the possible romance brewing for her friend. Then she made a request for help to be happy for both situations. Before she realized what she was doing, Justine was softly whispering what almost sounded like her second prayer of the day.

Having not been able to sleep once the sun decided to make its appearance for the day, Justine let Carrie Anne sleep and made her way to the sitting area in the turret. Outside the window, Justine had a perfect view of the tree tops, where birds came and went, busy doing what they were made to do.

The moment she awoke, she had realized what day it was and what she would be doing this morning. What lay before her was unavoidable. Charlotte would be expecting her. Carrie Anne would prod her to do the right thing. Justine was cornered. She had to go to church.

Church. Until recently, it had been a word that evoked security and serenity. A place where she could find healing and offer worship and repentance. Could she find that peace today? Cast off her cares onto a Lord who would care for her? Shaking her head slightly, she didn't think it was possible.

The verse from 1 Peter seemed silly now. Her burden, her care, was the loss of her family. The difficulties she had been dealt from God's hand couldn't be corrected by placing them there again. If she rolled off that burden, it would simply be trading back and forth with Him. God wasn't to be trusted. She would simply have to manage on her own.

Rising from her perch, Justine went through the motions of getting ready, dragging her heart into submissive obedience the whole way.

Sunday morning. Growing up, Garrett had always relished the thought of attending church with his family. But now as a grown man, sometimes he felt almost childish riding to church in the same carriage as his parents. Oh, he loved them, but deep inside, Garrett wanted to be the head of his own household. To eat breakfast with his wife on Sunday mornings, then accompany her to their carriage, with a child or two or ten in tow.

Sighing, Garrett looked at his parents seated across from him on the ride into town. He should be grateful for them, and he was. But this longing in his heart seemed to grow exponentially with each passing day.

There were young ladies in the congregation he knew would jump at the chance to be courted by him. Some of them were even beautiful, but none of them caused him to look twice. These were women he had known most of his life, and he wanted no part of what they had to offer. They were raised to take care of themselves first, to care more about the latest fashion than about anyone else. Social standing was top priority in their lives. No, none of those girls would do.

Louis pulled the carriage up to the steps leading to the massive stone building. Garrett helped his mother down, all the while watching for Justine out of the corner of his eye. Would she be here today? Mother had said she and Carrie Anne were coming to call this afternoon. The thought made his pulse jump, and he realized he was doing it again, seeing Justine as a potential mate. He'd been down this road before. When would he learn to wait on the Lord's timing?

All thoughts of waiting flew right out the window at the sight of the young woman as she arrived. She and Carrie Anne must have walked, for he saw them making their way to the church on foot. But it wasn't their mode of transportation that caught his attention. The sun's rays seemed to be made just for Justine this morning in her pink gauzy dress. Its soft rose color gave her skin a healthy hue, while the sun's rays lit her hair to nearly aglow. If not for her turning her head to speak with Carrie Anne, Garrett would have been able to see what that pink color did to her eyes. He'd have to find out later.

"Mr. Cole. Mrs. Cole. How do you do?" Justine tipped her head in greeting to him and his parents as she walked up the stairs with her arm in Carrie Anne's. *Get a grip, man.* He was at church, here to learn about the Almighty, not ogle at beautiful widows. It had been ages since he had heard pastor speak, and he wouldn't let Scripture bounce off his ears this morning just because Justine happened to look particularly fetching.

Justine wished she could tug her hat lower on her head so she could hide behind it. If she kept her eyes down, no one would know that her heart was being squeezed with an iron band.

Walking through the church doors had sent her emotions into a twister of flurry, one feeling getting tangled up in the next until she couldn't untie them anymore. Peace wrapped up with uncertainty, longing entwined with anger. She was spiritually parched, like the deer in Psalm 42, but if she took a drink, what would happen?

Seeing the congregation stand for the first song, Justine quickly joined them, her eyes trying to focus on the words of the hymn. Unfamiliar to her, it talked of blessing the name of Jesus. She wanted to sing along, but how could she in good conscience? It seemed wrong to sing something she didn't mean.

The pastor came to the front of the church as the music concluded, his easy smile and cordial manner making Justine feel more at ease. She wondered what passage of scripture he would use today. She silently pleaded with the man to make it something her battered heart could handle.

"We serve a God who is more powerful, more high and lifted up than our human minds can comprehend. He is the creator of all. Read along with me in your own Bibles if you will. Isaiah 40, starting in verse twenty-two.

"'It is he that sitteth upon the circle of the earth, and the inhabitants thereof are as grasshoppers; that stretcheth out the heavens as a curtain, and spreadeth them out as a tent to dwell in.'

"I'll jump down to verse twenty-six.

"'Lift up your eyes on high, and behold who hath created these things, that bringeth out their host by number: he calleth them all by names by the greatness of his might, for that he is strong in power; not one faileth'".

Justine's heart beat faster. The verses came from the same chapter Carrie Anne had quoted just before Jonathan's carriage exploded.

The pastor looked up from his Bible with a look of peace so deep Justine wanted to reach out and take it for herself. Oh, to have a close communion with God again.

"Consider a diamond for a moment."

Justine wasn't sure where the pastor would take this analogy, but her ears perked up.

"If you take a diamond and turn it one way, you will catch the light and it will shine. But that one moment of brilliance is not all the diamond has to offer. If you keep turning it, you will find many facets that shine many different ways.

"The God we serve is like that. One look at who He is and you see an all-powerful, awe-inspiring Creator who makes His dwelling in the heavens, who sits above the circle of the earth, and measures the water with the breadth of His hand. Amazing! Considering God in this light makes me want to worship Him for His glory and majesty."

The pastor's words evoked feelings in Justine she would rather not explore. But being sandwiched between an elderly man and Carrie Anne, she couldn't leave without making a scene. She glanced behind her to see if there was an escape route, but instead, something caught her eye. Garrett was slipping out of the row he shared with his parents and was making his way out the back door. Maybe the sermon was getting to him, too.

"Turn the diamond with me if you will," the pastor said as Justine faced forward again. "What do we see as we look at the second portion of this passage? We see a God who named every star, and because of who He is, all of them are accounted for. Every single one. How much more do you think He cares for us if He can do such a thing as this?"

Justine began to squirm in her seat as the questions in her heart taunted her once again. If God could make sure all the stars were there every night, why was her family not saved from their deaths?

Justine's gaze landed on the Bible that was open on Carrie Anne's lap. A verse stood out from the rest of the chapter. It implied that God's understanding was unsearchable. Could He really know the torture she was enduring? More importantly, did He really care?

The pastor continued to speak about different characteristics of God, and Justine dutifully sat through the rest of the service.

"As we conclude today," he said, "I want to give you an assignment for the week. If you have a Bible, take a piece of paper and put it in the back. On that paper, I want you to make a list of all the different facets of God you see in your life this week. Do you see His creative hand in nature? Write it down. Has He been merciful to you in your sin? You guessed it," the man said good-naturedly. "When you are reminded of who He is, jot it down and also note why you are particularly grateful for that attribute of God. Then finally, share some of your observations with a friend. I think you'll be surprised at what you notice about your Savior when you are really looking for Him."

He lifted his hands in an upward gesture and the congregation rose for the closing hymn. Turning her head as she stood, Justine saw Garrett slip back inside and stand next to his mother. His hair looked a little disheveled and curiosity about where he had been during the service made Justine miss the rest of the song.

# TWELVE

He didn't think it would be this easy. A simple lighting of the grenade, a quick calculation of timing, an accurate throw into Davidson's cab and that problem was solved. Now, one charming smile and he was in. Mrs. Dunsmore had been all too happy to oblige when he asked her for the key to the room. She probably thought cozying up to him meant he'd return the favor in the future.

He stood in the middle of the suite and caught a glimpse of himself in the full-length mirror. He took a moment to straighten his shirt and run a hand through his thick hair. He certainly did cut a dashing figure.

But now that he had gained access to her things, he needed to focus. Who knew how much time he had? Church could let out any moment.

First, he'd start with the dresser. He knew the money was here somewhere. It had to be. If it wasn't, he'd still find it and snatch it away from her as surely as he knew the back of his own hand. Jonathan had needed to be quickly disposed of—he couldn't stand competition—but he would take pleasure in making his widow suffer.

It didn't seem to be anywhere. Overturning one of the beds, he saw a wooden box, no longer than his arm and only about a foot high. He lunged for it, but at the same time, heard a noise coming from the front entryway. He grabbed the box and quickly ducked into the room next door. In the process, he tore his favorite vest on the bed post.

Just one more thing he would make Justine Davidson pay for.

As soon as the service ended, Justine saw Charlotte Cole weave her way through the congregation, heading in her and Carrie Anne's direction. Dressed in her Sunday finery, Mrs. Cole looked every part the society matron she was. A wealthy husband in the banking business, a large estate boasting gardens and horses, a handsome and successful son, and now, a grandchild.

Justine felt her heart tug at the sharp contrast between Charlotte's life and her own. Poor, without family, alone in a new country, void of any closeness with God. That was Justine. Despite her mental comparisons, Justine greeted Charlotte cordially. Justine decided it was time to stop wallowing in the misery God had given her. Time to take things into her own hands, to make a complete turnabout with her life. When she was old and gray, she wanted to look back and say that she had made something out of nothing. And this afternoon was the perfect time to start.

"Come now, girls. We've a carriage out front, and I know Cook is whipping up some of her culinary masterpieces for our Sunday lunch. We shall have such a wonderful time, encouraging each other in the Lord, just as the Bible tells us to do. If they're up for it, Anica and Bret will be joining us for dinner with baby Caleb." Her eyes flicked to Carrie Anne. "And Jeffrey, of course. Come along, now!"

Charlotte led the way to the carriage and before Justine could protest, Garrett had settled next to her while his mother sat opposite them with Carrie Anne. Charlotte said James had decided to ride next to Louis to leave more room for their guests. Why couldn't Garrett have sat up front? Or with Carrie Anne? Did he have to sit so close? There was room to scoot over on his side of the seat.

Despite her riotous emotions, Justine was looking forward to an afternoon at the Coles. Truly she enjoyed Charlotte's company more than just about any other woman she had known. Perhaps her mother's absence had created a void only another mother-figure could fill. Maybe Charlotte couldn't be that person, but she was becoming a friend, one that Justine was very grateful for.

As she pondered her friendship with Charlotte, Justine recalled the pastor's sermon. Was this one of the facets of God he was talking about? Justine could almost see through the shards of her broken heart to admit that maybe, just maybe, God had provided both Charlotte and Carrie Anne as friends to comfort her during this time. The facet of provision. Justine wished she could believe it.

"Mrs. Davidson, would you mind if we swung by the inn on our way home? I've only passed by and never been inside. It sounds delightful."

"That's fine by me, Mrs. Cole."

"Oh, please. It's Charlotte. Remember?"

"I'd love to show you our room, Charlotte." Justine said the last with a tease in her voice.

"Just as charming as I recalled," Charlotte said as the carriage pulled parallel with the inn. She reached out a gloved hand and placed it on her son's arm. "What a darling place. I will have to recommend this to James's business acquaintants. Wait. The Dunsmore Inn? Oh, I know Angelina Dunsmore. I don't know why I didn't make the connection before."

"We men will wait here," said James with a grin as the women climbed out. "I don't think I need to inspect lace curtains or hear a dissertation from Mrs. Dunsmore."

"We'll be back shortly," replied Justine, cutting a glance at Garrett as they made their way to the house.

The landlady was nowhere to be seen, so Charlotte, Justine, and Carrie Anne went straight to the second floor. When they reached the top of the stairs, Justine noticed the door to their suite was partway open. *How odd.* But then again, maid service was included in their room and board, so maybe it was being cleaned.

Charlotte and Carrie Anne came up behind her as Justine gasped in response at what she saw. One peek inside declared everything was about to change.

The room stood in disarray, clothes and personal items strewn everywhere. Justine saw her new gown and other clothing lying in heaps, along with Carrie Anne's garments. One bed had been flipped over. Every drawer's contents had been dumped on the floor next to chairs that had been turned upside-down. Someone had wanted something. Badly. I wonder if they got what they came for.

Justine stood in shock for a few moments in the doorway before stepping inside to inspect the damage.

"Oh dear," said Charlotte before slipping back down the stairs, presumedly to tell the others of the situation.

"What in the world?" Carrie Anne's soft voice carried to where Justine stood looking into the empty wardrobe.

"I have no idea. I know someone could have easily broken in. But the question is, why would they? It's not like we have anything to steal." But that wasn't entirely true, was it? Justine lifted the false bottom of the wardrobe and breathed a sigh of relief when she saw the purse that held the inheritance from her father. A peek inside told her it had remained untouched. Even though the perpetrator was gone, Justine felt the need to put the bag crosswise on her chest so no one would have access to it but her.

A slow walk around the room showed nothing was missing, yet it still somehow seemed as though everything had been taken.

Noise at the staircase caught her attention as Mrs. Dunsmore, then James, Garrett, and Charlotte came into view.

The landlady's face was in high color as she assured Justine that nothing of this nature had ever occurred at her fine inn. "You just have to believe me, Mrs. Davidson," she was saying. "After my maids set the room to rights, you can continue your stay with us." It was more of a question, Justine knew, but the woman made it sound like a statement.

Justine didn't know what she was going to do. Could she fall asleep in safety? Could she and Carrie Anne leave their room and not always wonder what would happen while they were away? She turned to look at her friend, knowing they both would suffer because of this ordeal.

Garrett and his father began to set the furniture straight as Charlotte gave each girl a hug. "Do you think anything was taken?" Charlotte asked.

"It looks like everything is here," said Justine.

"I'm glad to hear it. Even so, I insist you not sleep here another night. I don't think you would be safe," said Charlotte.

Justine knew what was coming next. Mixed feelings settled in her stomach as she glanced from Garrett back to his mother.

"Both of you must come to stay with us." As though Charlotte could see the argument about to ensue, she held up her hand, palm out. "I know what you are going to say, and I won't have any of it. The Bible tells us that we must extend hospitality to those in need, and in doing so, we have done so to Christ himself. Besides," she went on with a light laugh, "how lovely it will be to have two more women in the house to chat with!"

Carrie Anne and Justine stepped to the side to converse privately. "I think we should do it, Justine. Are you comfortable with going back to the Coles?"

Justine looked around their pillaged room once more and pressed her father's money closer to her side. "I just don't know, Carrie Anne." Justine wasn't sure she was in a good position to make be making decisions. "You decide."

"Mrs. Dunsmore," Carrie Anne said, addressing the landlady, "We are going to take Mrs. Cole up on her offer. And I am afraid I will not be assisting you in the kitchen tomorrow morning, either."

The older woman's face fell, but anyone could see she was admitting defeat. Who would want to stay in a room after they had been violated in such a way?

"We can have Mr. Smythe or Louis collect your things and settle your bill later today. Or would you feel more comfortable packing for yourselves?" Garrett's father wanted to know.

Justine glanced at Carrie Anne and was sure the look of emotional exhaustion on her friend's face matched her own. A member of the Cole's staff was perfectly capable of coming to collect their things. Right now, Justine had more on her mind than the wrinkles in her new dresses.

But as they made their way out to the carriage, something unsettling was making its home in the pit of her stomach. Not only did she wonder why someone would go through their things, Garrett's absence during church today made her wonder who did it.

Justine glared at Garrett from across the dining table until he felt like a worm waiting to go onto the hook. For one so pretty, the looks she gave could be murder. Purposefully trying not to squirm, Garrett stirred his vegetable soup and worked to focus on something other than the woman from whom he was receiving silent wrath.

They had arrived at the Cole mansion over an hour ago. Upon exiting the carriage, Justine and Carrie Anne had been shown to the guest room they had once occupied. Justine hadn't even graced him with a look, instead fleeing up the stairs to the retreat of the suite.

Truly, he couldn't fault his mother for offering the two girls a place to stay. But being near Mrs. Davidson too many hours of the day may not be good for his mindset. She was too beautiful for her own good. And his.

He had already been seated at the dinner table when Justine and Carrie Anne came down. They looked more refreshed, and Garrett had been pleased to see Justine was seated across from him. Now he wished she was at the other end of the table, for who could enjoy their dinner when they were being glowered at? Women. One minute they were allowing you to comfort them, the next, angry for who knew what reason.

"Did you enjoy the service?" His mother was posing the question to the group in general, but Garrett was curious what Justine would say. He knew the struggles she was having with her recent losses.

Justine looked down at her soup, but Jeffrey spoke up. "I have always been fascinated with diamonds, and this new way of looking at the character of God intrigues me. I think it's a perfect analogy. Miss Barnes, do you have an opinion on the matter?"

Carrie Anne looked up at the doctor with admiration in her eyes. "I agree completely. When I read the Bible, I see many different ways God works, and many different characteristics of His nature. I'm glad the pastor challenged us to look for evidence of Him this week."

As the conversation picked up around the table, Garrett didn't join in. Instead he watched Justine's face as she absorbed what was being said. Emotions ranging from confusion to sadness chased across her features. What he wouldn't give to be able to read her mind. She shifted her focus to what Charlotte was saying and caught him looking at her. Her face infused with red, but somehow Garrett didn't think it was because she was embarrassed. The sadness looked like it had been replaced with anger. Was she mad that he had overheard her prayer in the garden yesterday?

"When we got home, Anica told me she might be feeling up to joining us in the parlor for coffee after lunch. Shall we make our way there while I send a maid to fetch her?"

His mother led the way to the sunny parlor and soon they were settled in with coffee and dessert. Garrett noticed how Jeffrey and Miss Barnes ended up next to each other. He had hoped the same would happen with Justine. He wanted to straighten out whatever was between them. Instead, she had taken a chair by the piano, and her other side was occupied by the fireplace. Ah, well. At least from here he had a good view.

A movement at the parlor's entryway caught his attention as faces throughout the room lit up. Anica stood there with her new baby, her husband at her side.

"Join us," Charlotte motioned them in. "How is little Caleb this fine Sunday?" His mother cooed to Caleb as she eagerly took her turn to hold him.

"Doing well. He's a good baby, although he may have his days and nights mixed up right now," Bret said with a laugh. "That's all well and good for a day or so, but Anica needs her rest. To tell the truth, we have been thinking of hiring a nanny. Someone to care for him during the day so Anica can catch up on her sleep."

His mother was nodding her head in agreement. "Garrett, when you were born, your father employed a nanny to care for you in the same way. I say it's a wonderful idea, one with much merit. Bret, you must seek one out at once."

"I will, but no one comes to mind who is not already employed, and most importantly, someone whom we can trust."

"Forgive me if I am being presumptuous here, but I believe Carrie Anne would be a fine candidate for the position," Mrs. Cole said.

Bret and Anica exchanged a smile. "Miss Barnes, what do you think? After dessert, would you be willing to discuss details? You have such a sweet disposition. I would love to have you care for Caleb," Anica said.

Heads turned to the other side of the room as Jeffrey cleared his throat. "Not so fast."

Carrie Anne looked surprised and perhaps a bit disappointed that Jeffrey would disagree.

"She was too big of an asset in the delivery room and I enjoy her company too much to have her waiting around all day for Caleb to wake up from his nap." Jeffrey looked directly at Carrie Anne. "I was wondering if you might begin accompanying me on some house calls?"

Carrie Anne smiled and laughed nervously.

"Jeffrey, you rogue. Trying to steal her out from underneath us while we watch." Bret shook his head, laughing. "We'll quibble over this later. But just so you know, Anica and I intend to win."

Everyone could see Carrie Anne was delighted with the friendly banter. At Carrie Anne's insistence that she could do both, the topics turned to other matters while the baby was passed from arm to arm.

When it was Justine's turn, Garrett watched her closely. For a moment it seemed she would give her opportunity to the next person, but then she acquiesced. When she set down her coffee on a nearby saucer, Garrett could see her hand shaking. She looked into the face of the newborn and took him in her trembling arms. Garrett was proud of her courage.

His mother clapped her hands together and suggested, "Before jumping into rounds of whist this afternoon, let's go around the room and tell of one facet of God's amazing character that we have recently observed in our own lives. Anica, I know you missed church today, but would you like to go first? The pastor gave us some homework to do this week. He portrayed God like a diamond, with varying facets, different at every turn."

118

Anica appeared to be thinking for a moment, then a look of happiness came across her face. "I think my answer will be easy. How could I not thank Him for His gifts and recognize His generosity?" She gazed lovingly across the room at a sleeping Caleb in Justine's arms.

All eyes were already on the baby, so Justine was the natural candidate to go next. Garrett could see she was struggling to answer and her normally clear smooth skin had gone red and splotchy.

She looked about ready to bolt, so Garrett came to her rescue. "Here, let me take him. Uncle Garrett gets next baby rights."

"I'll go next," he said. And, looking at Justine as he spoke, said, "I thank God for friendship. For bringing new people into our lives. For letting us care about them."

Didn't he mean, care *for* them? Certainly, Garrett didn't care about her. He must have misspoken. He and his family had only done their Christian duty to care for two orphans, albeit grown ones.

Yet against what she would have expected, Justine was surprised to feel like she had been wrapped in a warm safe cocoon. It was as if someone had set her right in the middle of everything she had ever wanted.

This room, these people comprised what Justine had been searching for since her papa died. Home. That's what she felt here. Included and at home. She couldn't disagree that God's hand must certainly be involved yet at the same time the prospect unsettled her. Justine let her gaze move slowly from person to person.

Charlotte Cole. A woman who had taken Justine under her wing without a moment's hesitation. Carrie Anne, a constant, encouraging companion. James, Anica, and Bret. Three people whom she barely knew, yet who treated her fondly and extended continued goodwill.

Then there was Garrett. He stood holding the baby, looking like a proud papa himself. His joy and gentleness were palpable. Her suspicion of his involvement with Jonathan and now her ransacked room seemed incongruous with the reality of the person before her.

Plates clinked as they were being set on small tables around the room, and Justine realized the conversation around her was wrapping up.

"Carrie Anne, would you mind taking Caleb for an hour so Anica can catch a nap?" Bret was saying. "Maybe you and Jeffrey could use the new baby carriage to take Caleb out for some spring air?" The twinkle in his eye gave away his part in the matchmaking. "Then when he's ready to eat, perhaps the two of you would like to sit down to a game of whist?"

"I'll grab an extra blanket," Anica said, rising slowly from her chair.

"No, no," smiled Carrie Anne. "I've got it." Jeffrey joined her and the two made their way upstairs together.

"I'll be excusing myself as well. Charlotte. James," Justine said, addressing the wonderful couple, "I can't thank you enough for your hospitality."

The older woman surprised Justine by taking her in her arms and squeezing tight. She whispered in her ear the echo of Justine's thoughts. "God sets the lonely in families. I'm glad He's chosen to place you in ours."

# THIRTEEN

Gravel crunched under her feet as Justine left the gathering and took to the solace of the Cole's gardens. The trees seemed to beckon her with their flower-blossom arms, unfurling to hold her in a fragrant embrace. She inhaled deeply, letting the herbs and flowers caress her senses. She wanted to hold on to this feeling of belonging.

Family. *He sets the lonely in families.* It felt as though she had been lonely forever. Lonely growing up without mother or siblings. Lonely enough after her father's death to marry a near stranger.

She fingered a silky tulip. Late spring in Virginia had been bright and beautiful. A sharp contrast to Justine's dark and gloomy introspections. It seemed one moment her emotions found solace, the next, she dove deep into the wounds of the past. Her memories insisted on reaching as far back to what she was told about her mother's early death, all the way to today, with the ransacking of her room. Did her mind need to dredge up every other heartache in between? Like a long string of broken promises that hung over the Atlantic, Justine felt certain that not only would she carry them with her for the rest of her life, but more heartaches were sure to be added to the line.

Despite the tranquil surroundings in which Justine found herself this Sunday afternoon, despite the friendships she was building within this home, she knew true healing could only be found in God.

But even as she pondered this certainty, her emotions tugged on the long line of memories, insisting God had shown Himself unfaithful, and therefore could not be trusted. Ah, how she ached to feel so torn!

"I thought I might find you here," a deep voice caught her attention.

Turning, she looked at the man standing before her. The sun at his back lit his hair to a golden halo, but Justine wasn't sure if he was a devil in disguise. Was it mere happenstance their room was robbed while she and Carrie Anne were at church—the same time Garrett had gone missing during the worship service? His presence here now could mean nothing more than throwing her off his scent. Or was he being honest when he said he was grateful for their friendship?

"Mr. Cole, I thought maybe you and your father would continue the spiritual sparring that began in the parlor," Justine said coolly. She turned her back to him, hoping to signal her disinterest. As she heard him grow closer on the path behind her, she knew he hadn't taken the hint.

"Caleb is a beautiful baby, don't you think?" When she swung around, he held up his hand. "I do not mean any disrespect to your feelings, ma'am, just making a comment. I want you to know I know how hard it was for you to hold him today. I could see your struggle." Garrett hesitated. "Would you like to talk about it?"

Justine hadn't heard many lines from men in her life, but if she had, she believed this one would top them all. She had to hand it to him, though. He was a great pretender. How could he stand there and talk about feelings if he had just played the trespasser?

All right, she could play along for a minute or two. See how deep he could go in his little act.

She shrugged in response to his question. "I guess. Thanks for offering. But it seems none of this concerns you."

"Mrs. Davidson, Justine, if I may, I feel as though I have known you for a long time. Maybe it's because I knew Jonathan, too." He ran a hand across the back of his neck as he sat down on a bench and leaned forward on his knees. "When I heard you praying in the garden yesterday, I felt as though I could see into a place no one else knows about. It made me want to know you. Made me want to be your friend."

He looked over at her and Justine saw vulnerability in his eyes. Like he wanted to be known, too. No, that couldn't possibly be right—who would want their heart to be out in the open if they had something to hide, like a robbery or a ransacking? Maybe she would just have to probe a bit, if he was willing. See what she could find out.

"Do you read the Bible much, Mr. Cole?"

"Please, you must call me Garrett, if you will allow me the privilege of calling you Justine."

She had thought to ignore him on that matter, but it appeared he wanted to press the issue. "Very well, we shall be on friendly terms, you and I. Garrett."

He smiled, and, much to her dismay, Justine's heart warmed. This man's seemingly kind words and charming smile must not deter her from knowing his true character. An adversary who could sit here and pretend to be an ally while looking so very amiable was clearly dangerous.

"I do read often. Lately, I've been going through the Gospel of Luke. The passage I read this morning from the sixth chapter talked about a man building his house on the sand or the rock. I find it easy to remember because of the vivid word picture it paints. I can see it in my mind's eye.

"The storms of life are blowing and the house built on the sand fell down with great destruction. A massive downfall. Utter ruin. Like we see sometimes here on the coast when a hurricane comes our way. But the man who built his house on the rock with a solid foundation, had a house that stood through the storm." He paused. "It made me think about how deep my foundation goes and what it's made of. As any smart builder knows, the deeper the foundation, the stronger the building."

Justine's heart felt pricked as he talked about the familiar passage. She knew it well; her father had taught it to her as a young girl. She had always considered that the people who built their houses on the sand were the ones who didn't believe in God, and the people who had a rock foundation were Christians. But to look at her own life, the storms had blown, and where had they left her? Picking up the pieces of the shattered boards of her life, and a shoddy foundation on which to rebuild.

Garrett's depiction of the parable had been accurate, again piquing her curiosity about this man. He could talk out of both sides of his mouth very well.

"You're referring to what I've recently been through, are you not? I do believe you are trying to tell me something."

"Only God knows your heart, Justine. I was only trying to relay what I read this morning." Garrett paused. "What have you read recently?"

Justine felt herself color at the question. She should have seen it coming, since she had started the conversation about the Bible in the first place. But this wasn't the direction she saw this conversation headed.

"I haven't read since I left England. I haven't even gotten my Bible out of my trunk." She sat down next to him and looked at her lap, feeling her curls dance against her cheeks in the breeze. "I've never felt so divided in my life. God seems to want to be near to me, but His actions make me push Him away."

"Correct me if I am wrong, but do you mean to say that He chose to take your family away from you?"

Defiance swiftly snuffed out her melancholy mood. She swung her head up and could feel the fire behind her eyes. "Of course that is what I meant! God is all sovereign, isn't He? He could have at least prevented their deaths." Then just as quickly as her vehemence came, it left. "What's the use?" Justine hung her head. "I don't think I will ever understand."

Suddenly, she felt a warm strong hand grasp her own. She looked up and gasped in surprise, but quickly succumbed to her heart's betrayal. Wasn't this the man who had gone through her things and caused her to have to leave her home? How was it that same man could make her feel so safe with a simple touch? Justine turned to examine a spider crawling down the trunk of a nearby tree, feeling very shy under his scrutiny.

"Justine, do you remember our last conversation here in the garden?" At her nod, he continued. "I told you at that time I would be a listening ear, a friend. I want to extend the same offer to you now." He withdrew his hand and stood. "I wish I had the answers for the trouble in your heart. Seeing the pain in your beautiful eyes makes my heart break." She watched Garrett look up at the sky as he said, "I don't have

the answers, but I do know who God is. He's the One who created us."
He lowered his gaze and looked meaningfully at Justine. "The One who created you. He is a loving God; God *is* love. No matter what circumstances bring about our grief, He has promised to be there for us, if we will but turn to Him."

Justine stood and faced him. "It may seem clear to you, but I just can't make myself do that when I feel betrayed by Him. All my life, my favorite quality about God was His faithfulness. Now I find Him less than faithful. How can I serve a God like that?"

He gripped the upper portion of her arms. "Justine, listen to me. God is who He is, always. He doesn't change, even if we think He has. Our emotions don't transform God's character. He is the same yesterday, today, and tomorrow. The Lord binds faithfulness around His heart. It's simply who He is. He couldn't change it if He wanted to."

Tears threatened, but she stubbornly pushed them back. She would not cry.

Justine straightened her shoulders and Garrett's hands fell to his side once more. She would not let this constant unease in her stomach make her miss out on the rest of life. She would enjoy her new gowns, her new lavish surroundings, and mostly, her new friends. That is, if Garrett Cole could be considered a friend. At this point, it might very well depend on his Sunday morning alibi.

"Mr. Cole, I mean, Garrett, you have been a gentleman of your word this afternoon. You do, in fact, hold a certain ability to listen. I feel as though when we talk, I have really been heard. I want to thank you for that." She motioned toward the home. "Shall we join the others for an afternoon of cards? It's sure to get our minds off these weightier issues."

She smiled in spite of her heavy heart and led the way down the path back to the mansion. She caught a peek over her shoulder at this man she so often wondered about. Was his name Friend or Foe?

๑๛

The constable came and went that Sunday afternoon, leaving no answers in his wake as to who would ransack the room of two young women. Justine had heard Garrett tell his mother he'd left church because of a headache and had taken a walk around the block to ease it. Justine really didn't know whether to believe him or not. It would be very easy to make that excuse *if* in fact he had been going through her things.

There was nothing she could do right now to prove Garrett was the culprit. And if she found out he had behaved like a common criminal, she would be homeless once more. Her only consolation was that she'd still have her father's money plus the money from Jonathan's investments to fall back on.

Money. Maybe that was it. Maybe that was what Garrett was looking for in her room. She would do well to deposit it in a bank as soon as possible.

Justine leaned against the pillows on the huge four-poster bed, thinking how good it was to be back in this wonderful room where she and Carrie Anne had been welcomed to stay when they had needed the Cole's hospitality. Thankfully, her bleeding had all but stopped and Jeffrey Cole had given her a quick check-up after his walk with Carrie Anne, pronouncing Justine in perfect health. If only he could see beneath the surface to her torn heart. It still felt fractured and bruised, so easily slipping back into its old way of feeling.

She needed to stop thinking of her pain and instead try to enjoy the rest of the afternoon before her. Justine stood and straightened her new Sunday dress, making sure the fabric hung correctly and didn't show any wrinkles. Standing in front of the mirror, she took care to make sure every hair was in place. She wanted to make a good impression, especially on Charlotte. The older woman may have a soft heart, but she was still a prominent part of Virginian society, and Justine wanted Charlotte's opinion of her to remain in good standing.

After using the lavish bathroom, Justine shook her head. What modern conveniences money could buy. Maybe she didn't dislike change and innovation as much as she thought she did. Money certainly made things comfortable for those who had it. She could begin to embrace that lifestyle now that her financial circumstances had changed. And with tomorrow being Monday, she could open a bank account and deposit her father's inheritance to keep it safe.

Pausing in the foyer, Justine heard voices rising and dipping in laughter and repartee. She stopped short of the parlor doorway to listen to the exchange.

"There is no way you won that cribbage game!" She heard Carrie Anne say. "Now give me back my card, sir."

"I think *sir* is a bit too formal, don't you think, Miss Barnes?" Now Jeffrey spoke with a teasing note to his voice.

"If I can't call you sir, then you must call me Carrie Anne," came the breathy reply.

Justine peeked around the doorframe to see Jeffrey take Carrie Anne's hand in his own and give it a gentle kiss. All banter had ended and now the two sat across their game, gazing into each other's eyes.

Justine leaned back against the stairway wall. Ah, new love. Is that how it had been with her and Jonathan? She remembered being very drawn to him, but that infatuation had soon worn away. She had worked to keep it burning, but now she saw how Jonathan's secrets had doused the flames of their love, giving it no chance to grow. How could they build a marriage on anything but trust? And now that she knew the truth, she saw there had never been anything solid to begin with.

"Lost in thought, Justine?" Garrett's voice caused her to jump.

"I was just thinking of young love," she motioned to the sitting room.

"Ah, yes, the budding romance between my uncle and your dear friend. What could make for a more happy occasion?"

"How about a trip to the bank in the morning, with that bank note to accompany us?"

"Sounds like a good idea. Why don't we go in early before the customers start arriving? Get you set up with an account and make that deposit? Say around seven thirty?"

"Let's plan on it. You *do* still have the bank note…" Justine let her sentence deliberately trail off to see what he would say.

Red trailed up his neck at her insinuation, raising Justine's suspicions about his earlier whereabouts all the more.

"I assure you it will accompany us, ma'am." He dipped his head and made his way to join the game happening in the other room.

# FOURTEEN

One or two more, that's all he needed. Garrett set his hat more firmly on his head as he and the beautiful Mrs. Davidson exited the carriage in front of the bank. The seed of a plan had begun to form in the back of his mind, a plan really much bigger than he would have dreamed. A dream with a purpose. With just one or two more good investments and he would be set. Well, maybe not set, but closer than he thought possible to getting what he wanted.

He placed his hand at the small of Justine's back as he led her through the bank to his father's office. The two-story building's cathedral ceilings soared overhead while dark wood desks, wainscoting, and doorframes all boasted of booming business. His father had done well for himself.

He pulled out the necessary forms from the drawers in his father's desk and asked Justine to fill them out. "When the first teller gets here this morning, we will make your deposit. Did you bring your father's money with you as well? I would feel more comfortable knowing it was in safe keeping here at the bank."

Justine's eyes narrowed as she took in his comment. "How kind of you to think of my money's welfare, Mr. Cole." She patted her bag. "It's all right here."

He nodded. "Good." They both turned toward a sound in the hall and he saw Father was arriving for the day.

A quiet man, Garrett was used to his father's reserved manner. He found himself wondering what Justine thought of James Cole. Garrett stood to greet him and noticed Justine scrambled to her feet to do the same.

"Good morning, Father. What brings you to the bank this early?"

The older Mr. Cole settled himself in his leather chair behind his desk after Garrett offered him the seat. "I knew you had headed over here, so I thought I'd see if you had a few moments to talk about some business matters." He glanced at Justine and Garrett took the hint.

"Um, yes. Mrs. Davidson and I were just getting an account set up for her." Garrett poked his head into the hall. "But I see the tellers have started to arrive." He turned to Justine, hoping she would understand.

"It's no problem, gentlemen. I think if I can sail across the Atlantic on my own, I should be able to do some banking by myself just fine." She pointed out the window. "There's a charming dress shop across the way. Why don't we meet over there when you are finished?"

Garrett hid a chuckle behind his hand. He should not underestimate this one. Women may have the reputation of needing to be taken care of, but Garrett had a feeling upon closer inspection, Justine Davidson would not fall into that stereotype.

"Of course. I should be done shortly. I'll meet you across the street when I'm through." He held the banknote out to Justine and paused a moment before releasing it. He was grateful this piece of paper had helped make the connection to this intriguing woman. He could only hope he could keep the friendship that had been started now that his business with her had been concluded.

"Thank you, Mr. Cole," she said, reverting to his formal name. "I'm sure Jonathan enjoyed working with you." Garrett knew her choice to make such a statement had its cost.

He held her eyes a moment longer, then squeezed her arm. "See you in bit."

Justine smiled shyly then left.

Garrett turned to face his father across the desk. "I can tell by the look on your face you have something important to say."

James smiled. "I know how restless you have been in your work this past year. I must say, you lasted longer than I would have on the job. You are what I like to refer to as a traveling banker. Taking money in, traveling to deposit money here and there. Returning dividends to their proper owners." He gestured toward the lobby where Justine was conducting her business. "Even fetching young widows from faraway countries to ensure they are rightfully paid."

Garrett chuckled. "A traveling banker. I guess you're right."

His father went on. "I say all this because I know your heart has changed in these matters. Correct me if I am wrong, but I believe you wish to settle down soon?" His father leaned forward in his chair. When he got no immediate response from Garrett, he continued. "You know the banking business, son. You're a quick learner and you know what makes people tick. What would you say to a permanent position here at Waterford Cove Holdings?"

Garrett's heart began a certain off-rhythm *thum-thump thump-thum* in his chest. Here was his father, handing Garrett what he had long dreamed of. A job that didn't take him away for months at a time, a chance to put down roots. Permanently. He'd have the time to water those seeds that had been planted deep in his heart. This was even better than he had expected. But now that the offer had been formally made, he felt as though there wasn't enough air in the room. He tugged at his tie.

"Let me think and pray on this for a few days, Father. And we can talk some more this evening over coffee. I need some time to process what you said." The men shook hands, but before Garrett had completely left the room, he turned back. "By the way, what position were you thinking of?"

His father smiled. "Vice President, son. Right under me."

Garrett nodded his head, then stepped into the lobby. Vice President. Of this glorious bank. He took a deep breath to steady his nerves. Glancing around, he noticed Justine was nowhere to be seen. Probably across the street, spending her money on a new dress. He hoped it was pale blue to set off her exquisite eyes.

He looked over in the direction of the shop, hoping to see those chestnut curls glisten in the sunlight. Instead the sight he saw made his stomach sink. Eric Waverly had his paw on Justine's arm and the two were laughing as though they had been friends for a decade.

⚬⚬⚬

Justine saw Garrett jog across the street, headed in their direction. Her pulse jumped at the sight of his handsome shoulders filling out his finely cut suit. His blond hair was in need of a trim and it waved in the wind as if to say *hello*.

"Cole, how very good of you to join us this splendid morning. Mrs. Davidson was just informing me of her good fortune of late."

Eric Waverly inclined his head toward Justine and hooked her arm in his. His laughing eyes were mesmerizing in the morning sunlight. Then she caught Garrett's look, one she didn't quite know how to read. "Yes, I was just telling Mr. Waverly the brief history of how I came into some money recently. And how it now resides comfortably at Waterford Cove Holdings."

"Good fortune, I think not. But a blessing, nonetheless." Garrett turned to Mr. Waverly. "What brings you out this morning?"

"I was looking for you."

As Garrett's eyebrows shot up, Justine had to again wonder at the history these two shared. Last time she had seen the two men speak, it had not gone well. Garrett seemed genuinely surprised that Mr. Waverly would seek him out. Justine was, too.

"Shocked, I see. Well, you should know I have chosen to put all matters of ill repute behind me and become your friend after all. As they say, let bygones be bygones."

Garrett eyed him suspiciously. "Is that so, Eric? I had thought you should wish never to lay eyes on me again, yet here you are spending your morning looking for me. This is quite a turnabout."

"Well, if you must know, my motives are not completely pure. I was thinking of what you said the other day when I saw you outside my factory. You mentioned you are looking for investors for a new textile invention. I think I'd like to hear more, if the offer still stands."

Garrett's eyebrows furrowed this time. "It does," he said cautiously.

"Would the two of you care to join me at a restaurant across the way for some tea to discuss matters in depth?" Eric asked.

As Justine watched the interchange, she hoped the heat of the late spring sun wasn't turning her skin pink. That along with feeling like a third wheel made her start to squirm. "I have yet to make my final decision in the dress shop, and I'm sure you gentlemen would rather discuss these things at length without feminine ears in attendance."

"You're very gracious, Justine. Shall we plan on meeting at the carriage in an hour's time?" Garrett asked politely.

"Certainly."

Mr. Waverly bent over her hand and kissed her knuckles. "Forgive me for making you uncomfortable, *Justine*." He said the last as if mocking Garrett's use of her Christian name. "We shall meet again on Friday when I have the honor of being your escort at the ball."

Justine nodded her head and the two men made their way to the restaurant to discuss their business. Justine watched them walk away, noting how each man held an air of confidence about himself like a cloak. One with sandy blond hair and affable brown eyes. The other with hair as black as ink on parchment, setting off distinguished green eyes. She knew little enough about each to judge their true character, but she felt certain she would have a chance to do that soon—with both of them.

Turning, Justine headed back into the upscale dress shop. Before she had noticed Eric Waverly outside the window and went to join him, she'd had her eye on a certain gown.

"I see you have come back to admire the dress again. Would you like to try it on, my dear?" the saleslady asked. How differently she was being treated now that she wasn't wearing her old clothing. If only people knew the roots she had come from. But they need never be privy to that information. Justine was reinventing herself and she liked where things were headed.

Justine eyed the hemline and imagined what it would feel like to walk into the ball wearing this. Its sky-blue silk was the perfect backdrop to the silver trim that adorned the neckline and short sleeves. With her hair swept up high, she might just steal the show. And now she could afford to do so.

$\circledcirc\circledcirc$

"What's in the box?" Garrett asked, pointing to the parcel sitting next to Justine in the carriage.

"Just a new dress." Was it just him or was Justine trying to downplay what was most likely an expensive purchase?

Next to their carriage, a velocipede whizzed by at a great clip. It resembled the one he had seen in England outside Justine's small flat. He had always been fascinated with them and had picked up a couple of different versions in his travels. He eyed his companion. An afternoon spent at her side on a couple of bicycles sounded divine. Especially after his meeting with Eric and knowing he would have to go away for a time.

"Just look at that person. He's about to get himself killed on that thing!"

"On the contrary, he looks like he's done this before and is having the time of his life."

"I suppose you are one of those people who relish the fact that our world is filling up with new inventions all the time." She waved her small hand at him. "Of course you are. If you didn't have inventions, you wouldn't have investors, and then where would you be?"

"Guilty as charged, ma'am. You liked the root beer I bought you on the *Blue Flag*, didn't you?" Garrett challenged her. "Don't tell me that wasn't delicious." Garrett watched the bicycle turn the corner and go out of sight. "I think new inventions are an amazing display of the minds God has given mankind. His infinite wisdom has given us finite reasoning on such matters. Every perfect gift, as James chapter 1 says. Why would you not welcome that?"

She held up her hand again. "Wait. You think God has given people the ideas for these dangerous contraptions? What about those machines that hurt children in the factory owners' attempts to make more money?"

"I have never claimed men are good. Only God holds that title indisputably. God may give people ideas, but they make their poor choices on their own. By the way, have you given what we encountered on our tour of the town anymore thought?"

"If you are referring to the plight of those poor children who work in the factories, yes, I have. My heart nearly breaks when I think of those two children's faces who hang around the Dunsmore Inn. What is to become of them? Shall they work in a factory all their lives with no hope of a future? And what of their parents? I suppose some of them are orphans. Like me. But when I start to think about it, I find my mind going in circles. What could I possibly do for them?"

The carriage rumbled along until it started up the Cole's drive. Garrett looked out the window lost in thought. He had often wondered the same thing. What could one man do that would make any difference? The question seemed to be knocking at his heart's door quite frequently lately, and he felt more and more ready to answer the call. If what he was planning came to fruition…

Turning back to the present, he addressed the intriguing girl sitting across from him. "I'm working on something to be able to answer your questions. But let's let the matter drop for the moment. I have a surprise for you." He crooked his finger, beckoning her to wonder what he had up his sleeve.

# FIFTEEN

Justine could not believe she had been talked into this. Before she could stop the chain of events, Garrett had called to Louis and he had pulled the carriage to the stables behind the mansion. The pure excitement in Garrett's expression had caused her to want to see what he had in store for her. And before she knew it, she was atop the very epitome of invention, the bicycle.

Her legs reached the ground comfortably enough with her skirt hiked up a bit in the back, and much to Justine's amazement, the seat didn't feel as small underneath her as she had anticipated. Still…

Garrett was circling her in the barn, showing her how it was done. Justine's heart quickened when he turned the bicycle sideways and slid up next to her in a daring halt.

"All right, let's see what you've got." Garrett hopped off his bike and went to stand by her side.

"What I've got? Well, let's see. Money in the bank, a beautiful dress for the ball, and a new life here in America."

"Very funny. Put your right foot on the pedal and keep your left on the ground. Then push the right pedal down and you'll start moving. When you do, keep pedaling slowly, but not too slowly. You need to keep your momentum to stay upright." Garrett's warm eyes held her gaze and she found she couldn't quite look away. "I'll be right here next to you so you don't fall. I won't let go until you're ready. I promise."

Who was this man? A thief, maybe. Or an investor making the lives of innocent women and children miserable by the inventions he supported. Possibly a con artist, preying upon young, rich widows. Or was he just a handsome man who had come into her life and truly cared for her welfare?

Justine broke their eye contact and focused her reddened face on the pedals. She tried not to think of poor Mr. Navin back in England, who had once fallen on his backside right in front of her flat. Of course, Garrett made it look easy enough, but he had the advantage of trousers, while she suffered to straddle the poor victim in her skirt.

"Justine, you can trust me." Garrett said as he stood next to her and put his hand on her shoulder.

Something in his tone made her think he was speaking of more than just a velocipede. And as she returned his gaze, she knew deep in her heart that Garrett Cole was no thief, that she could believe him when he said he'd had a headache during church. In fact, she conceded to herself that she had believed him all along. But trust him? Yes, just not with her heart.

The Cole mansion sat on a piece of land that had been in the family since the turn of the century. Pride of ownership showed in the gardens and beyond. To the north of the garden was an open area blooming with wildflowers. The property was bordered by groves of trees on three sides, with a creek running west to east, looking, Garrett presumed, for the ocean.

Garrett's chest swelled as he thought of the land he was blessed to live on. He had always pictured a house of his own nestled on the back portion of the acreage. It had never been practical nor necessary before. Who wanted to commit to the cost and upkeep of a home that was rarely used? But now. Now, he was on the threshold of taking on such a charge. He pictured himself there beside a wife and children. A lot of children. He sighed, knowing his thoughts were just wishful thinking. He looked back at Justine following on her bicycle. She was doing surprisingly well. Her hair had come undone and was flying out behind her. She was truly a sight to behold, and she rode with such grace it nearly took his breath away. He gulped as he realized it was Justine he pictured in his house-to-be. It was Justine he saw standing at the door with a toddler on her hip and a baby making her glow with new life. Sweat broke out on his forehead, and he had to focus on the trail to rein in his thoughts. They were taking him to dangerous places.

Garrett and Justine came to a fork in the trail and slowed their cycles to a stop. "Enjoying your ride?"

Justine giggled lightly. The sound of her laughter made Garrett want to hear more of it. "Here I thought this invention was the enemy. But I am not too proud to admit I haven't had this much fun in ages." Her blue eyes were bright with excitement as she surveyed their surroundings. "You can't even see your house from here. What do these trails lead to?"

Garrett pointed to the east. "I'll let you in on a little family secret. If you take the one on the right, it's a straight shot to town." He nodded his chin to the one directly ahead of them. "This one you will just have to take to find out. But before we do that, I want to show you something."

Garrett turned to the left, leading the way, knowing Justine would keep up. Even the occasional bump or rock on the path didn't seem to faze her. What a lady.

The trail Justine followed Garrett on wove through tall grasses for a minute then up a small incline. "Leave your bicycle here," she heard Garrett call over his shoulder. "Come. Let's walk a bit."

He had already laid his contraption on its side and was helping Justine to balance. He held her hand then placed it in the crook of his arm after she had dismounted.

The first time they had walked together, it had been like this, Justine remembered. Just before boarding the *Blue Flag Line*. Carrie Anne on one side, she on the other. How tumultuous her feelings had been that day. Pride at starting out across the ocean independently. Sadness at leaving everything behind that would remind her of her father. Anger at Jonathan for meeting that woman.

At the time, Garrett had simply been Mr. Cole. An untrusted stranger turned benefactor. Now, she felt she knew him better. Could see what he was like on the inside. She was almost comfortable with him and knew that was a huge step in the right direction.

"Over there," Garrett was pointing at something Justine couldn't quite see. "That's what I wanted to show you." Their linked arms propelled her up the rest of the slight incline to a place where the terrain flattened out. A beautiful field spread before them, bordered by trees just getting dressed in their summer finery.

"What?" Justine looked all around but saw nothing of special interest.

Garrett released his arm from her hand and strode ahead. He shocked Justine by spinning in a circle with his arms outstretched. It reminded Justine of her response to their turret room at Dunsmore Inn.

"This. Right here." Garrett looked her straight in the eyes, and she saw something there that threw her emotional equilibrium off balance.

"This is where I'm going to build my home."

Uncomfortable at being made privy to something so personal, Justine looked around the property and tried to picture Garrett's future in her mind's eye.

"This land has so much potential, don't you think?" Garrett wanted to know, no—cared to know, what she thought? She considered that a great honor.

"Absolutely." Looking at it again through the lens of his question, Justine instantly thought of St. Alban's Orphanage run by Mr. Navin. If only the children there had acres to roam with fields and woods to explore. East Wharf didn't boast such amenities, and the orphanage would never be able to afford them, even if they were available.

But here. Oh, but here.

"If this was your land, what would you do with it?" he asked.

"Mine?" Had he read her thoughts? What would he think if he knew what had instantly come to mind? She decided to be forthright. "Well, I was thinking of St. Alban's Orphanage where I used to volunteer. In East Wharf," she clarified.

"Yes. Mr. Navin. I met him."

"You did?" Justine was surprised.

"Outside your old place." Her face must have registered her confusion for he went on. "I went there looking for you. Remember, I had Jonathan's investment payout. Mr. Navin is the one who helped me find you in the end. By the way, what made you think of the orphanage?"

"This land. I can just picture a huge home." She walked forward about ten paces. "Right here. Four stories tall, complete with turrets, bedrooms, school rooms, and these acres of fields and woods for homeless, parentless children to play and learn and grow." Justine stopped her lengthy discourse and looked shyly at Garrett. "Just wishful thinking for those two kids we saw."

"No, you're right. And there are many others as well." Garrett came and stood directly before her, his voice lower and more intimate than before. "It's a good idea, Justine." His eyes looked back and forth into her own as if he was on a desperate search, seeking the next clue to whatever it was he was after.

"But why stop at fields and woods? Come. I want to show you what else there is to see."

They walked their bicycles the rest of the way, but the extra effort down the center path was worth it. A small pool of water fed by a rushing creek awaited them at the end of the trail. Fish were easily visible as they took a break from their fast journey to calmly bask in the shelter of the shade.

Unbidden thoughts came at the picture of life this painted for Justine. She was like the fish in the middle of the stream, the ones who never found the respite of the pool. Always swimming, always searching. Justine felt like that most days. Ever since her life went from simple to complicated, she felt like she couldn't find that rest, couldn't catch her breath.

Lost in thought, Justine didn't realize Garrett had leaned his veloci-pede against a giant magnolia tree and was seated on a flat rock next to the pool. Much to her surprise, he had taken his boots off and was dan-gling bare feet into the water. He looked up to catch her look of shock and laughed out loud. It was a deep, jolly laugh that resounded in her heart.

"What on earth?"

He patted the rock, indicating she should join him. "Give it a try. But I warn you, it's cold!"

Justine shook her head, smiling, but settled her skirt discreetly around her so she could slip off her stockings and shoes. She knew she was blushing, but one glance at Garrett relieved her embarrassment. He was leaning back on his arms with his eyes closed, clearly enjoying the warmth of the spring day.

The fish darted out of the way as she cautiously dipped in her big toe. Not wanting Garrett to see her ankles, she took the plunge and put both feet in, then covered as much skin as she could with her skirt.

The spring water was frigid but awakened something in Justine's heart that had been dormant for too long. She glanced at Garrett from the corner of her eye, noting how his shoulders filled out his shirt. He was man, through and through. Seeing him in this rugged envi-ronment with that look of contentment on his face sent her mind in alarming directions.

Justine closed her eyes, too, wanting to examine the feelings this day had brought about. First trepidation, then delight on the velocipede. Puzzlement turned daydream when she saw the land Garrett intended to build on. A deeper accord between her and Garrett. Now the chilly water making her feel young and so alive. She didn't want the day to end.

A noise in the bushes behind them caught Garrett's attention. He glanced back but didn't see anything out of the ordinary. Probably a squir-rel or a rabbit wondering why these strangers had taken over its habitat.

"Remember the pastor's sermon about the different facets of God?"

Garrett took note of how Justine's face changed expressions at the mention of her heavenly Father. Garrett decided to plunge ahead anyway. "Last night I was doing some reading before bed and came across a passage I wanted to share with you. After all, part of Pastor's assignment was to share our findings with someone else."

Garrett paused, watching Justine dip her hand in the cool water. When she didn't say anything, he went on. "It was in Colossians chapter two. Paul was talking about how after we receive Christ as Savior, that's just the beginning. I love that about God. He's always working on us. Paul says we need to be rooted and built up in Christ and strengthened in the faith.

"It reminded me of the conversation we had about foundations. That even if our foundations are shaky, our roots in Christ can go deeper. And as they grow deeper, we keep growing up in our faith." Garrett laughed softly. "Sorry, I feel like I'm the preacher now."

Justine looked pensive as she studied the water. "Don't be sorry. It's a lot to process. I still feel so hurt by God. On one hand I want to be close to Him again; I want to grow. On the other, I never want to talk to Him again. I guess you've given me something to think about." She seemed to hesitate. "Can I ask you a question?"

Garrett's heart beat double rhythm as he waited. Maybe she was ready to trust God and move ahead with her life. He'd been praying to that very end. He nodded for her to continue.

Justine swirled her big toe around in the clear pool. She seemed to be gathering courage for what she was about to say. "I wanted to ask you about my husband." Justine looked at him.

Garrett laughed nervously. That was not was he expected her to say. "What did you want to know?"

"Just about your relationship with him. How well you knew him. And if you have any idea who would want to harm him."

Those were loaded questions, to be sure, yet it seemed there was something else she wanted to know but wasn't asking. Should he reveal Jonathan's secrets? Or was it better to remember someone for who you thought they were, and not the harsh truth of reality?

"I had known Jonathan for a couple of years. Once we made a long voyage together to western England. That must have been before he knew you, though."

"Why do you say it must have been before he knew me?"

Here it came. Garrett took a deep breath and blew it out, looking up into the trees. Behind him came that sound again, and now the skin prickled on his arms at the thought that someone was watching them. But a sweeping glance didn't show anything out of the ordinary, so Garrett decided to go on. Maybe if Justine heard the whole truth, she could put the past to rest and live fully in the here and now.

"Jonathan was a go-getter. Always looking to make a way for himself. He did some things you could say compromised his integrity. It was when we came to Bristol that I met—" Did she already know?

"Who?" Justine asked cautiously. "Who did you meet in Bristol?"

"It was then I met his wife, Margaret."

"Is this some sort of a joke?" Justine's eyes had a wild look to them.

"No." He said the word low and calm. "There's more. We traveled up the coast a bit and around to Tenby, in Wales. That's where Jonathan introduced me to Helen. Then, when we got to St. David's—"

"Enough!"

Justine stood up, grabbed her shoes and ran as fast as her feet could carry her.

She burst through the trees lining the creek and into the open meadow. She didn't pause to look back when Garrett called her name. She ran toward the main house until she had to pause to catch her breath. This was worse than she had thought, but at the same time it made so much sense. It explained why Jonathan was away most of the time. Even if he had divorced this first wife before he met Justine, Garrett was making it sound as if her worst assumptions about her late husband were true. He did, indeed have a woman in every port. He had given them his best and Justine had gotten the leavings.

144

"Justine!" A man called out her name, but she didn't turn and look. "Mrs. Davidson!" She started to run again but he grabbed her arm, bringing her to an abrupt halt. Couldn't he see she wanted to be alone?

She turned to remove her arm, but when she looked, it was Eric Waverly's touch she was shrugging out of, not Garrett Cole's.

"Mr. Waverly," Justine said breathlessly. "What are you doing out here?"

Justine took a moment to compose herself after her jaunt through the field. She looked down to discover grass and weeds clinging to her new skirt. Her feet were bare and covered in dirt. A hand put up to her hair revealed it had gone awry as well. This was not how a lady should present herself. She must see to keeping her emotions tucked neatly away, too. Be more careful in the future. Mr. Waverly, after all, was a person with whom she would do well to mind appearances.

A glance over her shoulder revealed Garrett fairly stomping through the grass to reach them. Eric turned then and patted her hand as they started back toward the house, as if he had known her all his life. He had ways that made a lady feel all at once charmed and comfortable.

"Louis said you had taken the bicycles out for the afternoon, so I thought I would catch up to you."

"Was there something you wanted to see me about?"

"I always want to see you. But I actually came to speak with Garrett about some business we are conducting. It turns out I'll be staying on for dinner tonight too, courtesy of the generous Mrs. Cole."

Justine looked behind her and noticed Garrett had given up the chase and was walking back toward the bicycles. Eric and Justine made their way into the house, but she knew that even though it would be painful, her conversation with Garrett needed to find its conclusion.

# SIXTEEN

Mother!" Garrett said in a loud whisper. "I can't believe you invited that man into our home." It was one thing to do business with Eric but to have him at his dinner table was another matter altogether.

Garrett had found his mother in the kitchen, directing the cook in the course of the evening's meal, looking as if she didn't have a care in the world. She knew of his past with Eric, but if there was one thing about Charlotte Cole that Garrett longed to emulate, it was her ability to display the love of Christ even in an adverse circumstance.

Dusting off her hands, she regarded him with a look that he dreaded to know the meaning of.

He held up his hands in front of him in mock surrender. "I know, I know. You've taught me well, Mother, but that doesn't make it any easier to have that man in my home tonight."

Charlotte put her arm around Garrett as they walked from the kitchen and whispered in his ear, "Love thine enemy and pray for those who spitefully misuse you. I'll be praying for you, son."

As they entered the parlor, Justine and Eric were just coming in the front door. Garrett's stomach turned at the way Justine giggled and hung on Eric's arm as if they were courting. Garrett realized with a jolt that the way she was looking at Eric was the way he wanted her to look at him. As he forced himself to shake Eric's hand, Garrett had to wonder if he was more upset about his past with Eric or Eric's possible future with Justine Davidson.

☙❧

Dinner graciously brought itself to a close as the members of the party dispersed from the table. The women found their way to the parlor, no doubt to ogle over baby Caleb while the men retired to the wood-paneled library.

"I have to say, Eric, it was surprising to see you in my home this evening," Garrett said as the other man lit a cigar. Garrett and his father had never been given to the habit, and if he gauged the look on his brother-in-law's face correctly, it seemed Bret wasn't too keen on the smell either.

Eric waved the offending cigar in the air, as if to wave off Garrett's comment. "I may have been burned by you in the past, Cole, but a smart businessman knows when to jump in on the next big idea. I, of course, had heard of the new textile machines you are helping to put into production, but I had no idea I would be in on the initial investment. I can't say how much it thrills me to be one of the first to have a hand in this. Not only will it fatten my coffers when the machines start selling, but I'll hopefully be able to add its production to my own factory."

Garrett leaned forward, his hands together. "Are you saying you will also produce these machines?" Garrett hadn't thought of that angle. But of course Eric would want a piece of the action. Fabric, or at least the manufacturing of machines that brought usable textiles to the masses, was his business. Garrett wondered if Eric would employ children in his new venture. A picture of Justine flashed through his mind, one where she leaned out a carriage window, concern for orphans on her lovely face.

"Most assuredly. I plan on adding to the rear of the factory and hiring many more laborers." Eric's eyes held the distinct glint of a man in anticipation.

Even though Garrett itched to ask about Eric's opinion and usage of child labor, he knew Eric was a shrewd businessman and Garrett didn't think the question would be well received. Since they were about to do business together on a regular basis, Garrett wisely held his tongue but mentally plotted when he could pay a surprise visit to the factory to see for himself.

Talk then turned to other upcoming inventions of interest. The conversation normally would have attracted Garrett's attention and input, but his mind kept wandering to the girl in the parlor, the one with the giant-sized hole in her heart, the hole he helped put there earlier today.

Justine had forgotten how it felt to have a man make her feel special. Eric Waverly had caught her attention, and she had a hard time focusing on what the women were saying around the room. Baby Caleb was passed around, but Justine couldn't deal with the feelings holding the baby would conjure up. So, she declined her opportunity, instead occupying her hands with her cup and saucer.

Dinner had been a grand affair, almost perfect, had it not been for Garrett scrutinizing her from across the lavish spread of food. She counted her blessings again as she thought of her current situation. Beautiful dresses, a lovely home in which to stay, prominent society keeping her company.

Now as Justine sat in the parlor hearing the other women talk about what the next few weeks held, she fiddled with the ruffles in the dress she had changed into, contemplating her own future. Her situation looked good at the moment, but did it hold promise for tomorrow? How could she ensure she didn't end up like those women down on the wharf, or even that woman Garrett had given money to by the warehouse? Trusting someone else to care for her hadn't done her any good. Jonathan's care had left her not much better off than the poor souls who lived close to the industrial district. Justine shuddered involuntarily and ran her hands down her arms as she thought of being in dire circumstances again. She must carefully consider her options so as to not succumb to such a fate.

Charlotte Cole's voice broke into her thoughts. "Are you cold, dear? Perhaps you would like a maid to fetch you a shawl from your room, hmm?"

Justine took the older woman's suggestion as an opportunity to take her leave. She stood and turned to Garrett's mother. "Truly, I am all right, Charlotte, and I thank you for an enchanting evening. But I do I think I shall retire early. Good evening to you all." She nodded to Garrett's sister and made her way through the foyer to the staircase.

Her thoughts were playing tug of war with her mind as she began to ascend the steps. Part of her worried about how she could make the future secure with enough money and connections to the right people, the other part was still trapped in the loss and pain of the past. A deep ache squeezed her heart each time she thought about what Garrett had said about Jonathan's questionable ethics. Margaret. Helen. And there were at least two more besides herself. The woman Justine had seen him with the night he died plus whoever Garrett had been just about to name when she cut him off.

She sighed, wondering what else could possibly come up to surprise her about her late husband. When he died, Justine had felt loss. Now she felt pain at not only his deception about their money, but at his obvious lack of character. She didn't think she ever knew who he really was.

"Justine!" Came Garrett's breathless call.

She paused in her climb to the haven at the top of the stairs. She didn't think she had it in her to have another conversation right now. All she wanted to do was fall asleep and forget her troubles. Yes, all of a sudden, sleep sounded like the best solution to everything.

"Wait, don't go." Garrett's soulful eyes pleaded with her. Justine hesitated. "I wanted to finish our earlier conversation. Won't you step out onto the porch with me?" Garrett must have sensed her indecision. "Just for a few minutes?"

Justine felt her shoulders visibly sag. She may as well face the truth about Jonathan sooner than later. It wouldn't make the truth any easier to bear. And it really wasn't Garrett's fault he had been the bearer of bad news. She owed him an apology for running away like that. She descended the few steps she had climbed and followed Garrett onto the porch.

Once outside, Justine spoke first. "I believe you." It was a statement born of resignation, said barely above a whisper.

Garrett couldn't identify with how it felt to have your world pulled out from underneath you. But he did know the ache of watching life pass you by, seeing others realize and make your dreams their reality. Maybe pain was pain. And Garrett was taught that to have a friend, you needed to be a friend. With his work always taking him away, he didn't have many friends, so maybe this was the time to try out that theory.

Opening his mouth to speak, he scarcely got out the first syllable when Eric stepped out onto the porch. Biting back sharp words, Garrett gave the man a well-placed glare. Unfortunately, darkness hid his face and Eric seemed oblivious to Garrett's disapproval of his presence.

But according to Justine's bright response to Eric, she didn't mind him being there at all. In the shadows, he watched as Eric took Justine's hand and kissed it. Did she welcome Eric's attentions? But maybe he wasn't advancing on Justine at all. Maybe Eric was just being a gentleman and wanted to have a new friend. Eric had been pleasant all evening and had contributed good ideas about combining their interests to make this latest investment profitable for them both. Like Eric had said, bygones were to be bygones, after all.

Thankfully the dark-haired man didn't stay long. "I'd best be going. My business here is complete. At least for tonight. Good evening to you both," Eric said as he made his way to an awaiting carriage.

The porch of the Cole home ran the length of the front of the house and its southern exposure afforded a beautiful view of the long drive and bordering trees. Mother had seen to having special outdoor furniture made and Garrett remembered one year, when he was about ten, asking if he could sleep on the porch and pretend he was Daniel Boone, tromping through the wilderness with only the stars to keep him company.

Garrett smiled at the memory. Not exactly an adventure when he knew everything he needed was only a few steps away.

Justine had found a seat on one of the outdoor sofas and he boldly moved to sit beside her, all the while wondering how to comfort this young widow. How would she react if he tried to console her? He was, after all, the one who had told her the truth about her late husband.

Garrett watched Justine intently, trying to read her thoughts. She finally glanced his way, and in the nearness of her presence, he could see the pain in her eyes.

A soft spring breeze rustled the new leaves budding on the trees, teasing its way over to where they sat. Signs of new life were all around, but the death of who Justine had known her husband to be was as fresh as a new burial site. Oh, how Garrett longed to reach out to this beautiful girl, but he also knew the acid of betrayal had just been poured upon the open wound of grief.

"I, too, have known pain," he said, starting the conversation with his elbows on his knees, his hands steepled together. "Nothing like yours, of course. My own wounds are more akin to a long, slow burn. For years, I've had an injury of loneliness and of not being able to grasp God's elusive will for my life. There's been a deep grievance of knowing there's something more, something else I ought to be pursuing but never knowing what it is." He sighed, praying that his words would hit their intended mark.

But no response came. He could only offer wordless comfort now.

Finally, sleep. Justine felt so at peace, so at rest for the first time in too long. Her mind grasped to know the reason for her heart's unusual quietness. Something strong seemed to have her in its embrace and she longed to stay for an eternity. Yes, this was where she belonged.

From somewhere in her conscious thought, Justine realized light was piercing her blissful world. What would dare interrupt her paradise? Braving open one eye, she looked, only to find Garrett's arm around her and Charlotte Cole at the front door, the foyer lit up behind her.

"Oh. There you two are. We were just saying our goodnights."

"Yes. Goodnight, Mother." Garrett didn't seem too anxious to move. Justine would bide her time until Charlotte took her leave. "Time to wake up, sleepy head." Garrett Cole's intimate tone sent her scurrying to her feet so fast, she tripped over her hem.

The look in Garrett's eyes as he studied her unsettled her more than the state of affairs she found herself in. How he could sit there looking like the cat that swallowed the canary when he knew full well that he'd had no right to put his arm around her and keep it there?

"You're not angry with me, are you?"

Justine felt trumped. He may have offered her the comfort of his arm but she had kept it there by falling asleep. He was not to be faulted. Although she couldn't imagine how this looked to Charlotte. She hoped the household rumors would not run wild now, although she doubted Charlotte would start them.

"No, Garrett. The fault is mine. I guess everything just caught up to me. I'm tired. So very tired." She wanted him to read between the lines of what she was saying. She was tired of the shocking revelations. Tired of the hurt. Tired of trying to make sense of everything.

Garrett reached out and took her hand in his. He felt warm. Familiar. Justine felt her consternation turning to scrutiny as she braved a look at this man. There had been so many times since they met when she thought it was more than mere coincidence that brought them together. Times when he came at just the right moment, to her heart's rescue. Times like this when she thought she saw a little more of his heart bared before her.

Then again, what did she really know about this man, Garrett Cole? He was a smart businessman, that was obvious. He came from a wealthy family, and yet he sought more wealth. Why had he never married? Did he practice ethics when dealing with money? Did he use women as her late husband had done?

Garrett gave her hand a friendly squeeze. "Don't worry. This will be our little secret. And I'm here to talk whenever you feel like it. That's what friends do."

When Justine came downstairs the next morning, the house seemed unusually quiet. Carrie Anne had accompanied Charlotte and Anica to a brunch so that baby Caleb would be taken care of while the other women socialized. James Cole had gone to his bank, Bret to his work, and Justine didn't know where Garrett had disappeared to. She helped herself to a late breakfast then began a search for stationary and an ink well.

The scent of rich wood, leather, and old cigar smoke met her as she cracked open the door to a library on the first floor. A quick perusal of the room showed no desk, but curiosity waylaid her resolve to continue her hunt.

Leaving the door open behind her, Justine was overwhelmed by the sheer volume of books lining the walls of the room. Someone had taken great care in purchasing this fine showcase of literary work.

A table under the expansive window caught her attention. On it, a thick book lay open, lying in wait for its next reader to come by. Under the table was a stool, so Justine pulled it out and began reading.

The familiar phrases of Deuteronomy chapter four streamed like water off the page and into the thirsty places of her spirit.

*(For the* LORD *thy God is a merciful God;) He will not forsake thee, neither destroy thee.*

Justine closed her eyes as she pictured the people to whom God was addressing in the passage. His people, the Israelites. They had bowed down to idols and worshipped God's creation, rather than the Creator. They had tested and tried Him instead of trusting in Him. And what had been God's response? A promise and a covenant. Open arms in the face of their disbelief.

The people God was talking to sounded just like her. It was a hard truth to admit. Why had they turned their backs on God when He had rescued them from slavery? What else could they possibly want? She began to read again, a few verses down.

*Know therefore this day, and consider it in thine heart, that the* LORD *he is God in heaven above, and upon the earth beneath: there is none else.*

Frustration rose up in Justine. Of course she acknowledged God as God. What did He want of her beyond that? She shut the Bible hard, consenting with the voices in her head that told her she would never understand. That striving was in vain and ignorance was bliss.

She left the room, trying to escape the conviction in her heart that told her she could understand. Across the hall, Justine saw what looked like an office. A large desk dominated the center of the room while windows looked out onto the front lawn. Bookcases lined the wall to the right and heavy brocade chairs spoke of important meetings held there.

Justine spied a large potted pine tree in the corner. Its evergreen needles spoke of health and life, while giving off the fragrance of Christmas. The simple beauty of the tree brought her heartbeat back to normal and she stepped closer, its heady scent like a healing balm to her frayed spirit.

Fingering its smooth needles, she saw an object behind the pot that caught her attention. Something was tucked into the corner of the room where the tree resided. She bent to see what it was. Its shape was oddly familiar.

"What do you think you are doing, young lady?"

# SEVENTEEN

Justine whirled around, feeling like she had been caught taking a sweet from a candy store.

The butler stood in the doorway. "This is Mr. Cole's office. Please leave."

Justine put her hand to her heart, surprised by the man's reaction. Then again, Mr. Cole was a banker and might have very private papers in there, papers that held confidential matters regarding his customers.

"Do forgive me, Mr. Smythe. I was looking for some stationary. I'd like to send a letter to a friend in England. Perhaps you could assist me?" Justine hoped the distraction would quell any further rebuke from the Cole's employee.

He used his hand to direct her out of the room and led the way to a small sunny room down the hall. "This is Mrs. Cole's study and you may use it if you please. But, in the future, please refrain from entering Mr. Cole's office without permission."

The butler left the door open a crack when he took his leave and Justine settled herself at the writing desk with a shake of her head. Perusing the drawers, she quickly found everything she needed to complete her mission.

*Dear Mr. Flanning,*
   *Greetings from America. I hope this letter finds you well.*

*First, a sincere thank you for your efforts to find me before I left England. Knowing my father had made provision for my financial security gave me an unexpected opportunity to feel connected to him again.*

*The other matter about which I write is more painful for me to address. It is a personal request that I cannot complete without your help.*

Justine paused her pen in mid-air, taking a calming breath. *Don't panic, it's just a letter.* As much as she tried to tell herself that Jonathan was in the past, there was still a part of her that wondered about the man whom she had loved. She had ten questions to every one answer concerning who he had been. She needed to know the truth about his life. And his death.

*Since my husband's untimely passing, questions have been raised about his character, specifically regarding his business affairs and personal relationships. I am led to believe my husband was not the man he claimed to be. I would ask you to question the police about his accident. I don't know who would want him dead, but maybe they have more information for me. And finally, I have been informed of my late husband's extramarital relationships. I'm asking you to either confirm or deny my suspicions. I will compensate you for any information you can provide.*

*Please find a temporary address below and reply at your earliest convenience.*

*Sincerely,*

*Justine Davidson*

Justine put down the pen with a shaking hand. How could a man continue to hurt her when he wasn't even alive?

The last few days had proved more fruitful than Garrett had anticipated. Ironing out the details of his plans had kept him from being home much, but everything was falling quickly into place. He had quietly met with architects and city council members, keeping everything under wraps for the moment. Soon, all would be set to start building. His only regret was that this would be a sole endeavor.

Garrett handed over his horse to a groomsman and sprang up the steps to the house. He felt more energized than he could remember. This was it. This is what he had been being prepared for his entire adult life, he just hadn't known it. Yes, he was finally on course.

Justine had only graced him with a shy blush and quiet hellos since she had fallen asleep on his shoulder. As he came into the house, Garrett caught sight of Justine and Carrie Anne in the parlor, opening what looked to be shopping bags. He held his own bag behind his back, not wanting the girls to suspect what might be inside.

"Hello, ladies. Had the afternoon off from watching Caleb, Miss Barnes?" Garrett addressed the young woman but chanced another look at Justine's face. He hoped she would continue to be open with him, and he regretted his absence over the last few days. Perhaps if he had been available, they might have continued their discussions.

"Yes. Anica decided she wanted to spend the entire day with him, so this morning I accompanied Jeffrey on three house calls and then I couldn't say no to Justine. She promised to buy me some new clothes." Carrie Anne's bright face reflected her happiness but Garrett could tell Justine was tired by the strained look in her eyes. A walk in the garden might brighten her spirits a bit.

"Would you ladies care to join me outdoors for some afternoon refreshment?" Garrett noticed Justine cast a hesitant look in Carrie Anne's direction. "It's the first day of May, after all. We should be outside. And if you agree, I can pour a little charm on Cook and get some sweets sent out to us." He gave them his most pleading look, hoping they would agree.

Garrett watched Justine until she had the courage to look him in the eye. Hers shone a brilliant blue against her soft skin. Add to that what the warm day had done to her curly hair and the end result combined together quite nicely.

Thankfully, Carrie Anne spoke up before Justine had the chance to turn him down. "I think I'll lie down for a bit but Justine was just saying how she longed for some time in the garden, weren't you?" She looked pointedly at her friend.

Garrett moved quickly so Justine wouldn't have the chance to get away. "Wait right here."

In the foyer, he hurriedly put the contents of his bag into his trouser pocket then procured some goodies from the kitchen. With basket in hand, Garrett stepped onto the porch where he found Justine standing quietly against a pillar.

He took a fortifying breath and prayed for the right words to say. He was afraid his delivery of the news about Jonathan had withered their budding relationship.

"Come. Walk with me?" Garrett said as he held up the delectable offerings in the picnic basket.

Justine turned slightly and shrugged her shoulders. Garrett realized he would do anything to garner a smile from that beautiful face. Maybe he could pull her from her somberness if he chose his words carefully.

He started walking around the side of the house then headed in the direction of the little pool the stream created. He was grateful when Justine fell into step beside him. "Looks like you and Carrie Anne had a nice afternoon shopping. Did you find anything in particular you liked?" Perhaps speaking of something she clearly enjoyed would draw her out.

Justine's eyes brightened slightly at the mention of her new purchases, but quickly dimmed again.

*Lord, help me here.* Then a thought struck him. Maybe she wasn't upset about the other night. There could possibly be a more serious reason she wouldn't directly look him in the eye.

"Justine. Look at me." He stopped on the path, and his heart turned over at her expression. "What is it?"

"Oh, Garrett." Justine crossed her arms and looked at the ground. "I love shopping and when I am busy buying things, I feel happy. But then the joy disappears faster than it came." She shook her head. "I feel like I have this huge hole inside."

Garrett nearly smiled, but caught himself. It seemed God was already at work answering his prayers. *Give me the words, Lord.* Garrett knew He would.

"Justine, I think God is trying to tell you something. That hole in your heart you speak of can only be filled by God Himself. Believe me, I know." Garrett chuckled softly. He sighed and looked up into the clear sky. "I have learned the hard way that when I pursue my own dreams and desires, that 'God-spot', as I like to call it, only gets bigger." Then he tipped Justine's chin up until she met his gaze. Her blue eyes were filled with questions.

"You know, there is nothing wrong with nice things," Garrett said. "I myself enjoy a little luxury. We just have to be mindful of where our financial blessing comes from and return what God gives us back into His hands."

Justine had looked back down at the ground but she nodded just the same. He hoped he had given her some things to think about.

Garrett remained where they were on the path, the goodies forgotten. He dreaded what came next. "Justine, I'm leaving tomorrow."

She jerked startled eyes back to his. Oh, how he wished she wouldn't look at him like that.

"I thought you were happy to be back. You've only just returned."

Garrett hoped her inquisitiveness was a sign she might be coming to care for him. "Yes, my mother was just as surprised. But I must go. An opportunity has presented itself. If I can gain enough financial backing for this project, I may be able to hang up my traveling shoes. For good."

"Really? What are you thinking of doing instead?" Justine asked with open curiosity.

Garrett set down the basket and raked his fingers through his hair. He laughed self-consciously. "My father has offered me the position of second in command at the bank. I'm seriously thinking about it." He leveled her with his gaze. "I'm hoping to put down some roots when I get back."

Justine felt herself blush, but knew it had nothing to do with her lingering discomfort of falling asleep against this man's shoulder and everything to do with the way he looked at her as he said his last statement.

"Oh. I see."

Garrett rubbed the back of his neck. "Well, I suppose we'd better head over to our rock and enjoy our little picnic."

Justine noticed Garrett's reference to "our rock" and wondered if it was just a slip of the tongue. It wasn't as if this was their own special place. She settled down on it, this time leaving on her shoes. "How long will you be gone? Will I see you before you leave?" Justine couldn't stop herself from asking. She bit her lip and realized she was holding her breath as she waited for his answer.

He put his large hand briefly on her shoulder and she could feel delightful tingles all down her arm. "I'm not sure how long this trip will take. There are several factors that are a bit unpredictable, but I am not leaving the country this time."

Garrett opened the basket and distributed cookies and cold lemonade. "How about if I stop by the charity event tomorrow night before I go?"

Justine nodded shyly as she sipped the delicious drink. "I'd like that."

Garrett leaned back slightly on the rock and reached into his pocket. He withdrew a small box and held it out to Justine. "Before I go, I also wanted to give you this."

Garrett had gone out of his way to buy her a personal gift. Something he had thought about in advance then made an actionable plan. The thought was astonishing. Other than her father, she could not think of a time in her entire life when she had been the recipient of such exclusive treatment. Justine all of a sudden did feel like this was their special place. This was their moment. Their friendship.

"Go ahead. Open it."

The lid lifted easily and there, lying on top of a soft bed of white cotton, was a silver fawn. Its little legs were folded underneath and its bright curious eyes gazed back at hers.

"It's the necklace from Bijoux d'Artisan. I loved it from the first moment I saw it."

"I know. I find myself feeling the same way."

Justine looked up, wondering if he was talking about the necklace or something else.

"There's more. Go ahead, open it."

She lifted out the unique locket and opened its hinge, wondering what other surprises she would find there. Seeing what looked like a tiny scroll, she turned the deer over and the paper fell into her hand. It was so small, it seemed impossible that something could be written inside.

She laughed self-consciously, saying, "It's a good thing I don't need glasses." The entire width of the paper was no more than an inch and whoever had written the words must have done so with a special writing instrument. No quill and inkwell she knew of could do the job. She read out loud:

*As the hart panteth after the water brooks,*
*so panteth my soul after thee, O God.*
*My soul thirsteth for God, for the living God:*
*when shall I come and appear before God?*
*Yet the* Lord *will command his lovingkindness*
*in the day time, and in the night his song shall be with me,*
*and my prayer unto the God of my life.*
*Why art thou cast down, O my soul?*
*and why art thou so disquieted within me?*
*hope thou in God: for I shall yet praise Him,*
*who is the health of my countenance, and my God.*

"It's almost more than I can accept." Justine looked at Garrett. "Why did you do this for me?"

"This psalm, I think, was written for you. The Bible is God's love letter to us, after all. He wants you to know He's right there with you, day and night. Always." Garrett shrugged. "And maybe I hoped it would help you remember our friendship while I am gone."

"Thank you, Garrett. I do thank you." Justine slipped the locket over her head and adjusted the little deer whose back laid flat against her shirt-waist. "We'd better head back. I think I'd like a rest this afternoon, too." "As we walk, I have two things I'd like to say. A warning and a challenge."

At that moment, Justine felt she would say yes to anything Garrett asked, heed any warning. What he had to say was bold yet she gave both things serious consideration as they strolled back to the house, taking a scenic route through the gardens on their way.

In the very middle of the garden, Justine noticed the trunk of a tree she hadn't seen before. Someone had taken great care in carving five names in the bark. JAMES + CHARLOTTE. ANICA + BRET. The fifth simply read GARRETT.

Justine felt something stir in her middle and was startled to realize she was picturing her name carved next to his to keep it company.

# EIGHTEEN

The beautiful blue silk of the dress Justine wore made soft *whooshing* sounds as she walked into the grand hall. Sights and sounds assailed her senses as she took in her surroundings. Not even the welcome dinner aboard the *Blue Flag* could rival this grand affair. The arched ceiling of the hosts' home reflected the soft glow of numerous candles while a string quartet played beautiful tunes. A vast assortment of food was laid out for all to enjoy and everywhere she looked, ladies and gentlemen in their finest dresses and suits stood talking and laughing, while others swirled to the music on the dance floor.

Justine felt her heart flutter as she thought about having to dance next to all the seasoned socialites who were in attendance. Thankfully, Charlotte Cole had taken a few moments this week to show her some simple steps.

She fiddled nervously with her new locket. Would these people change their opinion of her if they knew this was the nicest piece of jewelry she owned?

What had she been thinking when she accepted Eric Waverly's invitation? She knew exactly what she was thinking. She wanted to be in this exciting world. To make connections with those held in high regard. To be seen and associate with the most prominent citizens in Virginia. To be escorted by a wealthy gentleman who made her feel special.

Justine looked around discreetly for a familiar face. Eric said he would meet her here at seven o'clock. A glance at the grandfather clock by the doorway revealed it was nigh unto a quarter past now.

Then, coming toward her with an air of anticipation was Garrett Cole. How handsome he looked this evening in his fine tuxedo. Justine felt her face grow warm under his gaze as he wove his way through the crowd, never once taking his eyes off of her. She wondered at her feelings for him just as she wondered how he felt about her.

But before he could reach her, another man stepped to her side. With her attention focused on Garrett, it took Justine half a moment to realize it was Eric Waverly. He cleared his throat twice before she could force herself to look away from Garrett's face. Then embarrassed by her obvious attention to Garrett, she made a deep curtsy, hoping it would hide her discomfiture.

"We meet again, old friend," Eric said to Garrett, as he put his hand on the small of Justine's back. Justine squirmed under his touch and hoped Garrett didn't think she welcomed Eric's attention. All of a sudden it was extremely important to her that Garrett know she wasn't interested in Eric. Her father used to tell her she had very expressive eyes. She tried to send Garrett a silent signal, but he quickly mumbled, "Yes. Good evening to you both," and never looked back.

Garrett stood in the garden outside the ballroom watching the sunset. He was thankful for his faith in the Creator at times like these. Helped to put things in perspective. He was also thankful this area appeared to be empty of lovers looking for a quiet place to rendezvous during the party.

Red hot anger flared when Garrett thought of the way Eric had put his hand on Justine like he had a right to her. How dare that Waverly! Then again, Garrett had yet to make his feelings known, and what man in his right mind wouldn't welcome the company of Justine Davidson? She had such a grace about her. The way she carried herself, the way she could look at a man and make all rational thought leave his head. Her spunk. Even her insightful, brooding questions about God. He should feel grateful for the time they had spent fashioning their friendship over the last few weeks.

But Garrett wanted to be more than just Justine's friend. Last night he couldn't sleep as he wrestled with these new feelings. He shook his head and laughed quietly. Yes, he was in over his head. Images of him and Justine courting, then getting married and having a family of their own had assailed him throughout the night and into today. Garrett shoved his hands into his pockets and began to stroll the gardens. What would it feel like to gather her into his arms and kiss her sweet face...

But as he rounded a hedge, it wasn't his lips that were alighting on Justine's but Eric Waverly's. Eric held Justine in his embrace as his hand slowly stroked her silky hair. Justine seemed to whisper against his mouth and Garrett turned away, sick from witnessing the intimate exchange.

In all his years of worldly travels, every tragedy and sadness he had encountered, every lonely place he held secret on the inside, the image of Justine passionately kissing another was the worst catastrophe of all.

Tinkling laughter and floating music from the party faded into the background as Justine fought against the feelings Eric's kiss brought back. She realized how hungry she was for the intimate touch of another human being. It somehow made her feel alive again. But reasoning got the better of her as she realized what was happening. Goodness gracious! Suddenly it dawned on her why Eric's touch had felt so good. Justine had been imagining Garrett's lips caressing her own. How soft they would feel as they made a trail down her neck...

"Eric, please stop," Justine whispered against Eric's lips.

Oh, dear. How had this just happened? However it had come about, it couldn't now be undone. Justine stepped back quickly from Eric, putting space between them. She brought her hand to her throat. "You shouldn't have done that, Mr. Waverly." He seemed to be trying to hold her captive in his gaze.

"My, but you are a welcome addition to my life," Eric said with a smile in his voice. "Please forgive my saying so, but your kisses are delightful, my dear." He held his hand out to her. "Do come back so I may come to know those lips more fully."

Justine shook her head. When he said he wanted to come outside to view the sunset, she had no idea this was what it would lead to. She would not let him kiss her again.

"I can tell you are attracted to me, my sweet. Don't be afraid. Your beauty has captivated me from the first day I saw you. I have been able to think of little else. Do forgive me for being so forward and if you won't kiss me again, then allow me the pleasure of a dance?"

Justine led the way to the doors, knowing fully that Eric was close behind. She supposed she should accept his offer to dance. But she couldn't look him in the eye and instead searched the room for Garrett. He was nowhere to be seen, even after she and Eric's third dance together.

Despite the feelings the kiss had left her with, she began to enjoy herself. Eric was a good dance partner. He was gracious when she stepped on his foot and had an easy laugh. They finally took a break and Justine made her way to get something to drink while Eric got caught up in conversation with someone along the way to the refreshment table.

Although the evening had been fun, something else was on her mind. Justine knew before she swept the room with her gaze one last time that Garrett wasn't there. He had said he would stop by the ball to say goodbye to her. Perhaps that's what he had been planning to do when Eric had showed up. Regret seized her heart as she allowed herself to acknowledge what she knew to be true.

Garrett was gone.

Garrett released a mirthless laugh as he packed his bags for his upcoming trip. The ball had barely begun when he had hastily taken his leave. He couldn't imagine enjoying the evening after witnessing Eric and Justine together in their clandestine meeting in the dusk of early evening. Tomorrow morning, he would wake before anyone else in the house and take his horse the first leg of the journey.

Funny how things could do a complete turnaround faster than he knew was possible. When he arrived at the ball earlier that night, Garrett could scarcely keep from bursting through the doors. The sooner he told Justine how he had come to feel about her, the better. He couldn't wait to reveal the new and exciting feelings he was having for this beautiful woman. He had thought if he could get her alone for a few minutes, Justine could make her excuses to Eric and spend the rest of the evening with Garrett. Then they could dance and he would have sweet memories to carry with him on his journey and much to look forward to upon his return.

He had even begun to think this might be the woman God had for him to marry. Ha! Garrett grabbed the nearest shirt out of the wardrobe and threw it into his valise. Clearly, Justine Davidson wasn't the kind of woman he thought her to be. If she could so easily fall to Eric's allure, a spell Garrett knew had been cast on too many women to count, she wasn't the woman of character he wanted as his wife.

Forget the plans to leave in the morning. He knew he couldn't be here when he heard Eric bring Justine home in a couple of hours. Shoving the rest of his items in his bags, he slammed the front door behind him and made his way to the stables. He saddled his horse, strapped on the bags, and kicked the mare into a canter. He raced out of town, leaving his feelings for Justine behind.

If time could prove to be a balm to his broken heart, and perhaps given the right circumstances, he may just let his mother play matchmaker with him and one of the young ladies at church. At least then his loneliness would come to an end.

As Justine lay in bed at the Cole mansion later that night, she smiled at the memories of the evening. She had never danced so much. Eric had graciously let others have their turn, but he always found his way back to her.

Her fingers touched her lips. When Eric had dropped her off, she would have bet money that he would try to kiss her again. But instead, he was the perfect gentleman and only offered her a courtly bow.

Carrie Anne, of course, had wanted to hear every detail of the evening. She sat in rapture as Justine described the dresses and music and ambiance of a society ball. Justine left out the kiss in the garden, knowing her conservative friend would not approve. Justine had taken joy in retelling of all the politicians, businessmen, and ladies of high regard she had rubbed elbows with. Only when Carrie Anne had asked if Eric Waverly was a Christian did Justine feel her joy deplete. Justine didn't know the answer to Carrie Anne's question, and was pretty sure she wouldn't like it if she did.

Getting involved with someone who didn't have a strong relationship with God was what had gotten her into trouble with Jonathan in the first place. Although Justine's current faith was on shaky ground, she knew if Jonathan had had a solid foundation in Christ, he wouldn't have crumbled so easily under the weight of temptation.

Squirming under her covers, Justine tried to get comfortable. It was getting warm on these late spring evenings. Maybe if she let a breeze in, she could get cool and finally fall asleep. But as she walked to the window in her nightgown, she knew the restlessness she felt had nothing to do with the heat and everything to do with what was going on in the secret places no one could see.

*If everything hadn't fallen apart, then I would be able to be content.*

And if that was the truth, then she would just have to put her world back together. And she would do whatever it took to make it perfect.

Thinking about Eric Waverly, her heart leaped with excitement that a man so attractive could possibly desire her company. Justine felt her face heat at the remembrance of his arms around her during the dances and his hasty kiss in the garden. Who was this man, and why was he interested in her? He was handsome, rich, and charming and could probably have any woman he pleased.

But if she were to make a life for herself here in America, it wouldn't hurt to have his attentions. He was, after all, a wealthy businessman who was clearly savvy with his finances, having just partnered with Garrett on an important investment. And since Garrett had left without another word to her at the ball, she could safely assume he held no interest in her like she thought he might.

Garrett.

What would he think of her and Eric's private interlude in the garden? Justine took a step back from the window as she remembered Garrett's warning yesterday. Garrett had told her Eric had a way with the ladies. Was she simply his next conquest?

She would never know unless she played it out. And if she did it right, she could form an attachment to Eric Waverly so she would never have to fear being alone or poor for the rest of her life. This could well be the answer to all of her problems. Then maybe her heart would finally be healed and whole.

# NINETEEN

W hy, I do declare," said Mrs. Dunsmore as she spied Justine at the jewelry shop. "That wouldn't happen to be a bracelet Mr. Eric Waverly purchased for you, would it?"

Justine was fully aware that Mrs. Dunsmore knew it was from Eric. The landlady had made a point of keeping her nose in Justine's newfound relationship with the factory owner. Justine still felt uncomfortable with their burgeoning relationship being the talk of Waterford Cove.

Over the last couple of weeks, Justine had found herself at the center of Mr. Waverly's attention. It seemed that every other day, Eric came calling, brought her lavish gifts or took her to a party.

His most recent present had been one that gave her pause about where their relationship was headed. Although Justine hadn't allowed Eric to kiss her lips since the night of the ball, when she opened a box last night that held the dazzling emerald bracelet, she allowed him to kiss her wrist when he slipped it on. She knew that small display of affection was only a tiny glimpse of what he felt for her.

"Day dreaming of that handsome man, I see." Mrs. Dunsmore elbowed her in the side.

Justine handed the bracelet to the jeweler.

"You're not returning that, are you?" Mrs. Dunsmore looked appalled.

"No, ma'am. I just needed a link taken out." Justine decided to avoid confirming the nosy lady's suspicions on where the bracelet had come from.

"No doubt you know he can easily afford to purchase such wonderful gifts. And with an attractive figure like yours plus an enticing bank account, why wouldn't he?" Mrs. Dunsmore laughed as she exited the shop. Justine stood at the window and watched as Mrs. Dunsmore made her way across the street to Waterford Cove Chocolatiers.

Anger burned in Justine's heart as she absorbed the not-so-subtle implications of her previous landlady's insinuation. Is that what everyone thought? That Eric would only want to keep company with her for superficial reasons? Was that all she was seen for? Part of her was flattered. Who wouldn't want to be admired for their beauty and wealth? At the same time, she wanted to run after the pompous woman and tell her that Justine Davidson was so much more than that. That she was a Christian. That she had a father and a family who loved her and a future filled with the simple joys of life. But her mental diatribe quickly died. For those things were no longer true of Justine Davidson.

"A package came for you today, old fellow." Garrett's long-time friend brought the parcel to the table where they were enjoying lunch al fresco. Thankfully his investment route took him past the home of Charles Houst and his wife, Genevieve. The couple always had a place for him when he came through town. And although Garrett enjoyed some of the opulent hotels he stayed in, it was also nice to be in the comfortable presence of good friends.

The Houst's home was nicely appointed, on a large piece of land overlooking a lake. Their lunch was laid out on an outdoor table set up to take in the spectacular views. But the wonderful panorama and homemade food didn't compare to the real reason Garrett was grateful to be there. He knew full well this was a place he could be himself, gain some perspective, no pretense necessary.

"Do tell us more about the lovely Mrs. Davidson. Why, Garrett, she sounds most delightful." Genevieve Houst beamed at him from across the table where she sat next to her husband.

"I've probably said more than I should. It's dangerous territory for me to dwell on her any more than necessary. I fear I must gain back some of my heart if I wish to give it away to another someday." Garrett picked up his fork, intending to dig into his peach cobbler.

Charles laid down his napkin, but didn't let Garrett off the hook. "What's this about another woman? Is there someone else who's been catching your eye? I know you've been looking for the woman God has for you for some time now."

Garrett shook his finger at his friend. "Don't get any ideas, now. There is no one yet. Just the anticipation of someone else, even if she is faceless at the moment." Hoping to divert the conversation away from such topics, Garrett finished his dessert quickly and picked up the package.

"Don't look so forlorn, my friend. God has someone for you, He just hasn't revealed who it is yet."

Garrett barely heard what Charles said when he saw the package's origin. It was from Waterford Cove. Justine had sent him something! His mother must have given her the address where he would be passing through. But upon closer inspection, Garrett realized it was his mother's handwriting. Disappointment assailed him but he tried to cover it by opening the box to inspect its contents. "It's from Mother."

"Charlotte. Always thinking of others. Knowing her, she probably sent you a letter and some yummy cookies from Cook." Charles peered into the box expectantly, licking his lips.

"Like you haven't had enough to eat already," Genevieve elbowed her husband.

"No, you're wrong about that. I'll never get enough of you, my dear," Charles responded with a glint in his eye and kissed his wife's lips. They both laughed with the intimacy of two people in love.

Garrett paused from his perusal of the box to study his friends' faces. They looked so content. What he wouldn't give for that kind of closeness with another. He had thought it might be with Justine, but images of the kiss she and Eric had shared continued to haunt both his waking and sleeping hours.

Digging in the box, Garrett paused. *What in the world?* He pulled out the predicted cookies and set them on the table. Underneath lay a letter and a photograph of a woman. Setting the letter aside, Garrett couldn't take his eyes off the picture.

The young woman wore her light hair hanging loose. The hint of a smile played at her lips. And she had the most pleasant eyes. Turning the photograph over, it read "Summer Edwards, North Carolina, 1890." Suddenly, recognition dawned on him. He had seen this woman before. She had come to visit his church with her aunt last summer. At the time, she had worn her hair up, not around her shoulders like in the picture. Garrett laughed softly that he would remember such a detail.

Surely his mother's letter would explain the reasoning for the picture being included in the package. Garrett's curiosity was certainly piqued.

"What does it say?" prompted Genevieve.

Garrett filled them in while still scanning his mother's handwriting. "My mother is playing matchmaker again. She has tried to set me up with countless ladies in the past." And he knew why she was at it again. In his flurry to leave Waterford Cove, Garrett hadn't taken the time to say goodbye to his parents, but he had written them the next morning. His letter hadn't given all the details about Justine, but he had explained his need to get away and gain perspective. He was grateful now he had also told Mother he'd be going by the Houst's.

"This is a picture of a young woman I met last summer." He showed them Miss Edwards' image. "It says here that she has come to the area again to stay with her aunt and that my mother has made her acquaintance at church. It describes her as having a strong relationship with Christ and a heart for the poor and needy."

Charles laughed. "And she's beautiful. Sounds like the perfect woman for you. All that is needed now is your approval. What do you say, old boy? Ready to settle down and start a family of your own?" Charles put an arm around his wife and smiled down at her. "Trust me. Best thing I ever did."

Garrett stared out at the lake, thinking he was more than ready. More than ready to begin the next chapter of his life, to have someone by his side who would share his passions and calling. More than ready to walk beside someone who would be the other half of his whole. He winced, thinking that Justine was no longer an option for him. It seemed only fair to his heart to move on.

With a sigh of resignation, he knew what he would do. Tonight, he would pen a letter to his mother asking her to pass on a message to Summer Edwards. One that included his intentions of pursuing a courtship with her when he returned to Waterford Cove.

But as he lay on his pillow later that evening in the Houst's guest room, it wasn't the lovely Summer whom he pictured by his side for the remainder of his days, but the courageous, beautiful widow he had met next to a shattered carriage on a cobblestone street in East Wharf, England.

The man walked into the tailor's shop on Waterford Cove's Main Street. This errand had eluded him for some time now, but it was time to make it right. The green vest was his favorite and he intended to see that the tear was repaired correctly. It had been a busy couple of weeks and he hadn't had time to see to such details. But he knew he had Justine in the palm of his hand now. An important night was coming up and he wanted to look his best.

"Haven't seen you in here for a while, sir," the tailor said as he approached the counter. "What might I do for you today?"

"See to it that this is fixed perfectly. You know how I hate to be disappointed."

The tailor grimaced and handed him a claim ticket. "I assure you we do the finest work here at Rush's Tailoring and will repair it so you never knew what happened." He paused, then added, "What did happen to it, by the way? Such a big gash," he said, fingering the fine fabric.

"Just an errand gone awry. And mind your own business. I'll be back this afternoon to pick it up."

"This afternoon? No, sir. I cannot possibly fix it that quickly."

"Make it happen." The man slammed the door behind him, but soon had a whistle on his lips. He was getting close to the culmination of this little orchestration he was planning. And he couldn't wait to experience the grand finale.

⟡

Even though no one had imposed it as requirement, Justine had been attending church with the Coles for the last couple of Sundays. It seemed strange to not be able to talk about the sermon with Garrett on Sunday afternoons or be challenged by his gentle questioning.

In some ways, she felt as though she were mourning the loss of Garrett, as though he had died. *You're silly,* she thought, *he's just an acquaintance. And he'll be back someday.* But, oh, she missed him and looked forward to the next time they took a stroll in the garden or went to their special rock.

And yes, Justine admitted silently, she had chosen to come to church today because she wanted to sit where Garrett normally sat with his family, hear the words from the pastor he would have heard if he were there next to her. Justine wondered what these feelings meant for her relationship with Eric.

Jeffrey had stopped by to pick up Carrie Anne, and the two of them waved as they made their way to Jeffrey's carriage. Justine was happy for her friend, but wished she had someone at her side to enjoy this beautiful Sunday morning. Eric surely wouldn't be caught dead attending a church service, of that she was certain. During their time together, he had made his disdain of religion apparent. And one look at his beguiling eyes made it easier to believe him when he said religion was for the weak. It was in those moments when Justine was able to convince herself that his lack of interest in the things of God was of no consequence.

But in the light of day, it gave her pause. Then this morning she had woken with a strong urge to attend church with the Coles. Even after all that she had lost, she knew Eric was wrong. Religion wasn't for the weak; it was for those who knew they needed a Savior. Justine felt closer to letting her anger go, closer to being able to bless God's name again. Closer, but not ready yet. Maybe going to church again today, even if it was to feel close to Garrett, was a step in the right direction.

"Don't you look as fresh as the summer flowers this morning?" Charlotte complemented Justine as they made their way outside. "Perhaps there is a young beau at church this morning that may catch your eye. Oh, that's right. You have been spending quite a bit of time with Mr. Waverly lately, haven't you?"

Justine felt herself squirm at Charlotte's questions. Surely Charlotte knew Eric wasn't the church-going kind, and Justine realized how much the older woman's opinion of her mattered. Charlotte was a strong Christian, Justine knew. But it wasn't just a show like it was for some of the women she had met at fancy parties. For them, it was a social standing, a way of impressing people.

But Charlotte was different. She had an abundance of joy and peace that could not be mistaken. Justine knew Charlotte couldn't give away what she didn't have. A heart could not have an overflow if it was not first open and then welcomed what God had to pour into it.

They made their way to the church, Justine's thoughts bouncing between Garrett, Eric, and God. She was relieved when they arrived, so she could at least focus on the latter. She was getting exhausted trying to keep track of her jumbled thoughts these days.

After the singing, a young lady named Summer Edwards came to the front. She had shiny blonde hair and light green eyes. She spoke with an engaging manner, and Justine was immediately drawn to her.

"Good morning. My name is Summer Edwards. I have recently come to Waterford Cove from North Carolina to stay with my aunt. Some of you may know her, Miss Elizabeth Anton." A woman who looked too young to be Summer's aunt stood briefly and nodded at the congregation. "After meeting with some of you in our assembly here and speaking with the pastor, he has approved a new ministry for our church to get involved with. As you may know, our town has a high percentage of orphans."

Justine's ears perked up at the mention of the children.

"It is not within our church's plans to start an orphanage at this time, but there are things we can do." She withdrew a sheet of paper and scanned her notes. "First, we can collect money to start a fund for an orphanage to be built. Second, we can gather donations to be given to the children, including food and clothing. Next, we can invite these little ones into our church to hear the gospel. And finally, some of you may feel the Lord leading you to adopt one or more of these children." She folder her paper into a neat square and moved to sit down. "If you feel moved by the Lord to assist in one or more of these areas, please see me after church. Thank you."

Justine's heart was pounding by the time Summer Edwards finished her speech. Barely hearing the pastor's sermon, she thought about the list Miss Edwards gave. Was there something in what she had named that Justine could contribute to? She had always had a soft spot in her heart for wee ones who didn't have anyone or anything. Could this prompting in her heart be from the Holy Spirit? Probably not. He must not want anything to do with her since she had all but rejected Him.

"And this is how we love, because Christ first loved us," the pastor was saying. "And because of this love He has bestowed upon us, we can receive that love and become children of God. Our Lord then commissions us to pass that love on to others around us. Maybe you've had the chance to do that for someone lately.

"We will all go through hardship and great loss. But God uses the people in our lives to bring His love to us during those times. Jesus says, 'In the world ye shall have tribulation: but be of good cheer; I have overcome the world.'" The pastor paused and made eye contact with many in the congregation. "Could it be that this is another facet in the diamond of God's love for you?"

It sounded so simple, didn't it? Justine's cynical, hurting heart was trying hard to draw the parallel between God loving people so much that He could send His son to die for their sins and then allowing hurt and pain to enter their lives.

But upon closer inspection of the recent past, she could not deny how people had reached out to her. Carrie Anne, agreeing to come to America. Charlotte Cole, an example of a godly woman. Garrett, his companionship and strength present when she had needed it most. Not to mention the many material things that had been provided. First Class passage to America. A temporary home. Money to support herself. And, with the way things were progressing, a possible future with Eric Waverly.

Yes, she would have to admit, God had provided. So why did she feel abandoned by Him at the same time? There would be no easy answers, but she would set that aside and find Summer Edwards after church. Justine wanted to know the quickest way to take action with the orphan ministry.

Charlotte did the honors of the introduction. "Miss Edwards, I would like you to meet my dear friend, Justine Davidson. I do believe she was out and about the two times you've come by. She arrived from England this spring and is staying with us for a spell."

The young woman curtsied with all the refined class of a lady. Her clothes were impeccable and she held herself with a certain grace. But although her high upbringing was almost palpable, Justine sensed an adventurous spirit about the young lady. She had an independence about her, a confidence that said she would take on whatever came next and even do it with a smile.

"It is a pleasure to make your acquaintance, Mrs. Davidson."

"The pleasure is mine. And please, call me Justine."

"Only if you'll agree to call me Summer."

Justine tipped her head in agreement and asked if they could take a short walk around the church. "I wish to discuss with you what you mentioned earlier in the service."

"You two ladies take your time," Charlotte offered. "We'll meet you at the carriage out front when you are ready."

As the two younger women started walking, Justine began to ask questions about how Summer saw things progressing with the orphan ministry.

"I just arrived in town. But in coming here, I was looking for something worthwhile to occupy my time. Charlotte and I have met for tea, and she has informed me of the orphans and their work in the factories along the coastline. I was appalled when I learned many of them are injured at work and have nowhere to sleep, and what they eat they find in the refuse bin."

Justine noticed tears come to Summer's eyes. Justine could relate. She felt the same way about the children.

"Summer, what can I do? I want to help in any way I can." Justine remembered the day Garrett had given her and Carrie Anne a tour of the town. They had seen the factories, and Justine had heard some of them employed children. Maybe that's where she could start. But no, that would be like shooting one bullet at a thousand stampeding elephants. What good would it do? She could barge into every factory, but who would listen to her?

"One of our biggest needs," Summer was saying, "is financial." She shook her head. "If only we had the funding we needed to build an orphanage. But what am I saying? It is going to take years to raise money for something like that, not to mention construct a building that would house so many children. And who would run it?" Summer laughed, a tinkling sort of sound. "There I go, not having faith even as small as a mustard seed."

"Oh, I know all about that. Don't worry; you won't be judged by me. I have had my fair share of lack of faith." They had made a full circle around the church and were now nearing the front. "I have some ideas forming in my head, Summer, and I think I might be able to help." What she was thinking was crazy, but she just might be courageous enough to pull it off. "Like Charlotte said, I am staying at the Coles. Would you like to come for dinner tomorrow evening? I'm sure Charlotte won't mind. Then we will have the chance to talk about this again."

"Well, well, well, what do we have here?" Eric Waverly sauntered up to the two young ladies. His eyes perused Summer from head to toe, and Justine was tempted to be jealous. But then again, Summer was a very attractive woman. Still, it made her feel uncomfortable.

"Eric Waverly, meet my new friend, Summer Edwards."

Summer extended her hand for a small shake, but Eric took the liberty to kiss the back of her hand.

She withdrew it discreetly and looked at Justine. "I look forward to speaking with you further, Justine. I am certain we will be able to do much together to help the orphans, especially those who are forced to work in the factories. Good day, Mr. Waverly."

Summer hadn't gotten two steps away before Eric hissed loud enough for Justine's new friend to hear. "What's this about helping orphans? My girl is too good for that. I will hear of no such thing."

Summer caught Justine's eye as she walked away. How embarrassing. Didn't Eric know it was good form to be with a woman who was kind and helped others?

Trying to hide her red face, Justine cleared her throat and smoothed her skirt. "Eric, what a surprise to see you here." As she looked up, he caught her around her waist and pulled her to him. Justine could see over his shoulder that the Coles were waiting for her in the carriage.

"I couldn't wait until tomorrow to see you, my darling. I was hoping to steal you away for the afternoon." He bent down slightly to look her in the eye. "Hmm? What do you say, my dearest?"

Justine suddenly felt very uncomfortable in Eric's presence. Maybe it was because she could feel the Cole's watching them. "Thank you for the offer, Eric, but I already have plans for the day."

It wasn't a lie, exactly. Now that Eric had proposed to spend the day together, she tried to think of something, anything, to get away. Her plans suddenly included continuing the challenge Garrett had spoken to her of the day before he left.

"Maybe next time?"

But Eric wasn't to be let down so easily. He grabbed her arm and Justine winced. Wiggling free, she began to walk away. "Goodbye, Eric."

He raced to get in front of her, halting her progress.

"You're mine, you know. That bracelet you're wearing. That diamond hair clip. That new purse. All the parties I've taken you to. You're my girl now and nothing will change that." He smiled. "You might be able to elude me now, but I promise I'll always be around. Always."

Justine didn't respond and stepped around him. When she finally settled in for the ride home, Justine wouldn't look anyone in the eye. Her thoughts tormented her. Who was Eric Waverly and where had the charm and attractiveness gone? Justine tried to appease her conscience by telling herself he was just having a bad day.

But what if he was just now showing his true nature?

# TWENTY

It was an interesting challenge. Justine pulled her Bible out of the bedside table drawer and flipped to where the chain of the deer locket held her place in the book of Matthew. She was in chapter six now.

The day before Garrett had left, when he had given her the locket, he had done two things. Warned her about Eric Waverly and challenged her to read her Bible every day while he was gone. He said that he, too, would be reading, and they agreed to be in the same passages, though they were miles apart.

The first week, Justine had spent in the Gospel of John. It had been good for her heart to be reminded again of home when she had first opened to the book and found the flower she had pressed there. She had stroked the dried petals and remembered her father and all he had meant to her over the years.

Then the words of John, especially around the middle of the book, tested what seemed to be the farthest corners of her heart. God was trying to sweep them clean with His Word of life, but Justine still felt herself holding back.

Now she was in chapter six of Matthew, right in the middle of the Sermon on the Mount. She could almost see the eyes of Jesus. He was looking directly at her and telling her to follow Him. Reminding her to seek Him first and not to worry about clothes or how she looked or what she ate or drank. He promised to take care of all that if she would but trust Him. The question was, could she do it? And did she want to? Trying out her fledgling faith, Justine whispered the Lord's Prayer from the passage. "Your kingdom come, Your will be done," she repeated again.

Justine silently read the rest of the chapter, thinking of Garrett somewhere hundreds of miles away, reading the same thing. Was he giving his worry to the Lord and laying up treasures in Heaven? She hoped for his sake that he was.

"Your kingdom come, Your will be done," Justine whispered again as she drifted off to sleep.

"You look divine!" Carrie Anne exclaimed as she helped Justine with her day gown. "I know I said I wasn't interested in the finer things, but I'm trying not to be a bit envious of you going to the mayor's home for luncheon. But remember what Jesus said, 'When thou makest a feast, call the poor, the maimed, the lame, the blind: And thou shalt be blessed.'" Carrie Anne fluffed the rose-pink skirt of Justine's dress. "I suppose that doesn't apply to you since you're not the one hosting today."

Justine gazed at her reflection in the mirror in the guest room at the Cole mansion. She heard what Carrie Anne was saying but her thoughts were on other matters. Even though Garrett had been gone for weeks now, she still thought of him daily. When would he return? Would he still want to be friends with her? Oh, who was she fooling? Even her image in the mirror seemed to mock the mask she tried to put on.

Sometimes when she was alone in the garden or at her and Garrett's special rock, places where they had spent time getting acquainted, she would permit herself to subscribe to the truth. Truth that included wanting a future not with Eric, but with Garrett.

Ever since Eric had treated her roughly in the church yard, she hadn't been able to shake an eerie feeling about him. She had tried to not be alone with him since, a fact he did not seem to appreciate. He still came calling, despite Justine's coolness, and had yet to apologize for his rude behavior in front of Summer Edwards and the Coles. Even Jonathan in all of his lies had never been harsh or forceful with her. She consoled herself that, in reality, it was the only time he had ever done such a thing. The other times they had spent together had been almost magical. She should give him another chance.

Now she was headed to the mayor's home for the social luncheon of the year, and she knew the invitation had come only through her association with Eric Waverly. Justine felt like a fraud. If she couldn't say to the mirror that she wasn't even sure she liked the man, how could she say to a group of elite ladies that she wanted a future with him?

As Louis delivered her to the mayor's massive brick home, she compared the two men who had become part of her life. While Eric had a presence about him that commanded attention, Garrett had a gentle strength she anticipated encountering again and again. Eric's forceful kiss the night of the ball only made Justine long for the taste of Garrett's lips. Both men were smart businessmen, but Garrett's love for the Lord made Eric's attitude seem haughty and prideful at times.

Justine sighed and fiddled with her necklace, not her precious gift from Garrett, but a recent trinket from Eric. Everywhere they had gone together, it seemed the man had people in the palm of his hand. The ruby pendant at her neck attested to his efforts to get her in the same position. And she was tempted to succumb to his attentions. He was handsome, wealthy, and very well connected. It was rumored the mayor treated him like family.

Since arriving in America, Justine had slowly grown accustomed to being around women of impeccable dress and manners. But as they neared the gate to the home, butterflies assailed her stomach. Ladies in magnificent dresses were milling about in the late morning sun as she approached the front steps.

"Justine!"

She looked around to find the source of the soft, feminine voice.

"Summer, how nice to see you again." Justine tried to hide the red she felt coming into her face. "Please forgive me for canceling our appointment to talk about the ministry. I truly wanted to take part, but…" Justine left her sentence hanging, not certain what to say. Eric had come calling the day after the incident in the churchyard and had staunchly prohibited Justine's involvement with the orphans. He had been quite persuasive.

But no one new, least of all Eric, that every day this week she had placed herself on special assignment. Using Garrett's bicycle from the stables, each morning she had taken Garrett's shortcut to town. It indeed was a straight shot. She took her own money and stopped by a bakery and packed her shoulder bag full. Crossing it over her chest made it easy to carry and she would pedal all the way to the industrial district, passing by the Dunsmore Inn first.

The first time she had not seen the two street urchins who begged at the inn's back door. But every day since, she had found them. They would poke their heads out of a nearby alleyway, and once she had gained their trust, they began to smile at her. She had so many children now between the inn and the factories that she'd had to rig up a system for carrying extra bags of food. It had been a good week, but now thoughts of Eric's disapproval sapped her joy.

Summer put her hand on Justine's arm. "Do not worry," she said in her friendly manner. She had a way about her that brought Justine comfort. "We need to be submissive to the men in our lives. This, I understand." She had a small smile on her lips as she said it, like she had a great secret she was holding inside.

"Why, Summer, do you have a man to tell me about?" Justine felt as though she had known Summer for many years, rather than such a short period of time.

Summer's cheeks turned pink and she looked down at her pale green day dress. "Well, it is not common knowledge yet, but soon enough… Maybe I shouldn't say anything."

Now Justine really wanted to know. Summer was fairly new to town, but perhaps her aunt had arranged a courtship with an eligible bachelor. "You can tell me, Summer. You know I'm a newcomer as well and I really don't know that many people."

Summer laughed softly as the two made their way to the garden at the back of the house where the women would take their lunch then hear a word from the Mayor Burkett. "Don't try to fool me, Justine. Many people seem to know who you are. And everyone knows Eric Waverly. You're here today, aren't you?"

"All right, you have me there." Justine echoed Summer's laugh. "But I still want to know!"

Summer took a seat at one of the opulent tables canopied by a large honeylocust tree. Justine joined her, an anxious expression on her face. Summer settled her green skirt around her and looked at Justine with a sparkle in her eyes. "It's Garrett Cole."

Justine felt her face turn pale.

Summer rushed on. "Oh, I hope this wasn't too much of a shock. I know you're staying with the Coles. Do you know Garrett well?"

Justine thought she managed a nod, and she knew her face was quickly going from white to pink. Did she know him well? Not well enough, it seemed, that she wouldn't be aware of an important detail such as this. Justine's heart felt like it was in her stomach, and the food being set before her only made it worse.

Then her mind started to put together a timeline. Garrett had left before Summer had arrived. When had this courtship happened? Justine thought she might choke on her thoughts, so she took a long drink of iced lemonade, a treat on such a hot day.

"Have," Justine cleared her throat, "have you known Garrett long?" She took another long drink.

Summer waved her hand in the air. "No, no. We truly have only met once. Last year, in fact. But through the matchmaking talents of my aunt and Charlotte Cole, and, of course, some help from the Lord, Garrett has sent me a message that we will begin a courtship when he returns on Monday."

Monday? Garrett was returning in two days? Justine's heartbeat picked up just thinking of seeing him again. But then again, he wouldn't be interested in seeing her. He would have eyes only for Summer. Justine looked at her friend from the corner of her eye, taking in Summer's lovely yellow hair piled high to show off her equally lovely features. No, Justine could not imagine that Garrett would even have a moment to speak with her now that Summer would be in his life.

Summer seemed to be looking expectantly for Justine's response. "Oh, how wonderful for you both," Justine said absentmindedly as she scrambled to piece everything together. Surely Garrett had known of this before he left. Or perhaps he had sent correspondence from one of the stops on his trip. Maybe it had been love at first sight for Garrett and Summer. Maybe Justine had merely been a friendly diversion for his love-sick heart while he waited for his true love. In the end, Justine realized, it really didn't matter how they met or when it all took place. What mattered now was her own future. And the fact that it would not include Garrett.

Summer laid her hand on Justine's arm. "So? Any thoughts?"

Justine could not lie. She would not. Summer need never know her feelings for Garrett.

At Justine's silence, the other woman went on. "Even if you can't be involved in the orphanage, I'd love to get your take on making the ministry a success."

Goodness! How long had Justine's mind been wandering? A servant came by and refilled her glass and she took her time adding some sugar to sweeten it further.

Clearing her throat again, she said, "Of course. Please give me a week or two to put some thoughts together. I apologize again for not being able to meet with you before about this."

"You are far too apologetic, my friend. I know your heart in this matter. I can see it in your eyes." She sat back in her chair and folded her hands in her lap. "The eyes tell all, you know."

Justine looked down suddenly, not knowing what it was she felt she had to hide. Maybe her feelings for Garrett and the fact that she wished she was in Summer's shoes. Looking up, Justine squared her shoulders and decided she would stay on the subject of the orphanage and hope Summer wasn't as good of a judge of people as Justine feared.

"You are right in saying my heart is in this ministry. I would love to contribute financially." Justine took a bite of fresh fruit, looking thoughtful. "It was in England when the plight of poor children first laid hold of me. Since arriving in Waterford Cove, I have seen for my-self the need here. I'm anxious to help." Justine hesitated.

"But?" Summer prompted.

"I would like to remain anonymous in my contributions."

"Of course."

Justine pushed her barely touched plate away. It would be easier if no one caught wind of her early morning jaunts just in case her esca-pades got back to Eric. But she could help financially. Maybe even con-tribute in cash. To remain undisclosed was the wisest course, especially since she and Eric could continue their relationship now that Garrett would be with Summer.

She and Summer began going from table to table making small talk with the other women. Justine sincerely hoped Summer would gain more supporters today for this new endeavor.

And as for her feelings of fraudulence about being Eric's lady, she could socialize with confidence now. With Garrett and Summer's imminent courtship on the horizon, Justine's only choice would be to attach herself to Eric Waverly. She would fabricate a life for herself with him that would make her forget all of the painful things of the past. Garrett included.

"You have a letter from the post today, Justine." Carrie Anne situat-ed herself on the bed and held out a large envelope.

"Just put it on the nightstand, Carrie Anne." Justine's hands fiddled with her hair as she sat in front of the mirrored vanity. "Oh, I just can't get these curls right."

"You know you can always ask me to help," Carrie Anne said with a smile. She came behind Justine and fussed until she got the look just right. "Where are you and Eric headed tonight? And if I may ask a per-sonal question, is it getting serious between the two of you?"

Justine looked down at her hands. They used to look quite calloused and worn. But her arrival in America combined with the discovery of new wealth had afforded her to rely on others what she used to do for herself. She would wear long ivory gloves tonight, but that didn't hide her delight at the change in her skin. Ah, what a little money would do.

Yesterday she had left the Cole mansion with romantic thoughts of Garrett Cole coursing through her mind. She had returned with the knowledge of his relationship with Summer and a new resolve to never feel abandoned again. She was just plain tired of it. First her parents, then husband and baby, and most recently, Garrett. Not to mention God. He clearly had no interest in staying by her side. Her circumstances were evidence of that. She felt her newly softening heart toward Him growing hard once again.

Justine straightened her shoulders and admired her new gown while Carrie Anne fastened the ruby necklace at her throat. Eric insisted she wear the jewels he had given her when they were going to be seen in public together.

Her future was becoming more secure. She would simply take matters into her own hands and hopefully someday be the wife of Eric Waverly, the most charming man she had ever known. She would be engaging and beautiful and refined and win his heart so she could guarantee the kind of future she deserved.

"To answer your question, we're going back to Rue De Flores. And yes, we are quite serious. He never hesitates to let me know how beautiful he finds me or to lavish me with generous gifts. I dare to say he may propose soon."

"But Justine, what of his relationship with God?"

Justine flushed slightly. "He has no interest in the Lord, but he is a man of virtue and high morals."

Carrie Anne met Justine's gaze in the mirror. Justine knew what her friend was thinking before she even said it.

"If only that were enough, Justine. I know you and the Lord have hit a rough patch this year, but if you spend time in His Word and in prayer, you will realize His ways are best. He is the one and only thing in our lives that is constant when things go wrong. He has a good plan for your life. And might I be so bold as to say that plan doesn't include you marrying someone who doesn't share your faith."

Justine began to protest, but Carrie Anne silenced her with gentle pressure on her shoulders. "I will leave you with this thought, my dear friend. God has *always* had His hand on you, whether you knew it or not. He never lets go, Justine. Never. Through anything we could go through in this life, He is faithful and His love is unwavering. And whenever you are ready to turn back to Him, He will take you back with open arms and never let you go."

She watched her friend walk quietly from the room. Could Carrie Anne be right? Justine did long for the love and faithfulness Carrie Anne spoke of. She had tried to follow the rules of what God said and look where it had gotten her. But since she took matters into her own hands, she finally felt a little more peace. She was finally in control of her future.

Dismissing the bothersome thoughts, Justine crossed the room to the side table where Carrie Anne had dropped the post. The return address from Brookefairshire caught her attention.

Justine carefully opened the letter. She glanced at the bottom of the missive to confirm the signature. It was signed "Mr. Flanning." Her heart began a double-time rhythm as she read the script.

*Dear Mrs. Davidson,*

*I am of the hope that this letter will find you quickly. I took the liberty of paying the captain of a ship a high wage to deliver this with his shipment to America. I prayed that would be faster than sending it by post. It was imperative that this letter reach you as soon as possible.*

Justine's heart dropped to her stomach. She placed her hand on her chest as she wondered what her father's banker and lawyer could have to say that was of such import. She knew it must concern her inquiry about her late husband. But what sort of information would he have that would need to reach her quickly? She took a steadying breath and read on.

*After receiving your request regarding your late husband, I used my connections in the legal circles to look into his past. I know you had your suspicions about him, so I hope what comes next does not shock you overly much.*

*It appears Jonathan used his job at the pier as a cover up to purchase and transport illegal goods from many coastal towns along England's shoreline and even to and from America. Of course, he didn't usually do the deliveries himself, but he was the main man on most jobs. I also inquired of the constable in charge of the investigation of his death. I hope what I need to put down in pen next has already been deduced by your bright young mind.*

*The police gathered the remains of the hansom cab and came across fragments of a grenade, the kind that would be difficult to acquire but assures unquestionable harm or death.*

*The constable told me they have contacted the manufacturer of the grenade to learn its burn time. That will help determine if the bomb was already in the cab when Jonathan entered or if a bystander threw it into the cab. In short, as you already know, it is certain your husband was murdered.*

*The police are asking if you know of anyone who would want him dead or if anything unusual happened at the scene of the accident or shortly thereafter. Please send word as soon as you are able.*

*You know how much your father's friendship meant to me. That is why I feel it my responsibility to advise you to be careful. It is not certain that the person who is responsible for Jonathan's death may not somehow also chose to go after you…Especially now that you have your father's money.*

*Sincerely,*
*Mr. Flanning*

Justine sank onto the bed as she absorbed the words of the man her father had trusted with his will and wealth. If her father had placed his faith in Mr. Flanning, she was certain she could, too.

The initial shock of the letter was wearing off, so she reread Mr. Flanning's request for more information about Jonathan's murder. Was there anything unusual that could offer the investigator a clue? She tried to relive those last few moments before and after Jonathan's death.

She remembered she had seen Jonathan on the wharf, speaking to that woman and then to Mr. Cole. Garrett had purchased Jonathan's cab home, whistling to one that was nearby. The hansom had moved out of sight and moments later, the loud explosion. Then running to see what happened.

When Justine came to the scene of the accident, she recalled watching as someone removed Jonathan's body from the cab and laid him in the street. She was kneeling at this side when a man had come up beside her. Wait. That had been Garrett Cole. She had never considered his presence there before.

But he had been there. She was sure of it now. And then he had paid for passage and boarded the same ship as Justine. Now she was living at his house, and he had complete access to her bank account. It was the perfect set up. Mr. Flanning had warned her the same person who had killed Jonathan may be after her, too. For revenge or maybe money. Oh, heavens!

No wonder Garrett had been so nice to her. He was trying to get close enough to her to either do her or her bank account harm. Thoughts of their moments together assailed her. How could she have been so blind? The time on the dock and then again at the door to her cabin on board when he had offered to take her bag. Or when he happened to be the one to help her when she wasn't well upon arrival in America. And how conveniently he had come to her emotional rescue when she was in distress.

He must have wanted to keep Jonathan's money, so he disposed of him when he had the chance. Oh, he must have had a few good laughs on how well he had pulled the wool over her eyes. It was a good thing he wasn't coming back until tomorrow. She could ring his handsome neck. He was a pretty good pretender. Garrett had her convinced on more than one occasion that he was a devout Christian trying to help her and be her friend. He never would have had to follow her and give her the money. Justine never would have known about it if he hadn't told her; Garrett must have had a romantic tryst in mind all along. She would never forgive herself for falling for him. What a bad judge of character she had been. It was her situation with Jonathan all over again.

Well, Eric would be here any minute. And as long as she kept her early morning food deliveries and her involvement with the orphanage a secret, everything should go fine.

Justine couldn't believe she had at one time compared Eric and Garrett. She had Garrett so built up in her mind that Eric lost without a fight. But now that she knew Garrett had been a phony all along, she saw Eric entirely differently. And she couldn't wait to be a more permanent figure in his life.

Tonight would be a special night with Eric. She was sure of it. Not only would she work on pursuing a relationship with him, she would ask him to be her protector from the villain Garrett Cole. Eric would have the right connections in which to prove Garrett was the guilty party in all of this. Then Garrett would get what was due him.

# TWENTY-ONE

Garrett's trip had been more successful than he could have hoped for, allowing him to come home a day early. He had enough backing for this investment to see a hefty return. And the textile machine that had initiated this trip was proving to be a mighty big hit with the industry. He wouldn't be surprised if he received many years' worth of income off this one invention. It was just what he had prayed for. Now he could join his father at the bank as vice president, begin to court Summer Edwards, and settle down permanently in Waterford Cove.

As Garrett let his horse wander down the path that led to the field behind his parent's stone home, his mind wandered to the day he had taken Justine out here on the bicycles. She'd been having such a great time that day, and he had ruined it by telling her about her husband's many indiscretions. Why had he brought her more harm? What a fool he had been.

What he should have done was take her hand in his and tell her what he thought of her. That she was a precious woman of God, that the Lord could heal her hurts if she would just let him. How he was beginning to see her as a dear friend, and how he hoped God had something special planned for them.

As the house came into view, he wondered why he was even giving her another thought. She had made her choice, and it was clearly Eric

Waverly. The kiss Eric had given her had been made in the shadows, but Garrett had seen longing on Justine's face. Her whispered affections, even though he couldn't hear them, had convinced him he needed to move on.

And so, that's what he had done. Now that he was home, he would propose to Summer. No sense having a long, drawn out courtship. He knew what he needed to know. Summer was interested in the same things he was. And she was a Christian. A beautiful one at that. End of story.

Garrett's horse drew near the stable, and Louis came out to take care of the animal and to greet Garrett.

"Good to see you home, Mr. Cole."

"Nice to be home, Louis." Garrett dismounted and peered out the barn's door. "Who's that pulling away in the carriage?"

Louis's eyes took on a guarded look, and Garrett feared he didn't want to know the answer. "Mr. Eric Waverly again to take Mrs. Davidson to dinner."

Garrett swallowed. He really shouldn't care. But he did. "Does he come often?" He bit his lower lip, hating to know the answer.

Louis tied the horse to a ring in the stable wall and began to unsaddle him. "None of my business, but if you ask me, he comes too often for my liking."

Garrett nodded, affirming the man's opinion. Eric had been trouble from the first day they had met in school when they were just boys. He hated that this final investment trip had been instigated by the man's partnership.

Their most recent feud began a couple of years back when Eric was clamoring to be the top investor in the machines that would take the typewriter from something only a newspaper would own to an everyday household item.

Garrett had not accepted Eric's generous offer of partnership, and instead had given his favor to Jonathan Davidson because of Eric's lack of integrity. If he would have known about Jonathan's less than savory business dealings before they signed their agreement, Garrett wouldn't have included Jonathan in the deal either.

He shrugged as he walked to the house. No one could foresee the future except for the Lord, and Garrett knew he couldn't go back and erase who the main investor had been. If the only good thing that came from the entire affair was that Justine was financially taken care of for the future, that was good enough for him.

He greeted his mother with a warm hug and a promise to catch up with her later, then poked his head into his father's office. "Sir? You have a minute?"

"Garrett, come in. Just finishing up some paperwork. Good to have you back."

Garrett seated himself across the desk from his father. "I must say, I'm tired, but there's something on my mind that can't wait. I wanted to ask if your offer of vice president is still on the table?" Garrett steeled himself for his father's answer, but he needn't have feared.

A smile lit James Cole's face in response. "I was praying you would accept. Does this mean we can make it official?"

"It's official. Let's talk in the morning about the details." He stood from his chair. "Thank you, Father. This is an answer to my prayers."

The two men shook hands and Garrett retreated to his room. He needed a few moments to himself before beginning his evening.

As he gave himself a fresh shave and a new change of clothes, Garrett pondered what Eric and Justine might be doing right at this very moment. In his mind's eye, they were dining in opulent splendor at one of Waterford Cove's finest restaurants, laughing and planning the future. After dinner, they would venture out on a walk, hold hands, and gaze into each other's eyes.

Garrett could feel his ire rise just thinking of the two of them together like that. Justine must surely be blind to have fallen for Eric's charms.

Well, he would show her who had some charms. He stormed from his room and down the stairs all the while muttering to himself. The more he thought about Eric and Justine together, the madder he got.

"Mother! Father! I'm going out. Don't plan on me for supper!" Garrett yelled just before he slammed the door behind him.

He had somewhere to be and it couldn't wait a moment longer.

Eric straightened his newly repaired green velvet vest as Justine climbed into the carriage with him. So far, this evening had gone better than he could have anticipated. He just had one more thing on the agenda, and then it would be considered perfect. A diamond engagement ring weighed heavy in his pocket. When it graced Justine's slim finger by the end of the evening, he would be able to breathe a little easier.

Not only had Justine been talkative and responsive to him all throughout dinner, she had confessed she had information about Garrett Cole's possible involvement in her late husband's death. What a nice little twist. He had already planted evidence pinning the murder on Garrett. And now, even before someone had found it, Justine was already convinced. Perfect.

*Why, yes Justine,* he thought, amused, *I do have connections that could prove Garrett is guilty. He was there at the scene of the accident? Oh, you poor dear, I would be happy to do whatever I can to help bring his conviction.*

He put his arm around Justine's shoulders as the carriage started to roll away from Rue De Flores. Justine looked especially radiant tonight. Her cheeks glowed a soft pink and her hair framed her features in the most extraordinary way. Too bad he would have to snuff out her life while she was so young.

But he wouldn't do that yet. No, he would have a little fun first. Marry her, bed her, then take her money, or should he say Jonathan's money, as his own, and go on his merry way. And since he would have rights to her financial accounts as her husband, no one could come chasing after him. Yes, it was all working out better than he had planned.

But what a tragedy it would be when the maid found her dead in their bedroom, her wedding gown on the floor. He squeezed Justine's shoulder, and she looked up at him with trusting eyes.

But first, let her find the box. "Justine, my dearest. I was thinking about that beautiful evergreen in the corner of Mr. Cole's office. I saw it when we had our meeting in there a few weeks ago when I joined you for dinner."

"Yes?"

"I was thinking how nice it would be to have one of those for my own office. I'm going into town on some errands tomorrow. Would you go in there tonight and see if it has a label so I know what kind it is?"

"Sure," Justine said hesitantly.

"I'd be most grateful."

A slow smile tipped his lips as that little detail was taken care of. He turned his thoughts to the wedding night. Too bad this little beauty would have to leave the world so soon. If he didn't have revenge on his mind, he might just keep her around and enjoy her a little longer.

He gently stroked her shoulder with his hand. Too bad indeed.

Garrett tied his horse to the hitching post outside Summer Edwards's aunt's opulent home on Lumière Square. He hoped Summer could spare a few moments of her time this evening.

As he had ridden to her house, Garrett contemplated his next steps. Summer was a lovely young woman from a wealthy family. She was of marrying age and, from what he had heard, displayed spiritual maturity in her decisions. He couldn't wait to get to know her better. If he has his way, he'd marry Summer before a month or two could pass. He hoped their conversation tonight would lend itself to speaking of their possible future together.

He might be rushing things, but he didn't care any longer. Justine's heart was taken by another; he was lonely, and the perfect woman had come to his attention. What bigger sign did he need than that?

A maid answered the door to the stately residence, smaller than his parents' home, but similar in appointments. Garrett was shown to a formal parlor while Summer was fetched.

Soon she appeared in the archway, a vision in pink satin. Garrett's breath caught as he took in her beauty. He stood and tried to compose himself as he made a formal bow.

"Good evening, Miss Edwards. Do forgive me for stopping by unannounced."

Summer's singsong voice carried over to him as she spoke. "Oh, Mr. Cole, once you have come to know me better, you will find I do not worry over such things. Please, feel free to be yourself around me." She blushed slightly. "And I hope you will afford me the same offer."

"By all means. You must be surprised to see me here this evening since I was not to return until tomorrow." Garrett swallowed hard as they each found a chair to occupy.

"If I may be forthright, I felt I could not wait another minute to begin our courtship. And if I can say so freely, I feel mighty blessed to have your consent to such a favorable arrangement."

Even as he said the words, his heart screamed *Traitor!* He silenced the voice by focusing on Summer's red face, comparing Justine's soft pink blush to Summer's unbecoming scarlet.

Summer toyed with the gloves on her hands. "Your mother and my aunt speak quite highly of you."

"Would you mind taking a walk with me, Miss Edwards?" Garrett motioned toward the archway that led to the foyer. He thought of all the times he had asked Justine to walk with him. How natural it had been to have her at his side. How deep their conversations had been. How much he had looked forward to the next time.

He sighed as Summer allowed him to escort her out the front door. He didn't think it would be inappropriate to walk with her as long as they stayed within the square of homes on this unique block.

As they strolled, Summer told him of coming to Virginia from North Carolina, how she longed to spread her wings now that she was out from under her parents' watchful eyes and how glad she was to have a chance to get to know her aunt. She also told of the orphanage ministry she had helped to start at the church and her dream of seeing it have a large impact in Waterford Cove.

They made two loops around the square, each speaking of their interests and families. Summer was an intriguing young lady. As she spoke, Garrett tried to convince himself that she could very well be the woman God had saved for him all along. As he made his way home later that evening, Garrett wondered if indeed he and Summer had a future together. He would pray about it for a day and Lord willing, the next time he saw her, he would have a ring in his pocket. But he would buy it somewhere other than Bijoux d'Artisan.

# TWENTY-TWO

Justine turned the diamond engagement ring over and over in her palm as she made her way to her room. She laid her cape on the bed and looked out the window. The sun was setting on the horizon, preparing to bring in the darkness of night.

Her prediction to Carrie Anne had come true: Eric had proposed. She hadn't accepted yet, but he told her to keep the ring, just the same. She never would have guessed when she left the shores of England not so very long ago that she would find herself attached to a man of Eric's caliber. She leaned her head against the glass, closing her eyes and trying to picture her life with him. It seemed exciting and made her nervous at the same time.

Justine shook her head and admired the diamond once again. This is what she had wanted. What she had strived for. A secure future and someone to share it with. She was in firm command of her life, and now she would never be hurt again.

So why wasn't she feeling secure or even happy? Sighing, she looked out the window at the coming twilight. She knew the answer, just as surely as she knew the dawn would come in the morning.

She had to think about something else, get her mind off of what her heart was trying to tell her.

Carrie Anne was playing cards again with Jeffrey in the drawing room so Justine began to tidy up the room before getting ready for bed. As she did so, she pictured Eric's face. He had been gracious and considerate throughout their evening together and seemed to be his old self again. There was no sign of the Eric who had forbid her to help the orphans or the one who looked at other women when they were together. His attention had been riveted to her and he appeared to hang on every word she said. His proposal had been sincere, if, in her opinion, a bit rushed.

Yet it still seemed odd to her that he would not want her to have any involvement with the new orphan ministry. As much as she wanted to impress Eric, helping them was something Justine was not willing to give up. She was planning on riding to town again in the morning to purchase bags full of food and distribute the goods to fill hungry little bellies. And she would keep going every single day. No matter what.

But now a weighty decision needed to be made. When Eric had pulled out the ring and asked for her hand, something within her gave her pause. Her heart should have started thudding within her chest, but instead it sank to her stomach. She disregarded the feelings as nothing more than anxiousness. Everything would work out; it would just take time.

Before she lost the baby, she had always prayed on a matter before making a decision. That must be the tugging she felt in her heart, a sense she should take this to the Lord. Would He even care about her relationship with Eric? Although she tried to tell herself God had no interest in her, deep down she recognized a grievous and uncomfortable truth.

God had always been there. Justine was the one who had deserted Him, not the other way around.

It was too hard to think about, and it was too late now. She felt an ocean apart from God and had no idea how to get back to Him.

This was the time of day she normally spent a few minutes in the Bible, reading what she and Garrett had decided upon. But not tonight. Feeling confined by her thoughts, she left her room. Maybe she would write Mr. Flanning back to thank him for responding to her letter so quickly and tell him what she remembered about the accident and

Garrett Cole's presence there. She also wanted to reimburse him for his trouble.

She made her way down the stairs, thinking of how Eric had promised to get on the matter of bringing Garrett's conviction as soon as possible. It was a good thing Garrett wasn't due back until tomorrow, otherwise she may feel obligated to stay in her room. As it was, she and Carrie Anne would need to find another place to live. She hated to think what the consequences of Garrett's actions would do to his dear family.

Justine slowed her steps as she passed the library on her way to the writing desk in Charlotte's study. Remembering the day she went in and found the Bible open under the window, she put her hand on the solid wood door. What was the verse she had read that day? Oh, yes. About God's mercy and how He would never abandon or destroy. Then an invitation to acknowledge God as Lord.

She paused at the door, wanting to go in. Such an enormous space separated her parched soul from a clear stream, just out of reach. Was it really that simple? Would reading the Scriptures with an open heart bring her to the footstool of the Almighty? Could she brave a step in God's direction and hope to have Him meet her halfway? She turned the knob.

Someone had reopened the Bible and flipped its pages to the fourteenth chapter of the Gospel of John. It's where she had been reading last week. Justine ran her fingertips over the words. Even being near the Word of God felt like it could bring restoration. But Justine knew the Scriptures were like food to the body. What good was a scrumptious meal set before her if she never partook of it? Suddenly ravenous for the truth, she read the words on the page illuminated by the moonlight coming through the window.

*Jesus answered and said unto him, If a man love me, he will keep my words: and my Father will love him, and we will come unto him, and make our abode with him.*

Justine paused as she considered these words. Was her heart Christ's home? *Yes, Lord. I know You're here.*

207

She had been the one to try and shut Him out. But God had stayed. His love had resided. His once crystal-clear voice was now a mere whisper. But, oh, how she longed for Him to speak openly to her now. *Speak to me, Lord.*

Rereading the verse, she focused on the part about love and obedience. When she was little, her father had disciplined her, and she believed it was for her own good. It was her faith in him that caused her to obey out of love. Faith was the catalyst for her growth at the loving hand of her earthly father.

Was it the same with her heavenly Father? Remembering all her papa had taught about her Savior, all she had read in God's Word, she knew. The answer was *yes.* Yes. It really was that simple. All she had to do was believe.

*I do believe, Lord. I do acknowledge you as my God. You've neither abandoned nor destroyed me. Show me how I got to be comfortable with the idea of being mad at you. How could I push you away so easily? What is in my heart that caused me to ignore Your teachings, Your Word, and build my foundation on the shaky ground of love of this world and anger at You?*

Pride.

The single, simple answer stared her in the face as she read His words from John once again. Christ's love was there for her. Had been there for her. Would always be there for her. No matter what. It was her fleshly pride that kept her from grabbing onto that love with all of her might.

Carrie Anne was right. God never let go. Not once, through all the times Justine had pushed Him away. He had never turned His back, never shut her out. Amazing.

Remembering the pressed flower in her own Bible, Justine thought about how sometimes death must come to bring life. As she prepared to give her heart back to Christ, she knew she could always fondly remember her family. No, it wasn't her past that needed to be eradicated. It was her pride. Her self-centeredness. Her love of material things and the temporary joy they brought. Her control of the future. They all had to die to let Christ reign again.

Her heart famished for her heavenly Father, Justine prayed. *Father, forgive me for running from You. I know You have never left, but I ask You again tonight to come reside within me. All I have is my small faith to offer and I pray You will accept it as a humble offering. Faith that You are still a good God, even though we feel pain in this world. Oh, how lonely I have been for You! Come dwell within me, Lord!*

Tears came for the first time since she had lost the baby. They streamed down Justine's face, a deep release of sorrow, a deep cleansing. She realized in that moment the most precious gift God could ever give in all of His multifaceted grace and love, was the gift of His presence. He was here. He would always be here.

Peace enveloped her like a loving, gentle embrace. Her heart sang within her at the freedom she felt. Of course, her Lord would take her back! She pictured Him with open arms, welcoming her home.

She smiled as she remembered the day she and Garrett had taken bicycles out to the creek that bordered his property. His words that day had challenged her grow spiritually, to be built up in her faith. How that would keep her foundation strong. She remembered changing the subject and asking about his relationship with Jonathan, but really, she was just uncomfortable and didn't want to look too closely at her heart.

She was ready now. Ready for God to take such a close look that if He saw anything that wasn't from Him, He had free reign to uproot.

*Lord, I want to be filled up with You. I want to understand Your love and obey You so my foundation is firm. There are choices I have made that I don't think are Your will for me. And some that I think might reflect Your desires. I lay all these things at Your feet and ask You to show me the way. Thy kingdom come. Thy will be done.*

Justine ran her hand across the beloved pages of the Bible. With renewed faith and purpose to do God's will for her life, she knew the next step. She must tell Eric she could not consider his proposal and then she needed to break off any ties to the man. Tonight.

As soon as she made the decision, newness in her soul flooded her with light. Justine saw with definitive clarity the path before her. It would be difficult and it would take more faith than she knew she had, but with the Lord walking with her, how could she lose?

Garrett's face sprang to mind, causing Justine to falter. With the evidence pointing to him being Jonathan's murderer, there was no hope of even a friendship between them. Or was there? Maybe she could ask him tomorrow when he came home what he was doing at the scene of the accident. Her heart hoped beyond hope that he had an explanation for being there, for all the coincidences that had brought them together.

Her feet made soft padding sounds as she made her way from the library. As she closed the door softly behind her, Justine looked across the hallway. The door to Mr. Cole's office was ajar, and Justine remembered the night she had gone inside. She hesitated as she began walking past it, down the hall. Then she remembered Eric's request that she look at the potted tree in the office. Something she couldn't quite put her finger on told her there was an unanswered question waiting for her if she went in.

Justine turned around and slowly pushed open the door, spotting the evergreen tree in the corner. Then she remembered what was bothering her. The object behind the tree. Time to find out why its shape had seemed so familiar.

Not wanting to signal the butler's curiosity, Justine opted to search in the dark. She knelt at the foot of the tree and felt behind it to see if the object was still there. When her hands brushed aged wood, Justine grasped its edges and brought it out.

The light of the cloudless night was enough for her to recognize it as her husband's box. A shiver ran up her spine. She tried to think of a logical conclusion as to what Jonathan's personal effects were doing here in James Cole's office, but she could not reach an answer. Somehow Garrett or one of the Coles had obtained it and was hiding it here. But why?

Justine knelt on the floor and, ever so gently, opened the box. The sight of Jonathan's coat on top took her back to the night she lost her baby. She remembered pulling out his coat and never digging any further. She expected at this very moment for her heart to feel like it was tearing in two again at the thought of her unborn babe. Instead she felt a quiet sadness, a hushed peace in her spirit. Justine knew then that God had begun the healing process.

Looking down at the box's contents, she felt almost afraid at what she might find. Could there possibly be a clue to Jonathan's death here? A lead as to who had wanted him dead? Conclusive evidence that would lead to a conviction?

Placing the coat next to her, Justine began to unload the box's contents. It held the coins Jonathan must have had on him when he died, his belt, and an envelope. Justine thought hard. When was the last time she saw her husband's box? It must have been the day she and Carrie Anne had moved into the Dunsmore Inn. She hadn't thought of it since. She certainly hadn't realized it was missing until now.

Justine held the envelope to the window to read. Every word on it had been typed. Looking at the upper left-hand corner, she saw her old address in East Wharf. The letter was written to Mary Bigby. *Who in the world is that? I think I'm about to find out.*

The words *Return to Sender* were also on the envelope, written in large bold type. Evidently, Jonathan's letter to this woman had never reached her. When Carrie Anne had packed up Jonathan's things, she must have gone to get the mail as well and put this letter in the box, along with everything else.

When Justine unfolded the piece of paper, she saw the letter itself had also been typed. It was dated two weeks before Jonathan's death.

*Dear Mary,*

*I believe my life may be in danger. Be on the lookout for a tall, blond man named Garrett Cole. He has been following me, catching up with me at every port, and I suspect he may try kill me in order to keep the investment earnings he owes me.*

*There's more to him than meets the eye. I'll be home sometime mid-April. Ask around and find out what you can. But be careful. He's dangerous.*

*Yours,*
*Jonathan*

Justine had suspected the same, but this letter confirmed it to be true. Garrett had killed Jonathan. "It can't be," Justine whispered into the moonlit room. Suddenly the shadows around her appeared ominous and she shivered. "Lord, help me."

Picking up Jonathan's coat again, Justine ran her hand along the front, remembering the man she barely knew. So many secrets. So many lies. Was Mary the same woman he had met that afternoon when he landed? The same one who had handed him something and promised to meet him in the dark of night?

Even though it pained her, Justine evoked the memory of the personal encounter. The woman had given Jonathan something, and he had folded it and appeared to stuff it up his coat sleeve. Justine held the coat straight out in front of her so the sleeve fell straight down. Nothing fell out. She put her hand up the sleeve. Nothing was there. But as she looked more closely at the cuff, Justine noticed it didn't match the other. It had a tiny button to enclose the gap that a small slit had made.

Her heart pounding, Justine undid the button and reached two fingers into the pocket, pulling out a folded telegram.

Something inside told her she was about to learn everything she needed to know about Jonathan's life and death. With shaking hands, she began to read.

# TWENTY-THREE

It was funny how an opinion a person held to so tightly could be tossed out the window so suddenly. Justine remembered the first time she'd seen Mr. Navin, the man who ran St. Alban's in East Wharf, ride his velocipede. She had vowed then and there nothing could induce her to climb atop such an apparatus. Then somehow, she had been talked into riding one of Garrett's the day he had taken her to the back of his property by the river pool. And now, because of her daily jaunts to town, she was so comfortable on one she had no trouble riding with all her might toward Eric's home, ready to confront him with her newfound information.

Justine pedaled with a fury born of purpose. And since she took Garrett's short cut to town, she was making record time. She dropped the bicycle quickly and ran up the steps to Eric's home, a home she had only seen from the outside.

A slender young woman, decked out from head to toe, answered the door. "Yes? May I help you?" Her blouse was cut too low for propriety's sake, and she leaned against the jam casually, as if she was very comfortable in the home.

"I need to speak with Mr. Waverly. Is he here?" Justine tried to peer around the woman but only saw a lavishly appointed foyer.

"He went down to the factory for a bit. Call on him tomorrow." The woman shut the door.

It was in times like these Justine questioned her own sanity. How could she know who to trust after what she had read in Mr. Cole's office? Everything was so muddled right now, she couldn't see straight.

That's why she had to find out the truth tonight. After she broke off her relationship with Eric and returned his presents, she would stay until she had heard the facts from his own lips.

As she neared the factory, she mentally reviewed what she had seen. The letter to Mary Bigby, asking for an investigation into Garrett Cole. The next, a telegram. It simply said: Warn Davidson. Threat on his life. Make inquiry regarding Eric Waverly.

Each document cast suspicion on the other man as the killer. And to add to the mystery was the presence of Jonathan's box in the Cole home. It felt like a giant clue was missing. Was the answer right in front of her but her heart refused to see it because she had cared for Garrett?

She got off of the velocipede and made her way to the door of the factory. Lost in thought, Justine started when she was grabbed by a pair of small grubby hands. They pulled her to the side of the building, hiding her in darkness.

Adrenaline running high, she looked down at her captor. Two dirty little faces peered at her seriously, each putting a single finger to their lips.

"It's you," the little boy whispered. "Are you here with more food?"

"Forget the food." The older of the two children, a girl, turned to Justine. "We knows you can help us. You's nice."

Justine tried to piece together what was happening. These were the two children who had inspired her entire mission. They were her first stop every morning near the Dunsmore Inn. But what were they doing here? And at this time of night?

Bending down so she could look them in the eye, Justine said, "Yes. It is me. I don't think we've been properly introduced. I'm Justine Davidson. What are your names?"

"This here's Nathan. He's seven." The little girl jabbed her grimy finger at her chest. "But I'm eight, so I'm the boss. I'm Minnie."

"It's very nice to meet you Nathan and Minnie. But what are doing here?"

"Why, we works here. Earn a half a penny a week if we don't mess up. We's gonna buy us a house someday if we work hard enough."

It was pure torture to know these children held such high hopes yet had no future before them. Never in all her time spent at St. Alban's had Justine encountered such heartache. She could hardly reconcile that these children worked here. At Eric's factory. No. It couldn't be. She had to see for herself; she just couldn't believe it to be true.

"Who do you work for?" Justine wanted to hear from their own lips who their boss was.

"Mr. Waverly," the little girl said with her head down. "Everyone who works for him is an orphan." At Justine's gasp, the little girl brought herself to her full height. "That's why we wants you to help us, help all of us at the factory."

Eric was preying on the fact that these children had no parents, no one from the outside who would look out for their interests. Purposeful, resilient resolution rose up in Justine's heart. Everything she felt the Lord had been speaking to her about starting an orphanage here in Waterford Cove came together in one final decision. She didn't care what anyone thought, not Eric or anyone else.

These children were looking to her to be their liberator. To rescue them out of the pit they were in. Only One could be their eternal Savior, but Justine would do everything she could to give them a new start on life. Set them on a new path. She knew full well the value in that. It's what her earthly father had done for her. It's what her heavenly Father had done for her. And now, it was the least she could do for these beautiful souls.

With the Lord's help, she would comfort these with the comfort she herself had received. She gladly looked forward to spending every last dime from her father and from Jonathan's investment so the orphans of Waterford Cove would have food to eat and a place to call home. She would build an orphanage with her own hands and work all day and night to care for the fatherless if that's what it took.

This was what God was calling her to do.

Hang the dresses and the balls and the notion that life was built around what others thought. All that mattered now to Justine was what

God thought of her, and she had a pretty good feeling He was delighted to call her His daughter.

Garrett walked through the gardens, thinking of the friendship with Justine that was birthed here in this haven. He longed to talk with her again, to tell her what she had meant to him. What she meant to him now. He wished he could take her by the shoulders and shake some sense into her for falling for Eric Waverly. Couldn't she see through him? Hadn't he warned Justine she was just another conquest to Eric that would soon be tossed aside for his next romantic scheme?

Garrett thrust his hands into his pockets and began to walk the path that wove through the middle of the garden. He paused beside the tree with his name carved in the trunk. Such silly notions. True love. What was it? What was it really? Simply knowing the facts about someone and choosing a logical mate, as he had done with Summer?

The answer in his heart was a resounding *No*. Was it knowing the true heart of someone, all their redeeming qualities, all their faults and failures, and yet loving them so much you wanted to see them grow and change into a better person? Was it wanting to spend the rest of your life with someone, knowing God had placed them in your path for a reason, to fulfill a common purpose? The answer in Garrett's heart was a resounding *Yes*.

These thoughts rolled through his head as his feet carried him through the garden and on to the stables. Marriage wasn't built on logic, but on sharing your heart and life with someone. And he knew now he loved Justine that way. With a true love that came from Christ. He knew it would take work, that it would not be easy to construct their relationship again, but he felt certain if he told Justine his true feelings, she would consider breaking off her courtship with Eric. He had to believe it was true. And at his first chance, he would apologize to Summer for leading her on.

Garrett quickened his pace, certain Louis would know where Justine was.

The misfit trio hid behind a stone wall that contained the refuse of the factory. Justine peeked around the barrier to take another look at the appalling sight. Row upon row of noisy machinery lined the dirt floors, while huge machines polluted the air with their stench. Children of all ages stood in rags at the assembly lines, their tiny fingers working to build the sewing machines.

At the rear of the building, a large alcove held a massive desk with a gold nameplate that read *Mr. Waverly*. Out of sight once again, Justine leaned up against the wall, not quite able to absorb all she heard and saw. Before coming inside, Minnie and Nathan had told her of the horrific working conditions and the fourteen-hour days the children put in. She knew at once this was why Eric had opposed her working with orphans. Why, if she got them off the streets, she would take away most of his workforce!

*Lord, forgive me for ever attaching myself to such a man.* She was grateful now her eyes had been opened in time.

"I am so glad I am not going to marry that man," Justine said to herself.

"Oh, are you now?" came a familiar voice right next to her.

Justine turned and found herself face to face with Eric Waverly.

Eric roughly pushed Justine across the work floor and into a chair by his desk. "What's this about not marrying me, my dear? Didn't you take my ring earlier tonight? Tsk, tsk, tsk, you are a confusing little lady, aren't you? First you want one thing, then another." He pushed his fingers into the soft flesh of her shoulder until he felt her wince. "Don't you know what you can have if you become my wife? Why, half of Waterford Cove will wish they were in your shoes."

Justine wouldn't look him in the eye as he knelt in front of her. He liked weakness in a woman. That meant he had the upper hand.

"Well, Justine my darling?" he prompted.

Eric saw Justine's eyes dart to the two urchins who hid behind a piece of machinery. "You pity them, don't you?" He slapped her face and bellowed, "Look at me when I speak to you, woman!"

Justine looked at him fearfully and he felt his ego balloon up. He was just getting started. "If you won't marry me, your fate is sealed."

"Why would I marry you? You're a monster who uses little children for his own purposes!"

He lifted a hand to strike her and she cowered before him. Rather than slap her again, he thought he would try another tactic.

With a gleaming look in his eyes, Eric looked out over his factory, his money-making masterpiece. He would take this puny woman for all she was worth before disposing of her. But she didn't have to know that.

"Let's say we make ourselves a little deal, you and me. You don't have to marry me, but you do have to give me my money."

"What do you mean by that?" Justine asked in a shaky voice.

"You are a rich lady, are you not? I know Jonathan made a nice bundle of money when Garrett Cole took that investment away from me and made a deal with your good-for-nothing husband." Seeing understanding dawn on her face, he continued. "I see you're piecing the clues together."

She started to get up. "You killed him, didn't you? For revenge?"

He laughed heartily, a smile lighting his face while he pushed her back into the chair. "That's right, Justine. That was *my* deal. *My* money. And some lowlife swept in and took what was rightfully mine. Don't think for a minute I won't get it back." He smiled at her. "You just happened to be a nice addition to my master plan to do just that."

She cringed and looked away. "You won't get anything from me."

"Actually, I think I will. Back to my deal. The only way to get my money now that you've put it in the bank is through my longest-standing enemy, Garrett Cole. We'll go to his house tonight. Get the bank keys. You'll walk into the vault and get me the money from your account. But why stop there? You can clean out some of the rest of the cash Cole has on hand, too. Not too much, though. We don't want them knowing it's missing for a long time. Call it interest on the money Garrett and Jonathan took away from me."

Justine shook her head vehemently. "The Coles are my friends. I won't rob their bank."

"Looks like you'll need a little motivation. No problem. I'll keep a gun pointed at you the whole time. And," he motioned with his hand to the children working at the line, "if you want what's best for these children, you will do exactly as I say. And don't worry. Maybe your money will allow me to let them go free and hire more, shall we say, appropriate workers." He paused for effect and bent down to look her in the eye. "If you don't agree, let's just say you're not going to be happy with the outcome."

# TWENTY-FOUR

When Louis told him Justine had taken a bicycle to find Eric, a forewarning signaled in his mind. It didn't feel right that she would sneak away like this after dark to have an assignation with the man. Eric Waverly was not a man Garrett would trust to be alone with a woman like Justine. Maybe she was in trouble.

*Hurry.*

The solitary word shone like a beacon of light, leading him onward. Garrett put his horse through his paces and was at Eric's front door within minutes. He figured that was as good a place as any to start. The woman who answered Eric's door told Garrett he wasn't home but that someone else had stopped by earlier looking for Eric.

"Who? Who stopped by?"

"I didn't get her name. What's it to me? The louse will just have his fun with her and come running back to me. As usual."

"Do you know where Eric is right now?" He felt desperate. *Hurry.*

"Where else would he be? If he isn't running around, he's at work."

Garrett raced from the wealthy neighborhood and neared Eric's factory with renewed determination. If he found Justine in Eric's arms, well, he didn't know what he would do. Either way, it didn't matter. Justine could be in danger. Even if she wasn't, even if she felt she loved Eric, Garrett knew he couldn't go another moment without her knowing how he felt about her. His heart told him she felt the same way about him. She wasn't like all the other women he had known. She wanted to do something to help the orphans and the homeless. She was trusting, even if sometimes that trust got pointed in the wrong direction. She was purposeful and determined and stronger than she knew. Independent, yet she needed him. What a lady. And Garrett couldn't wait to spend the rest of his life showing her how much he loved her.

So what if she was distracted right now by the trappings of the world? He knew her. He had seen the truth of her heart in her eyes when she spoke of the orphans. He knew she was trying to sort through the losses of her past. Garrett could only pray she would allow him to walk beside her through the pain.

He tried the front door of the factory and found it locked. He thought that odd since he could clearly hear the machines working inside. Going around the side of the building, Garrett found a door ajar and slipped in.

☙❧

Justine could feel the children looking at her as they worked. Every once in a while, one would catch her eye, then look away in fear.

And Justine knew all about fear. Sitting here in Eric Waverly's child labor factory, she was afraid. Afraid for the children who sweated at the assembly line. Afraid for what might happen if she agreed to Eric's demands to help him get the money. Afraid what would happen if she didn't.

But Justine also knew she wasn't alone. God was with her. He wouldn't abandon her, no matter what happened. His perfect love was casting out fear once again. Christ's love for her was a shaft of light cutting through the darkness. It left only illumination in its wake. God would reign victorious over every evil. She believed it.

She also now believed Garrett had nothing to do with Jonathan's death. This was Eric's doing. Revenge on both of the men he thought stole from him. Knowing Garrett was innocent filled her with a peace and a certainty about her future.

Lifting her chin to the enemy before her, she met his piercing green eyes and said with confidence, "I'll do it."

Garrett heard the words straight from Justine's own lips. She was agreeing to marry Eric. Garrett stood behind the refuse bin wall, but even over the din of machinery, Justine's response to Eric carried to his ears like the mournful cry of a raven.

*Lord, what were you thinking sending me here?* Garrett thought as he rubbed his head. Had he misunderstood? *I thought Justine was the one You had for me.*

Haughty male laughter filled his ears. "I knew you would make the right choice, darling. You always were a sucker for a child's face. You won't mind if I use that little weakness of yours to my advantage, will you?"

A small yelp carried over to Garrett, and he chanced a look around the barrier. His disappointment at hearing Justine's response to what he was sure was Eric's proposal turned to fury when he saw Eric's claw of a hand clamp down on Justine's small shoulder. The pained look on her face was all he needed to know that something was very wrong with this situation.

"Before we work out the details of this arrangement, Eric, there is one thing I need to know." Garrett could see Justine's hesitation and was proud of her for continuing. "What about the box I found in Mr. Cole's office?"

"Oh, you mean the one incriminating Garrett Cole?" She nodded. "Clever of me, wasn't it? Nothing like a little forgery to secure the future. One look at that letter and the police will have no doubt about who killed Jonathan." Eric laughed, a sound that made Garrett's blood boil. He didn't know what the man had planned, but it obviously included pinning Justine's husband's murder on him.

Garrett leaned back up against the wall out of sight as he let the information sink in. Garrett had been there at the scene of Jonathan's accident. There was money involved. Garrett had been on the *Blue Flag* with Justine, making it look like he followed her to America. He had her as a house guest. Her money was in his father's bank. And now, planted evidence pointed to Garrett killing Jonathan. It didn't look good.

Justine's mind reeled at the revelation that Eric was the one who planted the box at Garrett's house. "The day we took the bicycles out and you stayed for dinner. That's when you put the box in Mr. Cole's office."

"I knew I could pay off Smythe. You can always tell who can be bought with the right price. Just like Mrs. Dunsmore. Brilliant, if I do say so myself."

So that was why the butler had barked at her the time she'd been caught in Mr. Cole's office. Perhaps he had been hoping his reaction would cause her to wonder why he didn't want her in there and to make a plan to sneak back in. Well, if so, his plan had worked. And the less she thought about her old landlady's duplicity, the better.

Justine did, however, think about the hours she had spent with Eric. All the presents. All the parties. All the attention he had showered upon her. Every move Eric made had been false. His intention had never been to woo her, just to use her to get his hands on the money. He was so intent in his desperation he had murdered Jonathan and pinned it on one of the most kind and gentle men she had ever known. It made her want to retaliate with everything that was in her.

But one look at the children working the factory lines was all it took to convince her she had to do what Eric asked. Get the keys from the Cole's house and then get the money out of the bank. And she needed to act fast. Get everything done before Garrett came home tomorrow. She didn't want him in any danger.

"Just promise you will do as you said for the children. Let them go."

Eric shook his finger in her face. "It's not quite that simple, my dear. I want you." At her startled expression, he laughed. "That's right, I want you. And I mean to have you."

224

Eric ran his hand softly down her face. "First, I'll forge a marriage certificate. I don't know why I didn't think of it sooner. For what would the police think if they got a tip about the money changing hands? It would smell fishy and you know it."

He smiled at her and she wanted to smack the look off his face. "But if we are husband and wife, then no one will ever come after me."

Justine felt new panic rise up within her. She tried to form a prayer. *Lord, help me*, was all she could offer. She knew what came after a marriage certificate. Her mind desperately searched for another way.

"Just imagine you and me together after we have such a binding agreement." Eric pressed his lips firmly to Justine's and she tried to turn her head away. The wedding night was a nightmare she hoped she never encountered.

Garrett thought he was going to be sick at the sight of Eric's lips on Justine. That was the final straw. He didn't know what he would do, but he couldn't stand there and listen to this nonsense any longer. Eric needed to get what was due him, but how to prove it?

Before he could take a step toward the two, a figure came out of nowhere and jumped on Eric, bringing him to the ground. Garrett wished he had one of those new roll-film cameras that George Eastman had invented. The look on Eric's face as the he lay on the dirt floor in his fine suit was something Garrett would like to see again.

He rushed toward the scene in time to see a second man tie Eric's hands together.

"Just what do you think you are doing?" Eric demanded. "I'll have you know, I am the owner of this factory and you will let me go this instant!"

The burly policeman who had tackled Eric said, "Mr. Waverly, you are under arrest for murder. We've heard enough to put you away for a long time."

"You can't arrest me because you overheard some conversation," Eric argued.

The policeman smiled. "You're wrong. Thanks to these two," the man gestured to two children standing next to Justine, "we got here in time to hear your confession." He gruffly grabbed Eric's arm. "Come on, let's go. And while we are on our way to the station, why don't you explain to me what you had planned for this little lady."

Garrett caught Justine's eye as Eric was led away. He couldn't quite read her expression, but he thought it might be something resembling a hope and a future.

☙❧

Justine's heart leapt into her throat when she spotted Garrett. What on earth was he doing here? This was all too bizarre. Maybe he was in cahoots with Eric, a partner in this horrible scheme of child labor. But no, that couldn't be true. Eric had clearly tried to set Garrett up for murder. He wouldn't do that to a partner, would he?

Now that the true criminal had left the room, Garrett gazed at her with a certainty in his eyes that told her everything was going to be okay. That he loved her and wanted only her. Could it be true? No, Garrett had already chosen another.

She returned his gaze, trying to see past the surface. This was the man who had befriended her. Cared for her. Challenged her. This was the man whom she had thought of a hundred times in the last two weeks. With the roots of her faith reawakened and Eric Waverly no longer clouding her judgement, there was nothing standing between them. Nothing except Summer.

"Ma'am," said an officer who had just arrived on the scene with a few others. "I'll need you to give me your statement."

Justine soon realized Garrett would be wrapped up for a while as well, giving his own account. She answered the man to the best of her ability, but she felt the incident with Eric was already behind her. Her mind was on other things.

She could see the children had ceased their labor now that their slave master had departed. Huddled together in a bunch, they didn't seem to know what to do. But Justine knew with certainty what her next move would be. And she couldn't wait to put it into action.

The policeman finished up with her and asked if she needed a ride home. Her heart did double time as Garrett stepped to her side and put a gentle hand on her shoulder. "I'll take care of the lady," he told the man.

Suddenly shy, Justine stood from her prison chair to face Garrett. Here was an innocent man, free from the crimes she thought he had committed.

Justine could feel the eyes of the children on them as Garrett slowly stepped closer. She couldn't bring herself to look up into his beloved eyes, but she knew them like she knew her own heart. A heart that belonged to Garrett, had belonged to him for some time now. If he didn't return her love, she knew she would go on, but oh, how she prayed earnestly that he loved her too.

She felt the warmth of his hand as he lifted her chin. Eyes that had captivated her with their friendship and trust gazed back at her.

"Justine." Garrett's voice sounded husky to her ears. Her heart sped up and she held her breath as she waited for him to continue. But instead of the words she longed to hear, Garrett gathered her in his arms and held her tight for a full minute.

Oh, how good it felt to have this woman in his arms! He wanted to hold her always, to keep her safe. *Thank you, God! Thank you for keeping her safe tonight.*

A tug at his shirtsleeve made him pull back from Justine to find its source. A little girl, probably eight or nine, looked up at him.

"I guess we've got some business to attend to." He smiled impishly at Justine, hoping she understood there was more to say but it would have to wait.

But she looked solemn and whispered in his ear, "That's Minnie. She told me all these children are orphans. We can't send any of them home because they don't have one."

Turning his attention to the clustered group of children, he said, "Everyone gather round. I bet you could use some food and a rest. Am I right?"

Most of the children either nodded or came closer.

"It'll take a bit for us to get organized and find a comfy place for you all to sleep tonight, but let's start with this: you are all done working for Mr. Waverly."

Garrett and Justine shared matching grins as they looked at each other and at the cheering kids.

Garrett said privately to Justine, "I'll ride home and get Mother and Carrie Anne and Louis working on the details. They'll gather bedding and food for everyone and the kids and I will all hunker down here for the night. Tomorrow morning, we'll figure out a more long-term solution." Before he stepped away, Garrett couldn't resist running his finger down the side of Justine's beautiful face.

☙❧

"You guys outdid yourselves." Justine lay in her cozy bed next to Carrie Anne. The whirlwind evening was catching up with her but even though it was close to two o'clock in the morning, she wasn't ready to close her eyes just yet. "James and Charlotte must have some pretty great connections to assemble that many supplies so quickly."

Carrie Anne replied in her usual insightful way. "Like it talks about in Second Corinthians, 'He hath dispersed abroad; he hath given to the poor: his righteouness remaineth for ever.' God has blessed you, Justine, to abound in good works."

"I'm beginning to see that. God has been so good to me."

Carrie Anne turned on her side and propped herself up on her elbow. "Does this mean you've made peace with God?"

Justine laughed gently. "Peace. Yes, He's given me His peace. He is my peace." She sighed contentedly.

Carrie Anne smiled wide and lay back on her pillow. Her hand reached over and squeezed Justine's. "'These things I have spoken unto you, that in me ye might have peace. In the world ye shall have tribulation: but be of good cheer; I have overcome the world.'"

# TWENTY-FIVE

I thought Garrett would be here by now." Charlotte got up from the dining table where they were gathered for breakfast. She peered out the window at the bright summer morning.

"He's most likely still getting Carrie Anne and Jeffrey settled with the children," Anica said, reaching for the salt shaker. "I can't imagine better foster parents than those two."

"That's true. I guess I'm just anxious to hear how the night went. That dirt floor couldn't have been pleasant."

Charlotte sat back down but doubtless knew how her restlessness mirrored Justine's own. After just a wink of sleep, before dawn, Justine had gone to Mr. Cole's office and gathered the items she knew the police would be stopping by later to collect. She knew with the evidence she had in her possession, the testimonies from last night, plus collaborating with the police in East Wharf, Eric Waverly would not be harming anyone else, ever again.

Next, it had been on to Charlotte's study to pull out some stationary. First, she had written to Mr. Flanning, wanting to ease his mind and to say thank him for his help, an errand that had been interrupted the night before.

Then her hand had flown across a blank page as she got her thoughts organized on paper. Justine made a column of needs the children had and what possible resources she could use or attain to meet those needs. The biggest issue was where to house the children. They couldn't stay in the factory more than just temporarily. *Lord, please provide.*

It would take months, maybe a year to build an orphanage. Justine wrote down some figures and questioned if she had enough money to make that happen. Perhaps she could get others to contribute.

Her list in hand, Justine had climbed the stairs with satisfaction and gotten ready for the day, knowing Garrett would be there soon.

Breakfast had gone on without him, but now that he would most likely arrive any minute, Justine stopped eating and fiddled with the napkin in her lap.

"Oh, good. You went ahead and ate without me." And there he was. Garrett swooped into the room and took his seat with a flourish. He didn't look any worse for wear after spending the night hunkered down in his enemy's factory. Instead, he beamed at them all and took a huge helping of scrambled eggs.

Justine sat across the table from him and stole glances at him when she thought no one was looking. What a man!

Garrett caught her eye and smiled warmly. It was obvious he was pleased with how things had turned out. And truly, Justine was happy for him. He would be married soon and would provide a nice home for his new wife and the children they would one day have. It was time for Justine to move on. She couldn't stay there forever.

Looking around the table, she studied each face but Garrett's. Three generations of Coles gathered for a joyous time together around the table. James had his arm around his wife, looking content on this Monday morning. Anica was holding Caleb close to her heart, admiring her new son whose wispy hair was already coming in. Bret was talking about a new business opportunity that had come along. Charlotte radiated cheer and good will, her youthful face glowing with contentment. Justine wished she could stay in this happy circle. But this was the home of Summer's future in-laws. Whether Justine wanted to or not, she would have to say goodbye.

"Hello."

The deep voice came from somewhere behind her in the garden. Justine turned around slowly. She wanted to look into Garrett's face but was uncertain what she would find there. But, oh, how she had craved this man's companionship and the intimacy their deep conversations brought about. Now there he stood, his rumbling voice resonating in her chest.

"Are you up for a walk to the back of the property?" Garrett asked.

She looked up. It was not what Justine had predicted he would say. She thought he'd mention the children or possibly plan out who would take the next few shifts. Tell her of his plans to see Summer today. Even mention the events that had transpired last night. But perhaps those things were indeed what he intended to say. Maybe he just needed to stretch his legs while they communicated about imminent details.

He offered her his arm and they slowly made their way down the trail. The grassy fields had more wildflowers than when she and Garrett had been there together the last time. But instead of steering her toward the stream, Garrett turned left, leading them up the incline to where he'd asked Justine's opinion about the land they now stood upon.

They stopped at the place Garrett had once spun in a circle, envisioning his future home. A house he would now share with another. Justine swallowed hard. She needed to get her mind on other things. Happy things.

"Justine—"

"Garrett, I—"

Their voices coincided with each other and Justine laughed, a welcome remedy to her tension.

"You first," said Garrett.

"I was going to ask how you found me last night."

"God led me to you." Garrett stepped toward her and she caught her breath at the look in his eyes. It wasn't right for them to be out there together, alone, when he belonged to another. "I came home a day early.

When I heard that you went to see Eric, I wasn't far behind. I needed to talk with you."

Justine felt like she was on the precipice of her life, waiting to see if she would fall from the cliff or soar above the clouds. Fear coursed through her at what Garrett would say. Was he going to ask her and Carrie Anne to leave? Summer probably felt it was too awkward for him to be staying under the same roof as two eligible women. Or was it possible he felt about Justine the way she did about him? She held her breath. Waiting.

Justine couldn't take it any longer. She needed to speak first to keep from tumbling over the edge.

"Before you say anything else, I want you to know something that happened while you were away."

"No. Please. It has taken me too long to realize how I feel, and I can't keep it inside another moment."

He paused and tenderly brushed her hair away from her cheek. "Since the day I first saw you in East Wharf, God has been leading me to this moment. I believe he allowed me to be near you when you needed a friend, and I always want to be the one you turn to, Justine."

Garrett turned his eyes heavenward, took a deep breath, then looked back at her. "I know you struggle with your relationship with God after all the hardship you have been through this year, but I'm asking you to let me be the one to walk alongside you in this journey called life. We'll get through it together. Will you agree to allow me to court you, my love?"

It was impossible. He had promised himself to another. Justine had already conceded that her friendship with Garrett was about to become thing of the past. But this man standing before her—oh, how she wanted him to be her future. Taking a fortifying breath, Justine whispered, "What about Summer?"

Garrett silenced her lips with a gentle hand. "I wasn't sure you knew about that, but it seems you're two steps ahead of me. I'm sorry I caused you additional pain. If I had only known…No. It doesn't matter now. It has ended before it began. I stopped by her place on my way home from the factory this morning." Garrett took her hand in his.

"Before we can go on, there's something you need to know."

"What?" Justine hoped it was something they could resolve, for she wanted nothing more than to walk through life with this godly man.

He looked down for a moment, intertwining their fingers together. "Justine, I am done with my traveling. My father has offered me a job as vice president of Waterford Cove Holdings and I have accepted. I have lived fairly frugally over the course of my adult life, and staying with my parents between travels has allowed me to save a great deal of money."

He looked so nervous, Justine wondered what in the world he would say next.

Garrett met her gaze. "The thing is, I want to give away what the Lord has given me." He gestured to the land around them. "I want to give it to the children. Build an orphanage right here and spend my days nurturing those little ones in the love of the Lord." He swallowed hard, and his eyes seemed to search hers for an answer. "I know you love gowns and balls and the finer things of life, and I promise I will do my best to still provide them for you. Running an orphanage, we'll not be rich, but I'll still work hard to give you what you want. We'll always have enough."

After her heart's cleansing last night, the tears came easily. Silently coursing down her cheeks in a sweet wash of joy. She could hardly believe what she was hearing. "Oh, Garrett," she said, squeezing his hand. He needed to know the truth. "I don't care about that stuff anymore."

He looked incredulous. "You don't?"

She shook her head vigorously. "No. I don't." She wished she had the plans with her that she had written out before breakfast. Would that be enough to convince Garrett she'd had a change of heart?

She went on in a rush, not wanting him to think she was just saying these things to seal their bond. "Last night, the Lord finally got ahold of me. I've come back to Him, Garrett."

Garrett gave her a quick, happy embrace.

"God has shown me the path He wants me to take." Justine smiled wide, letting out some of the joy bursting from her heart. "It mirrors perfectly what He has spoken to you."

She dropped her gaze, suddenly shy. "I've been going early every morning to feed kids that look hungry. In fact, the two that ran to get the police last night are the ones who inspired this whole thing." Justine looked up to gauge what he thought. "Many others are in need, Garrett. God's been speaking to me about an orphanage, too. I want to spend every dollar I have to give them a permanent home. I'm hoping to get the orphan ministry Summer's helping to organize at the church in on my plans." Her happy heart took a plunge to the grassy meadow beneath her feet. "Summer."

Garrett tightened his fingers on hers and his response seemed to echo to the woods and back. "You are the only one for me, Justine Davidson. I will spend the rest of my life celebrating the fact that the Lord has called us to the same mission. Does this mean you'll let me court you?"

Justine could barely contain the joy she felt inside then asked herself why she should. God had answered prayers she hadn't even prayed, and then some. She pulled Garrett into her arms and he swung her around and around.

He set her on the ground and gently kissed her lips as the swirling world slowly settled around them. She took his hand and turned toward the house. "Come. Let's go start that walk together."

# TWENTY-SIX

Justine fingered the fawn necklace with the words from Psalm 42 rolled up inside as she admired hundreds of white candles that formed a perimeter around the makeshift dance floor. Each one cast its tiny light on the midsummer flowers blooming in the field behind the Cole's mansion as twilight began to descend. The effect was magical. A quartet had been playing for hours and it seemed half of Waterford Cove had turned out for the ground breaking ceremony of the King's Castle Orphanage.

"I've got a surprise up my sleeve," Garrett whispered in her ear. "I think you might like it."

*As if anything could top what I've experienced in the last five weeks,* Justine mused.

Kisses and praying and planning. Late night talks and early morning walks. The days had been bittersweet as she mourned what was past and celebrated what was to come. Finding new facets about her Lord caused Justine to worship in humble thankfulness. Learning more about Garrett only induced deeper admiration. She had loved every minute of the adventure with both her heavenly Father and her future husband.

Garrett led her to where the front door of the King's Castle would be and turned them to face the crowd. When he had everyone's attention, he welcomed his whole family up front. James and Charlotte.

Anica and Bret. Jeffrey, and even Carrie Anne. Once the eight of them each had a shovel in hand, Garrett asked all in attendance to bow their heads in prayer.

Even though today was the Fourth of July and joy was already in the air, Garrett's prayer seemed to seal Justine's bond with him even further. His ardent words to their heavenly Father overflowed with thankfulness in getting them to this stage with the orphanage so quickly, then moved on to asking a blessing for the children who would soon spend their days in the love and care they needed.

When he said "Amen," instead of plunging his shovel's tip into the waiting ground, Garrett set his tool down and did the same with Justine's. She looked past him to Charlotte and Carrie Anne. They smiled back secretively. No one seemed to be interested in digging up shovelfuls of dirt at the moment. Instead, everyone's eyes were trained on Garrett and Justine.

Garrett dropped his knee to what would one day be the doorstep of the orphanage and took Justine's hand in his own. "Justine Davidson, you are the other half of my whole. Will you marry me?"

He pulled a ring from his pocket that surely must have come from Bijoux d'Artisan. It had the distinct makings of a one-of-a-kind masterpiece only Mr. Dandurand could fashion. A very unusual diamond sat above the circlet of a wide silver band. The way the craftsman had designed it, rows of tiny, clear diamonds ran in waves on the band while the blue color and shape of the large diamond exactly resembled a droplet of water about to splash into a diamond brook.

Garrett slipped it on her finger and they both looked from her fawn necklace and back again to the ring. They couldn't have been a better match. Justine knew she would always be reminded that whenever her soul was thirsty, whenever she was feeling downcast, to turn to the only Source who could satisfy.

Justine brought Garrett up off of his knee and held him tight. She pulled back but didn't let go, saying, "I'll marry you any day you say, and then every day after that."

Garrett laughed at her exuberant answer. "Just what I wanted to hear." When he kissed her, the crowd cheered. Garrett and Justine grabbed their shovels again and soon eight scoops of dirt signified the beginning of a new life for so many.

The newly engaged couple walked through the crowd, receiving congratulations until Garrett got pulled away by someone wanting to give a sizable donation. Justine excused herself. "You go ahead and talk as long as you want. There's someone I need to see."

Justine found Summer Edwards, swaying to the music at the edge of the dance floor. Justine had long ago gotten over Summer and Garrett's brief courtship. Over the last several weeks, Justine and Summer had spent many hours together, first at the Cole's, laying out detailed plans for the temporary orphanage, then with the children, helping them get settled in their makeshift home.

"Summer! Thank you so much for coming."

"I wouldn't have missed it. Plus, now it gives me the chance to congratulate you." She quickly hugged Justine. "You two were made for each other. I couldn't be happier for you." Summer gestured to where the mansion would be built. "I know you and Garrett have been very busy to get everything in place so quickly."

"Yes. God has really opened all the right doors. We plan to be open to accept children just after the first of the year."

"But not before a much-needed honeymoon?" Summer teased.

Justine felt herself blushing and Summer laughed. "Yes, I think it might be best to marry before we officially open the King's Castle. And we'll try to sneak a honeymoon in there as well. I'm just glad the children have a temporary place to stay." Justine thought of how smoothly the purchase of the factory had gone and of all the effort and supplies the community had lent to turn Eric's factory into short-term housing for the orphans.

"I'm still in awe of God's handiwork when I think of all the things that have fallen into place. Please pass on my thanks again to the church for the food they have faithfully provided."

Summer nodded. "I will, but trust me, they know how grateful you and Garrett are for their assistance. We are all happy to help." Summer nodded to someone behind Justine. "Looks like someone else would like a word with you." She gave Justine a friendly smile. "I'll see you later."

Charlotte came up beside Justine and gave her a heartfelt squeeze. "My dear, try not to hold it against me that I tried to play matchmaker between Summer and Garrett. I'm humble enough to admit when I am wrong."

Justine laughed softly. "Oh, Charlotte, I would never. Your steadfast love and service to Jesus were some of my greatest inspirations to follow wholeheartedly after Christ. I am so happy I'm going to be a part of your family now. It almost feels too good to be true."

"Please, call me Mother." Charlotte smiled. "You are after all, like a daughter to me."

"Mother." It was a word Justine had never been able to use. Now, it would be as familiar as her own name. As Charlotte walked back to the gathering, Justine's eyes filled with tears. She thought of Papa and how his gift to her would now impact many lives. She thought of her own baby and how if he would have been born, he would have been so loved and wanted. But now, Justine would have the opportunity to share that love with dozens and dozens of children. *Yes, God takes away, but He also gives. Blessed be the name of the Lord.* She wished she was in church right now so she could belt out the chorus of the hymn she had held back on so many weeks before.

Justine looked around. God had given her so much. Family. Friends. A purpose to fulfill. Lives to impact. It truly was a miracle.

"What's this?" a deep voice said beside her ear. "My beautiful bride-to-be crying on our engagement night? You're going to have to dry those tears, because we've got an entire lifetime of happiness before us. Plus, I've still got something for you to see tonight." He took her arm and led her toward the Cole's garden, away from the crowd.

Justine smiled and wiped her eyes. "I'm just being sentimental. And I am so thankful for all God has given me." She turned to look at him while they walked. "Especially that He gave me you. But you already gave me an engagement ring. What else could you possibly do to make this evening more special?"

"You'll see. Look up." At that moment, the sky burst with the beautiful colors of fireworks. Justine had never seen anything so spellbinding. It truly was an enchanted evening.

"I was hoping the fireworks would give us enough light to accomplish something long overdue."

They had reached the garden where their friendship had first been engraved on her heart. Garrett took her hand and led her to a tree she had seen before. On it were carved the names of the Cole couples.

"Call me sentimental, too, but would you indulge me for a moment, my sweet fiancé?"

Justine smiled and watched as he carved the name JUSTINE right below GARRETT in the bark. Seeing her name joining his for future generations of Coles to see, a fresh joy washed over her. She tipped her chin up to meet his waiting lips and drank in the man with whom she would share her life and love, together following a God who would never let go.

# DISCUSSION QUESTiONS

1. Carrie Anne Barnes is known for quoting Scripture in the middle of conversation. How do you think this made Justine feel? If you know someone in your life who is like that, name a time when their words challenged you, helped you, or came at just the right moment to encourage you.
2. The feelings and questions Justine's miscarriage cause for her are loosely tied to my own miscarriage experience. I, too, asked God what He was doing and then hardened my heart to Him for many months.
   - Name a time in your life when you weren't sure what God was up to and then recall something good that came out of that situation.
3. Justine feels like God is playing a giant game of chess with her life and takes the *Blue Flag Line* to America in order to regain control of the board.
   - Talk about a time in your life when you weren't in agreement on what God was doing. What truth from God's Word or what attribute of God helped you to see that He never changes even though our emotions do?
4. The pastor of the Cole's church gives the congregation some "homework." Let's do the same.
   - Take a piece of paper and write down some of the different

facets of God's character that you're actively seeing in your life.
- Next to each characteristic, whether it's His goodness, faithfulness, provision, strength, etc., write why that attribute is so meaningful to you. Share your observations with someone else.

5. Justine often falls into the comparison trap. She covets what others have, thinking she would be happy *if only* she had material wealth or proper social standing. Name a time when you have thought, "I'll be happy when I have _____ or when _____ happens."
   - What does the Bible say about coveting and contentment? What is one way you can apply those principles this week?

6. Garrett says that one of his long-standing hurts is not knowing the Lord's will for his life. Do some digging in the Bible, finding out what God's will is for everyone who claims Him as Savior (Hint: start in passages like 1 Thessalonians 5:16–18 and Galatians 5).
   - Then answer this: In the past, when God's specific next steps for you weren't clear, how did you react? In the future, when your steps aren't clear, how will you react differently?

7. Second Corinthians 9:8 ESV says "And God is able to make all grace abound to you, so that having all sufficiency in all things at all times, you may abound in every good work."
   - Over the course of her journey, Justine comes to realize God has been a faithful Provider. Name an area of your life God has provided for you that at first you didn't notice.
   - Read the verse again and then answer this question: Name one way you could use the provision He's given you right now (friendship, finances, time, spiritual gifts, fruit of the Spirit, etc.) to "abound in every good work" to others around you.

8. God has given us so much of Himself—mercy, grace, life, truth, wisdom, peace, His Word, His presence, His Son…the list could go on!
   - Do a short mental exercise and go through that short list one by one and picture your life without that particular

thing. It wouldn't be a pretty picture! We desperately need each one.

- If everything else was taken away from us but we still had the precious gift of God's presence, we would have enough because it's through the gift of Himself that we have all the other things on that list. Take a moment to recognize God is always with you and then thank Him for it.

9. To open her heart back up to God, Justine first had to recognize what kept her from a right relationship with Him. God speaks to her one word: Pride.

- What has been the barrier between you and God in the past or what is it right now? It's an act of humility when we come before God, totally open, asking Him to weed out anything in us that doesn't belong, anything that isn't from Him. Be bold enough in prayer, right now, to ask God to speak to you. The results will be more than you could ever ask or imagine.

10. After Justine made her heart right with the Lord, two things happened: She was able to see clearly the good works God had prepared in advance for her to do (see Ephesians 2:10) and her relationship with Garrett was repaired and made better than it had been in the past.

- As God draws you close this week, respond with a great big Yes, Lord. The small act of putting our whole faith and trust in our Savior will always result in a clearer, more passionate purpose for Him and His will for our lives and deeper, more intimate relationships with our spouse, our family and our friends.

# DEAR READER...

I could read and write love stories all day long. How about you? Sometimes I wonder why we never get tired of them, then I realize maybe it's because we picture ourselves in the story. We want to be the one who is loved and treasured, secure in the safe arms of someone who will love us unconditionally.

There's a repeated theme from Genesis to Revelation—God wants you and will go to any length to draw you close to Himself. Relationship existed in the Trinity from before time began and because of Jesus, we will have eternal relationship with our God. There's no doubt about it—God is the author of relationship and it's His gift to us—with each other and with Himself. What a generous God we serve.

But if you are married, it probably didn't take long for you to realize you married a sinner, and so did they. Most of us live within our marriage relationship with a contract mentality rather than a covenant commitment. You do your part, I'll do mine. You broke your end of the agreement which gives me license to break mine. Our God is the original Covenant Maker and the only Covenant Keeper, and He asks us and inspires us to treat our marriage like the covenant it is.

When our husband-wife relationships don't go the way we originally thought they would, we tend to want to hide. But what if, in full view of the sin that exists between us, we stepped forward and shouted loud about a covenant God? What if others saw God's covenant love for us lived out in this one challenging yet freeing act of commitment: I will love my spouse the most when they deserve it the least. Try it and see what God will do.

No matter where you and your spouse have been, you can come out from the shadows of shame that have been cast by a contract marriage and step into the light of the Gospel of Jesus Christ being lived out in your home with this theme resonating daily within your heart: "Marriage is a covenant TO GOD that says, 'Lord, I will give YOUR best to this person, I will serve them, I will love them, I will be YOUR hands and feet in their world, even when they break their promise.'"

The Vows Written in Permanent Ink Contest is an opportunity to share how God's covenant love to YOU has affected your covenant to your spouse. The three couples who won the contest for *Roots Reawakened* not only got the opportunity to have their first names as the characters in the story, they wanted to share a bit of their marriage testimony with you as well.

It is my pleasure to introduce to you the real-life Justine and Garrett, Charlotte and James, and Carrie Anne and Jeffrey. It is their hope that their stories would give you hope for your own marriage and reveal glimpses of our covenant God's faithfulness.

### Justine and Garrett's Testimony

Garrett and I got married in our early twenties, and I was definitely searching for the fairytale "Happily Ever After." It didn't take long into the marriage (albeit our honeymoon!) before we both realized marriage is a lot more than that! Marriage didn't immediately meld us together. We are two very different people coming from two different families and the blending or *oneness* wasn't at all easy or simple. It required a lot of work—including conversations and openness, saying 'I'm sorry,' and praying for each other and ourselves. That work has continued, especially now that we have added kids into our family. It is truly a daily, and sometimes hour by hour, commitment.

In contrast to our own character sometimes, we are reminded about God's character. Nothing stops God from pursuing us. No sin is too great, no situation is a lost cause. We have to continually ask God to remind us of His love for us, and how, in His power, we can love our spouse the same way. First John 4:19 says, "We love because He first loved us." This was the Scripture we had on a large sign at the entrance of our wedding. We didn't know it at the time, but that truth was going to get us through some of the toughest days and weeks of our marriage. We cannot thrive in our marriage without God's continued work in us.

### Charlotte and James's Testimony

When we married fifty-seven years ago, I was barely twenty years old and my husband was twenty-six. I was young, naive, and in love. I knew this was the man I wanted to spend the rest of my life with. Our marriage was founded on Christ, and we entered it with the commitment that it would be "as long as you both shall live."

At first, we had to work through some issues such as family traditions and money management, among others. I was an only child and he was from a family of four boys. Understanding on both sides was needed and God did provide this. Common interest and a sense of humor have certainly helped along the way. Most importantly, we have kept the following Scripture verse in the forefront to help us through the difficult times: Romans 8:28 NKJV says "All things work together for good to those who love God, …who are called according to *His* purpose."

God has been with us in the good times and the bad. We have trusted in His goodness, and He has never failed. We have been blessed beyond measure. One of my husband's favorite sayings is: GRATEFUL, THANKFUL, BLESSED.

A Jesus-centered marriage is everything!

### Carrie Anne and Jeffrey's Testimony

As a young girl, I played and dreamed of being a wife and mummy.

In my twenties, this became a source of pain and anguish when God wasn't sending me a partner (in my time). I prayed and pleaded with God, but to no avail. Little did I understand the work He was doing in both of us.

I tried to be a good and godly single woman, believing it would happen someday. I served at my church with children and youth. I went on a six-month mission trip. (Oh boy, did God work on me then!) I even served as a leader in a singles Bible study. All still aching for my spouse-to-be.

During this time, the Spirit led me to pray for him and write letters that I gave him as a wedding gift. At age thirty-one, I met and became friends with a divorcé who was ten years my senior. When he called me five months later, I had a feeling.

The week following our first anniversary would be the beginning of the most challenging season of our young marriage. My husband worked on a farm, and we knew there were dangers in the job. On Tuesday, he was working with a very large bull and sustained a kick to his right wrist. This was not that big of a deal; he did go and have it checked out just to be safe. On Wednesday, while working with another massive bull, that animal lost his balance and fell onto Jeff. This was the start of a long and difficult journey. We had to trust and rely on our faith and knowledge of God's Word more than ever. Psalm 147:3 says "He heals the brokenhearted and binds up their wounds" (NIV). And in Jeremiah 30:17, "'But I will restore you to health and heal your wounds,' declares the LORD" (NIV).

Fast forward to 2021, we celebrated our ninth wedding anniversary and continue to grow in the God who brought us together.

### A last note from the author

There is still hope for your marriage. Who or what are you putting your hope in today? Place it in our covenant God who can teach you to love the most when your spouse deserves it the least. Lean in when you feel like pulling away. Pour out even when the only one pouring into you is God. You will see the fruit of your obedience to God's Word and you will be blessed.

"The steadfast love of the LORD never ceases, his mercies never come to an end; they are new every morning; great is *your* faithfulness. 'The LORD is my portion,' says my soul, 'therefore I will hope in *him*'" (Lamentations 3:22–24 ESV, emphasis added).

For more encouragement and truth for your marriage, visit vowstokeep.com where you will grow closer to your spouse and closer to the heart of God's design for your marriage.

Going shoulder-to-shoulder with you for biblically healthy marriages,

Tracy Michelle Sellars

# ABOUT THE AUTHOR

Tracy Sellars was born to speak the truth of God's Word to your heart. She and her husband of twenty years live in the rolling hills of Ohio with their three teenagers. Tracy can usually be found on her front porch with her computer or in the recording studio with a microphone, teaching the body of Christ how to passionately pursue both their spouse and their Savior.

She is from the beautiful Black Hills of South Dakota but has moved twenty-eight times (and she's enjoyed every one). The shortest stay was three months. The house she lives in now is the longest—eight years!

Tracy and David have owned and restored almost 100 wrecked and classic vehicles. Currently, as a family they are working on a 1941 Buick Sedanette, a 1983 Mercury Capri, a 1983 Mustang, and a 1960 VW Bug.

If Tracy could write a novel in the bathtub, she'd be one happy camper. Pick up Tracy's new historical romantic suspense novels and learn how to grow closer to your spouse and closer to the heart of God's design for your marriage at www.vowstokeep.com.

# Discover more great fiction at
# CrossRiverMedia.com

## ROAD TO DEER RUN
### Elaine Marie Cooper

The year is 1777 and the war has already broken the heart of nineteen-year-old Mary Thomsen. Her brother was killed by the King's army, so when she stumbles across a wounded British soldier, she isn't sure if she should she help him or let him die, cold and alone. Severely wounded, Daniel Lowe wonders if the young woman looking down at him is an angel or the enemy. Need and compassion bring them together, but will the bitterness of war keep them apart?

## SWEPT INTO DESTINY
### Catherine Ulrich Brakefield

Maggie Gatlan may be a Southern belle on the outside, but a rebel on the inside. Ben McConnell is enchanted by Maggie's beauty and fiery spirit, but for him the South represents the injustice and deprivation he left behind in Ireland. As the country divides and Ben joins the Union, Maggie and Ben are forced to call each other enemies. Will their love survive or die on the battlefield of South against North?

## SURVIVING CARMELITA
### Susan Miura

It was Josie's hands on the wheel, her foot on the pedal. Her fault. Now, sweet Carmelita will never see her fifth birthday. Where do you run when the world implodes and you can't function? Josie leaves her Chicago suburban home to stay with a cousin in Key West, unaware her journey is guided by an unseen hand. Unaware that a trailer park pastor, a battered horse, a pregnant teen, and a mysterious beachcomber might just set her on the path toward an inconceivable hope and redemption.

## LOTTIE'S GIFT
### Jane M. Tucker

Lottie Braun has enjoyed a happy childhood with her father and older sister. But the quiet, nearly idyllic life she enjoyed as a child ended with tragedy and a secret that tore the sisters apart. Forty years later, Lottie is a world-class pianist with a celebrated career and an empty personal life. One sleepless night, she allows herself to remember and she discovers that memories, once allowed, are difficult to suppress. Will she ever find her way home?

# Growing in Christ

... from the ground up.

# Discover more great books at
# CrossRiverMedia.com

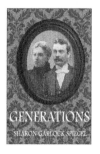

## GENERATIONS

### Sharon Garlock Spiegel

When Edward Garlock was sober, he was a kind, generous, hard-working farmer, providing for his wife and growing family. But when he drank, he transformed into a unpredictable bully, capable of absolute cruelty. When he stepped into a revival tent in the early 1900s the Holy Spirit got ahold of him, changing not only his life, but the future of thousands of others through Edward.

## CLAIMING HER INHERITANCE

### Debra L. Butterfield

A shooting, a stampede, a snakebite... Sally Clark has received an inheritance of a lifetime, but first she has to survive living on the ranch in Montana. Chase Reynolds is astounded that his father has willed one-third of their ranch to a total stranger. Who is this woman and what hold did she have over his dad? What Sally and Chase discover is beyond their imagination and wields far greater consequences than the inheritance.

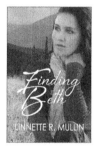

## FINDING BETH

### Linnette R. Mullin

Three years ago, Beth Gallagher lost her brother, Josh, in a tragic accident. Grief-stricken and estranged from her father, she turned to the one man her brother warned her about—Kyle Heinrich. Now she's discovered his dark side. She flees to the Smoky Mountians to clear her mind and find the answers she needs. Will she have the resolve to follow through? And, if so, what will it cost her?

## THE UNRAVELING OF REVEREND G

### RJ Thesman

When Reverend G hears her diagnosis—dementia with the possibility of early-onset Alzheimer's—she struggles with the fear of forgetting those she loves and losing her connection with God. But she soon discovers there's humor to be found in forgetting part of the Lord's Prayer and losing a half-gallon of ice cream. And she finds while the question she wants to ask is, 'Why,' the answer really is, 'Who.'

# Books that ignite your faith.

| | |
|---|---|
| HANDS FULL | FRICK |
| THE GRACE IMPACT | NANCY KAY GRACE |
| THE BENEFIT PACKAGE | CLYMER |
| ABBA'S ANSWERS | BUTTEFRFIELD |
| ABBA'S PROMISE | BUTTEFRFIELD |
| SURVIVING CARMELITA | MIURA |
| Marriage Conversations | KRAFVE |
| BETHANY'S CALENDAR | ELAINE MARIE COOPER |
| GROWING IN CHRIST | HYLTON |
| SWEPT INTO DESTINY | BRAKEFIELD |

Available in bookstores and from online retailers.

CROSSRIVERMEDIA.COM

## If you enjoyed this book, will you consider sharing it with others?

- Please mention the book on Facebook, Twitter, Pinterest, or your blog.

- Recommend this book to your small group, book club, and workplace.

- Head over to Facebook.com/CrossRiverMedia, 'Like' the page and post a comment as to what you enjoyed the most.

- Pick up a copy for someone you know who would be challenged or encouraged by this message.

- Write a review on Amazon.com, BN.com, or Goodreads.com.

- To learn about our latest releases subscribe to our newsletter at www.CrossRiverMedia.com.

Made in the USA
Monee, IL
06 October 2021

79430032R00144